TAKE IT
OR
LEAVE IT

I appreciate your support Enjoy (handwritten)

A novel by

TY

Ty (handwritten signature)

Library of Congress Control Number: 200902895

Request for permission to make copies or any part of the work
should be mailed to

Tytam Publishing
P.O. Box 1903
Newark, NJ 07101
E-Mail: tygoode1@aol.com or tygoode1@yahoo.com
Website: www.tygoode.com

Printed in China

What's good Nabiru? (Rafiyq, Ranisha, Darnell and Harry) you guys have single-handedly made sure that everyone in Newark knows about Newark's own...Ty! Thanks for the love!

To all of my aunts, uncles, cousins, friends and family, I appreciate all of your e-mails and messages. Thank you!!

To everyone who've read my book(s), thank you for the feedback and encouraging words. And thanks for spreading the word.

Shout out to all fellow authors-keep doing big things! It's all worth it at the end of the day.

If I have forgotten to mention anyone, please forgive me-I'm only human. You know what you mean to me. Charge it to the head and not the heart.

See you next time-
Peace!

Chapter 1

Simone walked through the apartment and made her way to the kitchen. She was preparing a bottle for her six-month-old daughter, Sabrina. Sabrina had been crying for the past twenty minutes. Simone didn't know what was wrong with her. She changed her diaper, gave her a bath and finally warmed up a bottle. She tested the milk on her arm as she headed back to the living room. She picked Sabrina up from her playpen and cradled her in her arms. She tried feeding her the bottle but Sabrina turned her head and continued to cry. Simone was worried. She did everything she could think of to get the baby to stop crying. She looked up at the clock and it read 2:30 am. Simone placed Sabrina back in the playpen before she rushed into her bedroom and shook her husband. Kareem mumbled something and turned on his other side. Simone shook him again a little harder this time.

"Kareem, something is wrong with Sabrina. She won't stop crying. Get up, baby."

"What's wrong? Maybe she just hungry," he said. Kareem turned away from her and buried his face under the comforter.

"Kareem, Get up! We need to take her to the hospital, now!" Simone screamed.

Kareem removed the covers from his head as he sat on the side of the bed. Simone was busy pulling on a pair of jeans.

"Where's the baby?" How long she been crying?" He asked.

"About an hour. I did everything I could think of. I'm surprised you didn't hear her," Simone added.

"Man, I was out of it," Kareem said as he went to the living room and retrieved her from the playpen. *"What's wrong with daddy's little girl? Why you makin' such a fuss? It's ok Poopy, daddy gon' make it better. We gon' take you to the hospital right now."* Kareem handed the baby to Simone while he slipped into a pair of sweats and his sneakers. Simone put the baby's jacket on and grabbed her insurance and other important information. Kareem grabbed his keys and escorted his two girls out of the apartment.

When they arrived at the emergency room of Saint Barnabas Hospital, they were shocked that there were only three people in the waiting area. Simone rushed to the desk and explained that the baby wouldn't stop crying. Kareem took the baby while Simone sat at patient registration. He remained standing and rocked her back and forth. He was frustrated that whatever he did wouldn't sooth his daughter's pain. He paced the room with Sabrina positioned on his shoulder and rubbed her back.

"Kareem, bring her over. They're taking her to the back right now," Simone yelled. A nurse opened the double doors and escorted the three to the back area. The nurse took the baby from Kareem and laid her on the table.

"Has she been dropped within the last 36 hours?" The nurse asked.

"Hell no!" Kareem yelled.

"Calm down please, sir, these are standard questions," the nurse insisted.

"Has she been given or ingested any type of drugs or chemicals?"

"No, nothing like that," Simone added before Kareem had a chance to speak. By the look on his face, she knew he was getting ready to curse the nurse out. "She just started crying and wouldn't stop."

"When did the crying begin?" The nurse asked as she scribbled something down in the chart.

"She cried a little last night but after I fed her and gave her a bath, she went right to sleep. And then tonight, she started before her nightly feed and wouldn't stop," Simone cried.

2

Kareem pulled her to him and kissed her on the forehead. "It's gonna be ok, baby," he consoled his wife.

"Ok, we need to get her weight, urine and a blood sample. The doctor will be in here to talk with you in a few minutes. Can you please remove her clothes?" She asked Simone.

Simone did as instructed. Kareem stroked Sabrina's hair as Simone held her and removed her pants.

"Hello, I'm Dr. Kroger." He said as he shook Simone and Kareem's hand.

"Nice to meet you Dr." They said in unison. Dr. Kroger asked several more questions as he wrote in the chart. Sabrina yelled and screamed to no end. Simone passed the baby to Kareem and excused herself from the room.

* * *

After two hours, Kareem returned to the outside waiting area with Sabrina wrapped in his arms. He spotted Simone sitting in one of the chairs and told her they were ready to leave.

Once back inside their apartment, Kareem put the sleeping Sabrina in her crib and joined Simone in the living room. "Well at least we know what's wrong with her. She's allergic to that cereal. I'll pick up a different kind in the morning before I go to work." Simone shook her head up and down.

"What happened? You ok?" Kareem asked.

Simone shook her head side to side. "I don't know, Kareem. I feel so bad that I can't do anything to help her. I feel like she misses her mother. It's possible that she could miss Shelly's touch, her scent, and her voice. Maybe that's why I can't get her to calm down sometimes."

"You are her mother! Stop worrying about that. It's been four months and we ain't heard a word from Shelly. Once we got married, Sabrina is your daughter too."

"I know she's my step-daughter legally, but I'm so attached to her. The last thing I want is for Shelly to come back and take her away from us. I don't think I can handle that kind of pain."

3

"Listen, you know what the lawyer said, since we have no way of contacting Shelly, after a year, we'll have sole custody and there won't be a thing Shelly can do about it. *She* abandoned Sabrina we didn't take her away from Shelly." He hugged his wife as she wiped the tears from her eyes. They went to bed and tried to get some sleep before Sabrina awoken.

Chapter 2

Tricia sat on her favorite sofa in her Mother's house. She pushed back and let the recliner extend. She looked up at the ceiling and exhaled. She knew it was time to move on with her life. Her mother went off with Marvin on a trip to Hawaii for two weeks. They were due to return home any minute.

Maryanne Hobbs walked in the door with Marvin closely behind her. She dropped her bags on the floor and went to hug her daughter.

"Hey sweetie, how are you?" Maryanne inquired.

"Hi Momma, hi Marvin, how was the vacation?" she smiled.

"Oh, Hawaii is beautiful! Tricia, you have got to go there and see for yourself," Maryanne beamed. Marvin gave Tricia a hug and sat on the sofa. Maryanne plopped down next to him and removed her shoes.

"Do you want to tell her, baby?" Marvin asked.

"Tell me what? What happened?" Tricia asked.

"We got married!" Maryanne beamed.

"What?! Momma, I thought you said you didn't want to get re-married," Tricia asked.

"I thought I didn't want to get married too, but I was not about to let this one get away." She blushed as Marvin kissed her on the cheek.

"Congratulations! This is wonderful news. I'm so happy for you two." Trish smiled but deep inside, she thought her mother's last comment was somehow directed towards her.

"So Tricia, how are you doing, really?"

"I'm fine, Momma. I'm just taking it one day at a time. I'm going to stay at a hotel now that you two are back…and married. I don't wanna be in the middle of some newlyweds," she laughed. Maryanne saw right through her daughter. She shook her head and rubbed Tricia's arm.

"Trish, it's ok to feel like being around us married folk will remind you that your marriage isn't working right now. And it's also ok for you to stay right here. This will always be your home."

"We know that you're going through a rough time right now Tricia, and whatever we could do to help, just ask. I think I might have a solution to our living situation," Marvin said.

"How so?" Tricia frowned.

"Well I can see why you may be a little hesitant about staying in the house with us," Marvin began.

"No, it's not just that Marvin. There is just too much history in this house." Trish glanced at a photo of her and Tarik before she continued. "Too much has happened here. I don't think I'd be able to move on if I'm living here. I'll start looking for a place as soon as possible," Tricia said.

Marvin shook his head up and down as if to say that he understood. "Well I still may have a solution. Maryanne, would you mind if you and I stayed here in your house for a few months? That way Tricia can stay at my house until she gets herself together. I know we agreed to stay at my place but considering the circumstances, would you mind if we changed plans for a little while?"

"Oh Marvin, that's a wonderful idea," Maryanne smiled.

"Tricia, would that work for you?" Marv asked.

"Oh my goodness, I couldn't…I don't want to inconvenience you two. You just got married and I don't want you rearranging your life on the count of me. No, I'll just get a hotel room until I find something permanent."

"Don't be silly. You are welcome to stay at my house for as long as you'd like. We'll be fine right here," Marv said.

"And besides, you can save up some money while you're staying at the house," Maryanne added, "Stop being so stubborn and just say thank you. Don't go making a mountain out of a molehill."

Tricia smiled, "Ok, I can see that I won't win this one. Marvin, I really appreciate this, thanks. And thank you too Momma. I should be gone in a week." She hugged them both.

Chapter 3

It was a beautiful Saturday morning and Tricia was packing the last box into her car. She was taking the last trip from her mother's house to Marvin's house. She wanted to be settled before she went back to work on Monday. She waved to her mother and Marvin before she drove away. She didn't feel like being alone so she called Simone.

"Hey girl, what's up? Now that you're a mother, we hardly talk," Tricia laughed.

"Yeah, Brina keeps me busy. I'm still adjusting though," Simone replied.

"You feel like some company?" Trish asked.

"Sure, come on over. Kareem is at work and I could use some adult conversation," Simone said.

"I'll be there in a few," Tricia said as she closed her cell.

Simone came to the door with Sabrina in her arms. She stepped aside and allowed Tricia to enter the apartment.

"What's up, girly?" Simone asked as she headed to the living room. Tricia walked into the apartment and closed the door behind her.

"Oh, look how big she's getting," Tricia said as she stretched her arms out and took the baby from Simone.

"Be careful Trish, she's a little agitated. She's allergic to the cereal we've been feeding her. We had to take her to the hospital a few nights ago. She's finally starting to feel better."

"Ohh, poor baby," Tricia cooed. She put a blanket on her lap and lay Sabrina across while she slept. "So what's up with you, mama?" She asked Simone.

"I'm maintaining. It's rough but I love being a mother. I think Sabrina has brought Kareem and me closer. My goodness, I have a family now. Sometimes it seems so unreal. That is until Sabrina starts acting up," Simone laughed.

Tricia smiled at her friend and shook her head. "I'm so happy for you. It seems like your dream is coming true. You've wanted a family for so long and now you have one. And you're happy as ever," Trish said.

Simone stopped laughing and stared at her sister friend. "Trish, how are you doing?

"Girl, did I tell you that Momma and Marvin got married?" She perked up as she changed the subject.

"What? When? They came back from Hawaii early?" Simone asked with excitement.

"No girl, they got married while they were down there. Momma said that she didn't want to let her man get away," Tricia's voice trailed off.

"And speaking of men getting away, what's up with you and Tarik?"

"Simone, don't go there. You know we are over. I haven't spoken to him in over four months," she said as she stared at the photo that hung on Simone's wall. It was a picture of the four of them at the club a few years ago.

"That's because you're being stubborn and won't call him. Trish, why won't you work this out with your husband? The love is still there on both parts." Simone tried to reason with her sister friend.

"Simone, I can't be with Tarik. I don't trust him. I don't want to be wondering what he's doing when he's not with me. He lied to me and I can't get over it. I'm thinking about a divorce. Marvin is going to introduce me to an attorney that can take care of everything." Tricia said that with such sadness in her voice, Simone teared up.

"Trish, I'm not going to push the issue. But I will say this and then mind my own business. Do you really want to lose your soul mate? You know that what happened between Melissa and Tarik was an accident. You know that he'll never hurt you again-especially in that way. Are you sure your marriage isn't worth

9

saving?" Simone took Sabrina from Tricia's lap and took her in the bedroom and laid her in her crib.

She left Trish to ponder her words for a few minutes while she answered her telephone.

"*Hello…*" Simone answered.

"*You have a collect call from Clinton's women's correctional institution from Tammy. Will you accept the charges?*" The operator asked.

"*Hell no!*" Simone slammed the phone. She made a mental note to put a block on the phone first thing in the morning. She couldn't help but to think what would have happened if Kareem answered the phone.

"What's wrong? Who was that?" Trish asked.

"Probably a wrong number. Somebody calling here collect," Simone answered. She couldn't believe that Tammy got her number and actually called her house. She went back to join Tricia on the sofa.

"Did I tell you that Marvin is letting me stay in his house for a few months?" Tricia asked.

"What's that all about? Aren't he and Moms gonna stay there now that they're married?" Simone assumed.

"Well they were, but Marv suggested that I stay there and heal-sort of speak. There are too many memories in Moms' house and I could save up some money if I stayed at Marv's for a few months."

"That's good; you do need time to heal. I'm so sorry you are going through all of this. If there's anything that I can do, don't hesitate to call me. You know I'm here for you," Simone said.

"I know. But I'm going to move on with my life. I've made my decision and now it's time to live with it. I'll be ok. I go back to work tomorrow so that'll keep me occupied for the most part." Tricia got up and grabbed her jacket. She went to the bedroom and kissed Sabrina on the cheek, "Feel better sweetie." She hugged Simone and told her she'd call her sometime during the week.

"Ok girl, take care and be careful." Simone said as she stood in the doorway.

"I will, tell Kareem I said hello," Tricia smiled.

"Ok, and remember…anything?"

"I know. Love you, too." Tricia got in her car and drove to Marvin's house.

Chapter 4

S helly wrapped the towel tightly around her body as she stepped out of the shower. She went into the bedroom that she shared with her lover, Constance. She and Connie had officially moved into their own apartment.

They met while Shelly was pregnant with Sabrina. Shelly was leaving the hospital one afternoon after a pre-natal visit and she decided to have lunch in the diner across the street from the hospital. She sat alone in the booth when her waitress came along, "Hi, I'm Constance and I'll be serving you today. How may I help you?"

"I'll have French fries with gravy, a double cheeseburger with everything, and a large lemonade."

As Constance took her order, she looked at the petite woman and smiled, "You must be hungry, huh?"

"I'm starving. I couldn't wait to leave that hospital so I could come over and get something to eat. These cravings I'm having will not be ignored," Shelly laughed.

"So how far along are you?" the waitress asked as she scribbled the order in her pad.

"I'm six months. But I feel like I'm nine months already." Shelly forced a smile.

As Constance walked away to place the order, Shelly sat in her booth looking like she'd lost her best friend. She sat and rubbed her belly and waited for the food. She was hungry and didn't want to lose her appetite by thinking about her life at the moment. She drank the glass of water and motioned for Constance to come to her table.

"Would you mind just bringing me a pitcher of water? I would hate to keep bothering you for water," Shelly suggested.

"Sure, no problem," Constance replied. She walked away and came back with the water and then she placed extra napkins on the table. She motioned for another waiter to bring the food to Shelly's table. Once the servers were gone, Shelly ate everything that was put in front of her. She was ready to order ice cream when Constance returned to her table.

"I don't mean to rush you but I'm getting off in five minutes and I don't wanna miss the bus. Would there be anything else before I write the check?" Constance asked.

Shelly thought for a moment and then shook her head no. She was a little embarrassed that she'd eaten everything off her plate. She took the check and gave Constance her tip.

"Thanks so much. And I'm sorry about rushing you," Constance apologized.

"No no, don't worry about it. I understand. Have a nice day," Shelly yelled behind her.

When Shelly went to the cashier to pay for her food, she ordered her ice cream to go. She paid her bill and walked out of the front door. Just as she was opening the bag with the ice cream she felt her stomach turn. Shelly knew all too well what was getting ready to happen so she tried to run to the nearby garbage can. She was a foot away from the can when she regurgitated on the ground.

"Shit!! All my food," she said aloud.

"Wow, now that's one I've never heard before. You sound more upset about losing your food than just being thankful that you made it outside of the restaurant," Constance laughed.

Shelly looked up at her and rolled her eyes. She didn't see anything funny. She just wanted to get home and lay down. She continued walking towards her car. Constance ran behind her and handed her a few napkins.

"Thanks, Constance right?"

"Connie, please call me Connie. I didn't mean to laugh but you have to admit, that's not usually the first thing a person says when they throw up."

Shelly smiled after she thought about it. "Yeah, I guess you're right. I did kinda wolf that food down." Connie walked with Shelly to her car and handed her a couple of wet naps. "Oh, thanks, I have some hand sanitizer in this car somewhere," Shelly mumbled.

"Oh damn! There goes my bus. I'm going to miss my own funeral," she smiled.

"I'm sorry, I didn't mean to make you miss the bus," Shelly said.

"It's ok, it's not like you did it on purpose. How are you feeling?"

"I stink. I wanna get home and get out of these clothes. Can I give you a ride since I did make you miss the bus?"

"You don't have to do that...the next one should be coming in about fifteen minutes or so." Connie said.

"I insist, let me drop you off. That is if you can stomach how I smell," Shelly smiled.

"No, I don't wanna impose. I'll be fine, go get cleaned up. Have a nice day," Connie replied.

"Well then I'll stay right here with you until the next bus comes. I really feel bad so you can't talk me out of it," Shelly insisted.

"Ok, have it your way," Connie added. They stood by Shelly's car and talked. They talked so long that countless buses had gone by without Connie realizing it. She glanced at her phone and noticed that they'd been talking for three hours. They were sitting in Shelly's car as if they were old friends.

Connie initiated the conversation and talked about her ex. She was going through something and needed an ear. Shelly hadn't talked about her feelings towards Simone or Kareem to anyone. She kept it all inside. Connie gave her the opening to vent. She told Connie all about Simone and Kareem. She even told her that she was once in love with Simone and was now pregnant by Simone's man. Connie was in awe. The issues she had with her ex-girlfriend seemed minor compared to Simone's life.

Once Shelly realized how late it was, she insisted on taking Connie home. Connie didn't refuse this time, she felt a

14

little more comfortable with Shelly. And that was the start of a beautiful friendship...until they consummated their relationship one month before Shelly gave birth to Sabrina.

Shelly turned around and saw Connie walking into the bedroom. Connie proceeded to the bed and kissed Shelly on the neck. Shelly smiled and stood.

"What's wrong?" Connie asked.

"Nothing, I'm good." She said as she continued getting dressed.

"Shelly, come on now, you've been distancing yourself lately. Every time I come near you, you move. What's up?" Connie inquired.

Shelly faced Connie and smiled. She shook her head from side to side and wiped an escaped tear from her eye.

"Con, I've been thinking a lot about Sabrina. I miss her and I really want to see her."

"Then why won't you call her father and make arrangements to see her? I'm sure he'll let you come and visit. I mean, she is your daughter."

"It's not that simple, Connie."

"Are you sure you're missing Sabrina and not her dad... *or her mom*?" Connie asked with raised eyebrows.

Shelly looked at her and rolled her eyes. "Please don't start with this again. I told you that my relationship with Simone and Kareem are in my past. But they do have my daughter so..."

"So, you'll always have a reason to be in their lives." Connie finished Shelly's sentence.

"I hate it when you do that, Connie! If there's something you want to say then just say it! Don't beat around the bush. And if you're gonna start with that jealous shit, then you can save that because I'm not in the mood!" Shelly turned away from Connie and walked out of the bedroom. Connie stood there and shook her head.

Shelly told her up front that she was bi-sexual. Connie was a proud lesbian but she was really attracted to Shelly so she thought like most women and figured that she could convert

15

Shelly to only women. She's now beginning to realize that Shelly is still in love with Kareem and she still has deep feelings for Simone. She hears something more in her voice every time they discuss Kareem and Simone.

Chapter 5

Tarik sat at his desk and went through the stack of mail that his secretary sat in front of him.

"What!? Is she serious?" He picked up the phone and dialed Tricia's cell. After four rings, the voicemail kicked in so he left a message: *"Hey Trish, it's Tarik, I just got the documents, give me a call when you get a chance."* He hung up the phone and stared at the papers for what seemed like eternity.

Tarik turned off his computer and packed his briefcase so that he could leave for the day. He was leaving an hour early because he could no longer concentrate on his work. He turned off the lights in his office and told his assistant that he'd see her in the morning.

Tarik got into his car and drove directly to Mom's house. He knew that Tricia was staying there and he thought it was time they had a face to face. He got out of the car and rang the doorbell.

Maryanne came to the door and smiled at her son- in-law, "Hey baby, how are you?"

"Hi Moms," he said as he kissed her cheek.

"Come on in baby," she said as she closed the door behind him. Tarik sat on the sofa and looked around for Tricia. He didn't see her car in the driveway but he thought there was a chance that she was there anyway.

"Would you like something to drink?" Maryanne asked.

"No thanks, Mom, I'm fine." He cleared his throat, "Uhm is Tricia around?"

"She's not here, Tarik." Maryanne said with a saddened look. She hated the fact that her daughter was so stubborn. She was just like her father, Fred Hobbs.

"Do you know what time she'll be in, I really need to talk to her?" He asked with urgency in his voice.

Maryanne looked at him with raised eyebrows before she spoke, "Tricia is not staying with us anymore, honey, she's been staying at Marvin's house."

"Marvin Woodsby? Why would she be staying there?" He was confused.

"Oh, I forgot. You don't know that Marvin and I got married a few weeks ago while we were in Hawaii," she smiled.

"What, you got married? Congratulations, Moms. You deserve all the happiness in the world," Tarik forced a smile as he hugged Maryanne. She sensed his mood and decided to change the subject.

"How is Melissa doing?" She asked. Tarik turned away, he didn't want Mrs. Hobbs to see the embarrassed expression that covered his face. "It's ok, Tarik. I'm not here to judge. And I'm not insinuating that you and Melissa are seeing each other. I understand that she's your friend and that you two made a mistake."

Tarik felt the color come back to his face. He didn't know where Moms was going with the conversation. "Thanks Moms, I wish Tricia were this understanding," he smiled.

"Me too," she laughed.

"Melissa is fine. She and Mike are engaged to be married. She's just waiting for Phil to sign the divorce papers. But she's really happy and the baby is doing great. Melissa says that he's sitting up and crawling already," Tarik smiled.

"That's good to hear."

"Moms, why is Tricia staying at Marvin's house?" Tarik asked.

"Well, she felt a little uncomfortable being around us newlyweds so she was going to look for an apartment. But Marvin and I suggested that she stay at his place so that she could save money and find her own place."

"Moms, I don't mean to put you in the middle of Tricia's and my mess. But she's not answering my phone calls and she's not returning my messages. Would you please give me the address to Marvin's house so that I could talk to her?" Tarik pleaded.

"Tarik, I really wish that you and Tricia can work it out but I don't feel comfortable going behind her back and giving you the address if she doesn't want to talk to you," Moms said.

"I understand, Moms. But I just received the divorce papers in the mail and I really need to see her."

"She sent you divorce papers? When?" Moms yelled. She was clearly upset with her daughter's decision.

"I got them today. She sent them to my office. Would you please call her now and ask her if it's ok to give me the address? I know that she'll pick up the phone when she sees that it's you calling," Tarik suggested.

"I can't believe that girl, Damn!" Moms shook her head and reached for the phone.

Chapter 6

Tricia answered as soon as she saw her mother's number flash across her phone, "Hello Moms."

"Hi Tricia, I need to talk to you." She said with a serious tone.

"Moms, what's wrong?" Tricia sat down.

"Why in the world would you be trying to get a divorce?"

"Why would he tell you that? I hope you're not calling to preach to me again, Moms. You know how I feel about my marriage and the sooner I end it, the sooner I can move on."

"Well, I think you're making a mistake and I also think it's time that you talked this out with your husband," Moms said.

"I don't have anything to say to him, Moms."

"Well you'd better think of something because he's on his way over there so you all can talk about this."

"Moms, you told him where I'm staying? Why would you do that?" Tricia was annoyed.

"Because when you decide to end a marriage, your husband at least deserves some answers. Tricia, all you have to do is listen to him. Tarik loves you and I don't want you to walk away like this. That man deserves some answers and you need to give them to him. Be civilized and talk to your husband. I know I may have overstepped my bounds and I'm sorry, but I had to make sure that you did everything to make your marriage work," she paused, "do you hear me, Trish?"

"I hear you. I still can't believe he's coming over here right now. I look a hot mess. I need to get decent," Tricia mumbled.

"You need to get decent for a soon to be ex-husband?" Moms laughed.

"Very funny, bye Moms."

"Tricia, you can fool everyone else in this world but I'm your mama and I know what's in your heart. I told you before, don't let your pride make you throw away a good man. They are hard to come by. And that's why I'm married, now," she laughed again.

"I hear you Moms. I have to go." Tricia said solemnly and hung up the phone.

* * *

Tarik rang the doorbell and waited nervously. Tricia peeked out the curtain and saw her husband standing there in a pair of beige slacks and a brown pull over shirt. She could tell that he'd just come from work. She ran her fingers through her hair once more and tucked her shirt inside of her slacks and opened the door. She stepped back and allowed him room to enter the house. "Hi," she said.

"How are you?" Tarik asked.

"I'm ok, I guess. Have a seat. Would you like something to drink?" Trish asked. She was nervous as well. She had been thinking a lot about Tarik. She dreamed about him just about every night. And the fact that he was standing at the door was making her weak.

"No, I'm good. But I do want to talk to you about those papers you sent me."

Tricia exhaled and grabbed a bottle of wine out of the ice bucket that she'd placed there as soon as she'd gotten off the phone with her mother. She poured herself a glass of wine and took a sip. "Are you sure you won't have a glass? This could be a long conversation."

Tarik gestured for her to pass him a glass of wine and she obliged. "Tricia, how could you just up and ask for a divorce?"

Trish sat down on the chair across from him. She sighed and looked his way. "Tarik, this wasn't an easy decision. I just don't see any reason why we should prolong the inevitable."

"Prolong the inevitable? We haven't even tried to work it out. Why you are in such a rush to end it? I thought by giving you some time, you'd see that you're making a mistake by walking away from us."

"No Tarik, you made the mistake, remember?"

"I remember us making mistakes. You still aren't willing to take any responsibility for your part in this? It's entirely my fault that we are in this predicament?" He smirked and took a sip of his wine.

"Tarik, I know I made a mistake. I am taking responsibility for my actions. I apologized to you for what I did. I know you said that you can accept what I did as an accident but I can't accept what you and Melissa did as an accident. How can I ever trust you again?" She was getting upset as images of Tarik and Melissa flashed in her mind.

"Do you wanna trust me again? Because if you do, you'll find a way. Why do you think it's so easy for me to forgive what you did? I forgive you because I know you, Trish. I know that you're not gay. I know that's not your thing. And I trust you when you say that it was an accident. But I guess you don't have that much trust in me, huh?" He sighed.

"Tarik, before all of this happened, I trusted you. At first I was very skeptical about Melissa, but you convinced me that you two were platonic friends. Then she and I became good friends-very good friends. And then to find out that you fucked her-the way that I found out-that's unforgivable. You and her lied to me. And to top it off, you didn't have the decency to use protection! You thought you were the father of her baby and had the nerve to be disappointed when you found out that you weren't. And I had to sit right there through that entire ordeal in front of everyone while my husband claimed to be the father to another woman's baby-a woman whom I considered a friend," Tricia cried.

Tarik went to her and sat down in front of her on the ottoman. He took his wife in his arms and held her while she fought his touch. Tricia didn't want Tarik to console her; she just wanted to be pissed. But Tarik wouldn't let her go until her crying turned to sniffles. He then got up and refilled their glasses.

Tricia kicked off her shoes and put her feet up on the ottoman. She laid her head back on the chair and closed her eyes. It was indeed going to be a long night. She took the glass from Tarik and gulped it down. She handed it to him for a refill before he sat back down.

Chapter 7

Simone walked into the bedroom wearing a one piece crotch less leotard. Sabrina was asleep early and she had plans with Kareem. She turned off the TV as soon as she entered the room. She made sure the baby monitor was on and then she crawled to her husband on the bed.

Kareem smiled and reached for her. She eased closer to him and kissed him on the lips. Kareem sat back against the headboard and Simone straddled him. He grabbed her shoulder length hair and pulled her head back and proceeded to kiss her hard on the mouth. Simone moaned and enjoyed his touch. It had been two weeks sine she and Kareem were able to make love. Either Sabrina was awake or Kareem was working late. Simone was extremely horny. And she was going to show her man just what he'd been missing.

She pulled his shirt over his head and rubbed his bare chest. She pinched his nipples and felt them react to her touch. She moaned as Kareem flipped her on her back and positioned himself on top of her. He kissed her neck and moved his way down to her breasts. The fishnet leotard was leaving very little to the imagination. Kareem found her nipple poking through a hole and met it with his mouth. He sucked it until she arched her back and guided him to the other one. Kareem gave the same attention to her other nipple while he caressed the area between her thighs.

Simone moaned and begged for more. She rubbed and made his dick come to a full erection. She tried to slide off his underwear but he grabbed both her hands and pinned them over her head. Kareem licked her stomach and went down until he found what he was looking for. Simone arched as his wet tongue touched her clit. Kareem held her hands above her head while he used his mouth to satisfy her desire. Simone immediately wrapped her legs around his neck as he licked her insides. She guided his head with her thighs as he took his time and teased her clit. Kareem licked the tip just enough to give Simone a tingling sensation. When he was satisfied that she was ready for more, he released her hands and spread her legs apart and stuck his tongue as far as it would go into her nectar. Simone gasped as she moved her body to mach his strokes. Kareem felt the juices pour down his lips and chin as Simone reached her first orgasm.

As Simone shivered and shook, Kareem slid down his underwear and stood over her. She looked up at him and moved to the top of the bed. She opened her legs and invited him inside her tunnel.

Kareem got on the bed and slowly entered Simone. He moaned as he rode her slowly. After a few minutes, Kareem grabbed her legs and placed them around his waist. Simone clung to him for dear life. She expertly matched his strokes as she never removed her legs. Kareem moaned and began pumping faster. Simone knew he was about to come so she looked at him and smiled, *"Come all over my face, baby. I wanna taste it."*

"Ooh shit...baby, I'm coming...I'm com...ing...aahhh." Kareem quickly pulled out of Simone and squirted his juices all over her mouth and breasts. Simone lay there as Kareem rubbed his dick in his juices that had decorated her mouth. Simone opened her mouth and welcomed his dick. She lay on her back while her husband stood over her and fucked her in the mouth. Simone used her jaws to grip his dick and made sure her tongue caressed the tip of his dick while she brought him to another erection. Kareem pulled away from her mouth and rolled her over onto her stomach. He dove in doggy style and fucked his wife until he came all over her back. Kareem collapsed on top of Simone until they heard Sabrina crying three hours later.

Chapter 8

Tarik was the first to awaken. He and Tricia stayed up and talked for hours. They ordered Chinese food and went through two more bottles of wine. Tricia joined Tarik on the sofa where they fell asleep. Tarik looked to his left and saw his wife sleeping peacefully. She tossed a little when he moved. He admired her beauty and smiled. Even though Trish had cried most of the night, she still looked amazing to him. He attempted to get up from the sofa without waking his wife. As he sat up and placed his foot on the floor, Tricia opened her eyes.

"Good morning," he said.

"Good morning, Tarik." She said as she covered her mouth and yawned.

"Do you have any plans for today? Cause I was gonna run out and get breakfast so that we can finish what we started last night," Tarik suggested.

"Tarik, I think I'm all talked out." She said as she looked around the room.

"I hear you. I just hate to leave things like this." He said as he waved his hand between the two of them. "We've been through too much, Trish. And it wasn't until last night that I realized how deep your pain is. I'm truly sorry for causing the way you feel," Tarik said.

"Tarik, I know you're sorry. And deep down I know that you'd never hurt me intentionally. I'm just having a very hard time moving past this," she paused, "And I feel that if all this time didn't bring me closer to forgiving you then nothing will." Tarik stared at her. He was not going to give up on his wife that easily. They both sat deep in thought for a few minutes. Tarik

26

looked over at Tricia and noticed the tears welling up in her eyes again.

"Baby, please don't cry. I love you. And I know you still love me," Tarik said.

"Tarik, me still loving you was never an issue. Of course I love you. I have loved you for a long time and I can't just turn my emotions off at the drop of a dime because I'm pissed with you," she retorted.

"I know that. That's why I hate seeing you so bitter and cold. I feel fucked up because I'm the cause of this. I don't want you to look at me and only see the mistake I made. As much as I love you, I'd rather be without you than to see you like this. Cause like you said, if time didn't heal your wounds by now, then maybe they won't." Tarik sat quietly in thought for a moment.

Tricia looked at him and thought about what her mother and Simone said and wanted to just be honest with her husband. "Tarik, I…" she exhaled, "we just…you should just go. I can't do this right now." The thoughts of him and Melissa would not disappear from her mind.

"Trish, please baby…I'm begging you to think about this. I don't want a divorce. I wanna be with my wife," Tarik pleaded.

"Tarik, please just sign the papers. There's no need for us to keep going back and forth. We can't be together!" Tricia stated. She didn't even bother to wipe the tears from her eyes this time. She did not want to end her marriage but she knew she would never be able to trust Tarik again. So she thought it best to just let it go.

"There you go being selfish again. You need to check yourself! You fucked somebody else, too! We both made mistakes but you can't find it in your heart to forgive me?" Tarik exploded.

"Tarik, you'll never understand how I feel about you fucking Melissa. And I don't intend to spend the rest of my life trying to explain it to you. Just leave!" She shouted.

"You know what? I never should've expected anything else from you. I know how you are and how you'll always be. And even though I love you in spite of you, be careful what you ask for! I'm a good man and I'm not gonna stand here and try to convince my wife of that!"

Trish had already made her way to the door. She turned the knob and flung it open. "Bye Tarik!" He walked towards the door and shook his head. He glanced back at Tricia as he crossed the threshold, "Yeah, ok." Tricia stood against the door after she closed it. She looked down at her wedding ring and twirled it around. She slid the ring off her finger and placed it on the chain around her neck.

Chapter 9

Kareem gathered the clothing that lay sprawled across the floor. He and Simone had been having passionate sex all week and he was cleaning up the evidence of last night's escapade. He was excited that Sabrina was sleeping through the night. He hadn't realized how much he missed Simone.

"What are you doing up so early?" Simone asked as she walked into the living room and sat on the sofa.

"I don't know. I just couldn't sleep. I was going to get a drink and saw all our mess and just started picking it up. Yo, you did ya thing last night."

Simone smiled. She tucked her feet under her ass and got comfortable. Kareem bent down and kissed her on the mouth. "Now you know this love cause you ain't even brushed ya teeth yet. You all smelling like garbage truck juice and I'm slobbin' you down," he joked. Simone laughed out loud and then covered her mouth as to not wake Sabrina.

"Shut up, just because you beat me to it for once now you wanna hike?" she laughed.

"Nah, I'm just playin'," Kareem chuckled.

"I need to talk to you about something." Simone said in a more serious tone.

"What's up? Talk to me."

"I'm ready to go back to work. My old job called and offered me a supervisor's position. And I wanna take it."

"But I thought we agreed that you'd stay home with Sabrina until she was at least a year," Kareem said.

"I know baby, but things are changing. We could definitely use the extra money for the down payment on our house."

"Simone," Kareem huffed, "why the sudden change? Why are you going against the plan? You know how I feel about day care."

"You didn't hear me out. I wasn't thinking about putting her in day care. I was gonna ask Moms if she would be willing to watch her. She's retired and she adores Sabrina."

Kareem relaxed a little. "Well what if Moms says no? She just got married and she may not wanna spend her days babysitting."

"Well if she says no then I'll tell the job that I can't accept the position. Moms is the only person I'll trust to keep our baby," Simone said. Kareem sat in thought for a while. Simone could tell that he was angry because she noticed his jawbone constantly jumping. She watched him for a few more minutes before she spoke. "Kareem, what you think?"

"Well you already made up ya mind. So ask Moms and see what she says."

"Okayyy. But why are you so mad? I know we discussed me staying at home but Sabrina is getting spoiled. And if I stay at home with her any longer then we won't be able to get anyone to keep her whenever I do return to work. She needs to be around someone other than us."

"I'm not mad, Simone. I'm just shocked because I thought we discussed this months ago. If you didn't want to stay at home with my daughter then you should've just said that!"

"Our daughter, Kareem! Not your daughter! And I was fine with staying at home but we need the money. We can't keep living in this apartment. Sabrina has more stuff than we do and there's no room to store any of her things. She'll be walking soon and where do you expect her to walk? It was only me and you for a long time and this place were big enough for us but now we have a baby and we need a bigger place as soon as possible."

"What? You don't trust that I can make enough money to get our house?" Kareem asked.

"No, do not go there! It's not about you making all the money. We're in this together. And I already said that if Moms says no then I won't take the job!"

"I just don't get it. You always said that you wanted to have children and to be a family. And now that we have that, you tryin' to run away from it." Kareem shook his head.

"I'm not running away from anything! Yes, I've always said that I wanted the whole thing, a family and a husband but I never said anything about sitting at home for the rest of my life. You need to understand that this was not in the plan. I am sacrificing and compromising to make sure that everyone is accommodated, but what about me? Why aren't you willing to compromise for me? All I want is to return to work to help better our financial situation."

"No, Sabrina wasn't in the plan but she's here now!" Kareem shouted.

"Kareem, don't try to make this about Sabrina. You know damn well that I love her like she was my own baby. I..." Kareem cut her off.

"Why? Because you fucked her mother?" And as soon as he said those words, he regretted doing so.

"Wh...what are y...you talking about?" Simone stuttered.

"Simone I know all about you and Shelly. She told me everything so don't even bother denying it!" Simone sat on the sofa in shock. She had no idea that Kareem had known about her relationship with Shelly. She looked in Kareem's direction as he was walking into the bedroom to a crying Sabrina. Simone didn't realize how much time had passed until she saw Kareem with Sabrina in his arms heading out of the door.

"Where are you going, Kareem? Where are you taking her?" Simone called after him as he reached the steps to the front door.

"I'm taking my daughter out for a while." He shouted over his shoulder.

"Kareem, don't leave like this. We need to talk." Her words fell upon deaf ears. Kareem never looked back or responded. Simone went back into their apartment and returned to her spot on the sofa. *"Shelly, that BITCH!"*

Simone had fallen asleep on the sofa as the tears wouldn't stop falling from her eyes. When she awakened, she called Kareem's cell phone and got his voice mail. She decided that she needed to keep busy to keep from worrying. Simone went to the stereo and put on Mary J. Blige' self titled Cd. As she cleaned the apartment, she let Mary's words sooth her pain. When the Cd got to track number ten and she heard Mary singing about her man having a visit from an old friend, she got dressed and left the apartment.

Chapter 10

Shelly walked into the apartment and saw Connie in the kitchen preparing dinner. She walked into the kitchen and kissed Connie on the cheek.

"How was your day? Connie asked.

"It was ok. My boss is driving me crazy, though. He thinks that my entire life revolves around his needs.

"What did Mr. Wakeman do now?" Connie asked.

"I don't even wanna talk about it. He's a trip, though." Shelly smirked as she made her way to the bathroom.

Connie stood over the stove and stirred the macaroni noodles. She was trying desperately to have a nice evening with her woman. She went into the bedroom and changed into a pair of black short shorts and an orange tank top. She slid her feet into her black three inch stilettos and made her way back to the kitchen. She finished making the macaroni and cheese and took the barbeque chicken out of the oven. Connie peeked into the living room to see if Shelly was on her way out of the bathroom. When she heard the shower turn on, she knew the coast was clear. She set the dining room table and fixed their plates. Connie went to a closet and removed four candles and set them on the table. She waited until the water stopped before she lit them. "Shelly, the food is ready. Hurry up before it gets cold," Connie yelled into the bathroom.

"Give me two minutes," Shelly yelled back.

"This is a treat." Shelly smiled as she pulled the wife beater over her head. She was wearing a pair of boy shorts that barely covered her ass.

"Well, I figured that we could both relax a little. It's been a little hectic around here lately," Connie smiled.

"Yeah, the tension has been a little thick these past few weeks. And I want to apologize for snapping at you. It's just that I don't think you understand how I'm feeling. And when I try to talk to you and make you understand, you always make it out to be more than what it is."

"I know and I apologize for my part. I promise that I'll try to be more understanding," she smiled, "now let's eat before this food get cold."

"This is lovely but we're missing one thing," Shelly said. She went into the kitchen and grabbed two beers. She sat a bottle in front of Connie. "We're all out of wine."

"This will do. Now eat your food so that I can have dessert," she winked.

"No baby, we're both having dessert. I deserve a treat too." Shelly said with a wicked grin.

Connie was the first to finish. She cleaned the table then ran dish water in the sink. She began to wash the dishes as Shelly was putting away the food.

When Shelly finished, she stood back and looked at Connie. She saw how the shorts were perfectly fitted to her ass. She admired Connie's figure. Connie stood 5'8". Looking at her from a side view, she was shaped like the letter 'S'. She had big breasts and a nice big round ass. Her hair was a cinnamon brown and it was rested a little past her shoulders.

Shelly went to Connie and hugged her from behind. She felt her nipples and rubbed up against her ass.

"Hey stop that. You need to let your food digest," Connie smiled.

"Oh really? How about I cheat and have dessert a little early?" Shelly continued to feel and rub up against Connie. She turned her around and kissed her. Connie began feeling on Shelly's breasts and kissing her neck. She pulled Shelly to a chair and sat her down. Connie stood over Shelly and placed her right leg on the back of the chair. She tugged her shorts aside and let Shelly have dessert. After Shelly sucked the life out of Connie, she laid her on the table and squatted over her so that Connie could return the favor. Connie pulled Shelly's ass down to her as she lifted her head and met Shelly pump for pump. Just before Shelly reached her climax, she sat on Connie's chest and buried Connie's head into her bush. Connie's tongue went into overdrive as Shelly moaned and released her juices in Connie's mouth.

Shelly got off of Connie and helped her into the bedroom where she grabbed a bag out of the nightstand drawer. The bag contained all types of dildos and other sex paraphernalia. Shelly pushed Connie back on the bed and smiled as she turned on a pink ten-inch vibrator.

Two hours later...

Shelly was the first to awaken. She put everything back into the bag and placed it back into the drawer. She put on her t-shirt and went into the kitchen. She grabbed a spray bottle of Clorox and began to disinfect everything. She grabbed a bottle of water from the fridge and went into the living room to watch TV. She heard the shower turn on and waited for Connie to finish her shower.

Chapter 11

Kareem entered the apartment and turned on the light. He placed a sleeping Sabrina on the sofa and removed her clothing. He called out for Simone and waited for her to answer. He picked Sabrina up and walked through the apartment searching for his wife. Kareem saw that she wasn't there and cussed under his breath. He put Sabrina in her crib and dialed Simone's cell number. The call went straight to voicemail. He dialed again and got the same results. He grabbed Sabrina's baby supplies so that he could give her a bath at the kitchen sink like he'd seen Simone do on occasions. As he was cleaning the sink, Sabrina began to cry. He stopped what he was doing and went to pick her up. Kareem positioned Sabrina on his shoulder and went back to washing the sink. He ran the water and dropped in some baby wash. He waited until the sink was half full before he went to lay out clothes for the baby.

Sabrina continued to cry while Kareem held her on his shoulder. He hadn't realized that she was hungry for food. He'd only grabbed a couple of bottles when he left but Sabrina had been eating baby food for two months. Kareem left in such a hurry that Simone didn't have a chance to tell him to take the baby's food.

It was now nine o'clock and Simone still wasn't home. Kareem got the baby dressed in a sleeper and called Simone's cell again. Simone's phone still went straight to voicemail.

Sabrina was crying uncontrollably now and Kareem didn't know what to do. He tried to rock her to sleep but that didn't work. He went into the kitchen and warmed a bottle. He tried to lay her down so that he could use the bathroom but

Sabrina was crying at the top of her lungs. He had to go to the bathroom so he placed her in her crib and went to the restroom. Sabrina's screaming was beginning to irritate him. Once he was done in the bathroom, he picked her up and took her with him in the kitchen so he could test the bottle; it was just right so he gently pushed it in her mouth. Sabrina stopped crying when she tasted the milk. But that only lasted for a minute. She turned her face away from the bottle and began crying again.

"Poopy what's wrong wit' you? Why you crying like this? It's ok, daddy's gonna make it better." He said as he rocked his daughter in his arms. He sat down on a chair then it hit him that Sabrina maybe wanted cereal in her bottle. He went to a cabinet and saw rows of Gerber baby food. He grabbed three jars and put them on the table. Kareem took Sabrina to her car seat and carried it with him back into the kitchen. He made sure the food was warm enough for her to eat then he put it in a bowl. He tied a bib to her neck and then fed her the food. Sabrina calmed down as she tasted the food. She ate the food faster than Kareem could feed it to her. He felt so bad that he didn't realize that his daughter was hungry.

Sabrina cried for more after it was all gone. Kareem opened the applesauce and fed that to her. When she was done, he fed her a bottle of water and laid her on his bed. He was ready to take a shower but he didn't want to let go of the bottle. Sabrina was asleep after drinking half the bottle. Kareem gently laid her in her crib and went to take his shower. At that moment, he really missed Simone. He didn't have a clue as to how to care for his daughter on his own. He was stressed and frustrated that Simone wasn't there. He got out of the shower and grabbed a beer on his way to watch TV. in the living room.

* * *

Meanwhile, Simone was sitting on Moms' sofa pouring her heart out. She had tried to call Tricia a few times but she only got the voicemail. She called Moms and asked her if she could stop by and was welcomed.

"Moms, I just don't know what happened. Kareem just snapped. He just started going off for no reason." Simone said.

"Simone please, now you know better than to come over here acting like you didn't do anything wrong. It takes two people to argue. Now what happened?"

"Moms, he really did just go off. We were having a nice time and I told him that I was offered my old job with a promotion and that I wanted to take it. He started yelling about who's going to watch Sabrina and how could I go against the plan and stuff like that."

"What plan?" Moms asked.

"Well when Sabrina first got here, we talked about me staying home to take care of her while he worked," Simone explained.

"For how long?" Moms asked.

"That's just it. We didn't really make a time limit on how long I would be a stay at home mom. I think Kareem was so sure that I wouldn't be able to get another job he just assumed that I would be home for at least a year. But that's not even the worse part. He accused me of not wanting to stay at home with *his* daughter."

"Excuse me?"

"Yeah, that's exactly what he said. He tried to make it about Sabrina when he knows that I love that girl like my own child."

"Simone, that's one thing that you two need to get straight. You have to sit him down and talk to him about that. He can't go throwing in your face that Sabrina is his daughter and not yours. First off, it's only a reminder that he cheated with Shelly in the first place," Moms said.

"I know. I wanted to nip that in the bud as soon as he said it but…" Simone's voice trailed off.

"But what? Come on Simone, talk to me. What happened?" Moms pushed.

Simone took a deep breath before she spoke. "He knows about me and Shelly."

"What does that have to do with anything?" Moms was clearly confused.

"He threw it up in my face that he knew and he said that Shelly told him everything." Simone said as she wiped teardrops from her eyes.

"Simone, you may not like what I have to say but I'm going to say it anyway. I understand how Kareem feels about you and Shelly."

"Moms, what me and Shelly had was a...ah...like a short lived love affair." Simone tried to explain.

"Well, just like I told Trish, your man should have heard that kind of news from you. You married this man with your little secret tucked away in your closet."

"But Shelly had no right to say anything to him. She was supposed to..."

"What? Keep it a secret? Did you really expect her to keep her mouth shut? She had the man's baby, Simone! She needed revenge on the both of you and by telling Kareem, she could kill two birds with one stone. So no matter how he found out, it's out now. You need to make this right with your husband."

"But what about how he hurt me regarding Sabrina?" Simone asked.

"You have every right to be hurt. But after hearing that he knows about your affair, can't you see that he hurt you intentionally? Kareem didn't mean anything by that chile." Moms took a bite of her cake and sipped her iced tea while Simone continued to shake her head. She knew that Moms had a point but it didn't erase her hurt. Although she would get to the bottom of this, she still planned to return to work.

"Moms, would you mind watching Sabrina while I went back to work? I know you're a newlywed now so if you really don't want to be bothered, don't be afraid to tell me," Simone smiled.

"Girl please, when have you ever known me to bite my tongue about anything? I would love to keep her. I'm retired but my husband isn't. I'll need something to keep me busy while Marv's working."

"Thanks Moms. Kareem will be so happy that you said yes. He trusts you and probably only you to keep Sabrina. Putting her in daycare was not an option," Simone beamed.

"Well, you still need to work that out with your husband, too. If you two agree then I will be more than glad to keep her. Just let me know if and when it happens."

Marvin walked through the door and hung his suit jacket on a hook.

"Hello ladies," he greeted the women.

"Hi honey," Moms said as she stood and kissed his lips.

"Hi Marvin," Simone smiled, "nice to see you again."

"It's nice to see you, too. How is it going?" Marvin asked as he stopped near the kitchen to hear her reply. Simone could tell that he was making small talk so she smiled and said that everything was good.

"Ok Moms, I'm going to be heading home now. Thanks so much for the talk. Oh…have you heard from Trish? I tried to call her a few times but her phone just kept going to voicemail." Simone inquired.

"I haven't heard from her. She's probably still pissed with me for giving Tarik Marv's address so he could go and talk to her. But that was a few weeks ago. She left me a message a few days ago saying that she was ok. You know how that chile gets when she's mad. She stays to herself until she's ready to talk about it. So I expect to hear from her soon," Moms answered.

"Ok, let me go home and face the music. I'll keep trying Trish to check on her," Simone stood, "Moms, thanks again. Love you." She said as she hugged Maryanne and headed towards the door.

"I love you too, baby. Let me know what you and Kareem decide."

"I will," Simone said as she walked to her car.

Chapter 12

S helly walked into the apartment and kicked off her shoes. She had finally mustered up enough nerve to call Kareem. She'd been rehearsing things to say when she called. She checked the bedroom to make sure Connie was not home. She wasn't ready to discuss the details of her decision with Connie and she didn't feel like being nagged about it. When she saw that Connie was not home, she closed the bedroom door and walked into the kitchen. She closed the bedroom door in case Connie walked into the apartment, she'd go directly to the bedroom thinking Shelly was inside.

Shelly went into the kitchen and picked up the phone. The first thing she did was dial *67 to block her number. Her heart beat faster and faster with every number that she dialed. She prayed that Kareem's cell number was still the same. She was nervous but being able to see her daughter outweighed her nervousness. She dialed the last number and waited as the phone rang.

"Yo?" Kareem answered after four rings. When he didn't get a response, he spoke again in a louder tone, "Hello?"

"Hello...Kareem?" Shelly asked.

"Who dis?" he asked.

"It's Shelly," she said in a shaky voice.

"Shelly? What you want, yo?"

"Kareem, we need to talk. I... ju"

"Yo, don't start with this bullshit again!"

"Kareem, I'm not calling to start anything. I...um...I just wanna see Sabrina. I was wondering wh...what is a good day for me to come and see her?" she stuttered.

41

"You ain't comin' nowhere near my daughter! Is you crazy or something?!" Kareem shouted.

"Kareem, she's my daughter. I have a right to see her."

"You gave up yo rights when you dropped her off on my doorstep!"

Shelly looked at the phone as Kareem had slammed it down in her ear.

"Shit!" Shelly shouted, "Fucking bastard!"

Connie walked into the apartment and heard Shelly shouting from the kitchen. "Who are you calling a bastard?" She asked as she put her purse on the table and sat opposite Shelly.

"Nobody." Shelly walked into the living room.

"Shell, what was that about? Who was that on the phone?" Connie asked.

"It's not important. How was your day?" Shelly asked as she picked up the cordless phone and dialed 1234 then hung up the phone.

"It must be something serious because you standing right in my face dialing a fake number so the last number can't be redialed." Connie was getting impatient.

"Con, just let it go. I don't wanna talk about it right now!"

"Why is everything an argument with you? You could've said that in the first place! But no-you sit here and make yourself look suspicious and guilty." Connie was clearly pissed by now.

"I'm not guilty of shit! And I don't have to explain every little thing I do to you!" Shelly exclaimed.

"I don't ask you to explain every little thing to me. I'm just trying to be here for you! I walked into the apartment and you were shouting and name calling, I figured something was wrong and I tried to help! Now you jumping down my throat like I did something wrong!" Shelly closed her eyes and took a deep breath. She shook her head and grunted. "I tell you what? Forget I said anything," Connie said. She went into the bedroom and slammed the door.

Connie returned from the bedroom twenty minutes later and walked straight through the living room without even looking in Shelly's direction. She walked into the kitchen and grabbed her purse. She mumbled the entire time she was in Shelly's presence. She picked up her car keys from off the key hook next to the door and walked out of the apartment.

Shelly went to the window and watched as Connie walked out of the building. She saw Connie wave at a neighbor and then stop to talk with her. She watched them converse for ten minutes and then watched Connie get into her car and speed off. Shelly saw that the neighbor eyed Connie's ass like she wanted to taste it. Shelly rolled her eyes and went back into the kitchen and fixed herself something to eat.

As she sat at the table eating a cheeseburger, she planned her next move with Kareem. She took a silent vow not to let Kareem or Simone get any rest until she was able to see her daughter. *This ain't over yet!* Shelly thought.

Chapter 13

Simone walked into the apartment and saw Kareem ending a call on his cell phone. She looked at him and sighed. She put her keys and purse on the table and joined him on the sofa.

"Hey," Kareem said. He had a disgusted look on his face.

"Where were you? What's wrong?" she asked.

"Just out doing some thinking," he answered.

"Where's Sabrina?" Simone removed her shoes as she waited for him to answer.

"She's in the crib," he looked at Simone, "so was you ever gonna tell me?" Simone closed her eyes. She knew that the conversation was inevitable and she didn't know what to expect from Kareem.

"I don't even know what to say, where to start," Simone replied.

"Well, you better think of something because I need some answers Simone. Try starting from the beginning." Simone sat on the sofa with her head hung low. She silently prayed that Sabrina would wake up and interrupt their conversation. "Don't sit there and look stupid! What the fuck! Talk!" Kareem yelled.

"Calm down before you wake the baby, Kareem. I know we need to talk. I…I…just…can we…do this in the morning? I'm tired."

"Nah, you can't even get that. So, when did you and Shelly start fucking?" Before Simone walked through the door, Kareem had thought he was calm enough to discuss the situation.

"Ok, the beginning? It all started with Tricia." She looked up at Kareem before she continued.

"What Trish gotta do wit this?" he asked.

"I had my first homo-sexual experience with Tricia. That was why we had the fight before the wedding and that's why she kicked me out of her bridal party." Simone sniffed. Thinking about it made her cry.

"What? You and Trish? How long have y'all been fucking?" He was clearly irate even though he'd known about Tricia for a while.

"No...no baby, it only happened that one time. It wasn't like that. It just happened and before it was over, we were fighting. We were drunk and once she realized I wasn't her man, she snapped."

Kareem looked at his wife in confusion. He was in shock.

"So that's why you kept saying that it was your fault? You pushed up on her?"

"Kareem, look I'm telling you about Trish because you have a right to hear it from me."

"Oh now I have rights? You didn't think I should have found out about Shelly from you?! I had to find out from her little sarcastic ass. It was obvious that she only told me to get back at you. But knowing that doesn't ease the pain or embarrassment!"

"Well I'll be damned. You should know better than anybody how she is. You told me the exact same thing when she told me about you and her. Yeah, I know, it doesn't ease the pain!" Simone was getting upset.

"No, don't try to flip this on me. This is about you and Shelly."

"Yeah, but it was only a me and Shelly because there was a you and Shelly! You want answers? Well so do I! Let's do it!" Simone demanded. "You told me that you were done with her. You said that she didn't mean anything to you. I found out that you and her was in a fucking relationship for over a year! And when I came home from prison, she walks in and drop off y'all daughter? Don't you dare sit here and accuse me of everything-especially when I didn't ask any questions about what you were doing while I was locked up. For all I know, you could have still been fucking her!"

45

"And I didn't ask you any questions about what you were doing while you were inside!"

Simone gasped. She was at a loss for words. She wasn't sure if Kareem knew about her relationship with Tammy and she sure wasn't about to be that honest. "This is bullshit Simone and you know it! So are you gay? Bi-sexual? What the fuck are you?" He shouted. They both got quiet when they heard Sabrina on the monitor.

Simone went to the bedroom and picked her up. She checked to see if she needed changing and as she carried Sabrina to the kitchen to warm a bottle. Kareem was right behind her.

"Answer the fucking question! Are you gay?"

"No Kareem I'm not gay! I'll admit that I was a little curious about women and I got with Shelly. But that was more about getting back at you for constantly cheating on me. And…" she paused, "I wanted to know what the fuck was so special about this girl that you stayed with her for over a year. So we got together. It happened and it's over. You're my husband. You're who I want to spend the rest of my life with." Simone said as she placed Sabrina in her car seat. Once she put the bottle in her mouth, Simone placed Sabrina's hand around the bottle so she could hold it herself. Simone was getting paranoid so she tried to calm down. She didn't want Kareem asking questions about her stay in prison.

Kareem was too upset to say anything about not knowing that Sabrina could hold her own bottle. He smiled on the inside knowing that his daughter played him. "Why didn't you tell me before we got married, Simone? Why would you keep this a secret?"

"Why did you ask me to marry you after you knew all of this? How long have you been holding this in? You were just waiting for a reason to throw this shit in my face?" She asked. "It's obvious that Shelly told you a while ago since you don't have any contact with her now," she smirked, "Or do you?"

"There you go again with that bullshit! I don't need a fucking reason to ask my wife about the bitch she was fucking!"

"The bitch *we* were fucking!" Simone added.

"Simone, you think this shit is a game? You knew about Shelly! It's not like you just picked a random woman, you fucked my chic!"

Simone chuckled and shook her head up and down. She tried to rock Sabrina to sleep. She laid her on her chest and soothed her back. Sabrina saw Kareem and cried for him to pick her up. She reached for him as he paced through the living room.

"She wants you, Kareem," Simone said.

She tried her best to remain calm but Kareem's last comment almost made her snap.

Kareem looked at his daughter and softened up a little. He took her from Simone and rocked her while he continued to pace.

"So she just went from being some bitch you were fucking to being yo chic...wow!" Simone got up from the sofa and headed to the bedroom.

"Nah, don't go nowhere, we ain't done yet," Kareem said. He knew he went too far with his last comment.

"I'm going to take a shower while you put the baby to sleep." Simone said and walked into the bathroom. "Maybe we can discuss this rationally when I come out," she yelled over her shoulder. Kareem's words had stung but she already knew how he and Shelly felt about each other.

* * *

Simone walked into the bedroom forty minutes later and saw Sabrina asleep in her crib. She slipped on a nightshirt and walked into the living room. Kareem was sitting on the sofa drinking a can of beer.

"Kareem, I know we need to finish our conversation but I don't wanna argue anymore. We can get past this." She sat next to her husband and rubbed his hand. They sat in silence for several minutes. "How long have you known about me and Shelly?" Simone asked.

"She told me right before you went to prison. But with everything we were going through, I couldn't really think about that shit," he confessed. Simone was glad that Kareem was calm.

"What made you say anything after all this time? Look at us, we're happily married and life is good for us right now."

"I know," he paused, "I didn't mean for you to ever find out that I knew. I ain't mean to blurt it out like that. I had time to think about us while you were away and I wasn't gonna let my pride keep me from being with you after you done swallowed your pride and took everything I dished out to you. I always knew you was gonna be my wife. I just had to get everything out my system before I settled down. But when Sabrina got here, I had to check myself. I wanted to get married and give you the family you always wanted. You deserve that much from me."

Simone was speechless. She saw the change in Kareem when she first came home. Sabrina made Kareem man-up. She'd longed for him to change for years.

"I hear you, but we need to get one thing straight. I don't appreciate you calling Sabrina your daughter as opposed to our daughter. That hurt, Kareem. I don't care how pissed you are, you are not going to throw in my face that you and Shelly had a baby while we were together. I love Sabrina and it has nothing to do with what happened with me and Shelly. And I'm not going to keep having this conversation every time you get pissed off! Now you know about me and Shelly, I know about you and Shelly-so it is what it is. We can either take it or leave it!" Simone stated.

"You're right. I'm sorry about saying that. I just got so pissed about you going back to work that I wanted you to be pissed too."

"Yeah, and about me going back to work," Simone began.

"I'm ok with it. Just ask Moms and see if she'll agree. I was trippin to even ask you to stay home with her all this time. I'm glad you are getting your job back. I know how hard it is for a person to get a job once they have a conviction. Congratulations, baby. And I'm not sure if I ever apologized for everything I put you through but I'm sorry baby. I love you." He leaned over and kissed her on the mouth.

"Thanks, I love you too, and Moms said yes," Simone smiled. They sat in each other's arms and talked for a few more hours before going to bed.

Chapter 14

Shelly sat at her desk and searched the internet for child custody lawyers. She was a paralegal and was done for the day. Her boss was already gone so Shelly decided to do her search at the office so Connie wouldn't suspect anything. Shelly found a lawyer not too far from her job and scribbled down the number. She could have easily gotten a recommendation from her boss but she didn't want anyone to know what she was planning. She would call Mrs. Sylvan in the morning to set up a meeting.

Shelly opened her cell and dialed Kareem's number. The phone rang a few times and then went to voicemail. Shelly listened to the message and waited for the beep. *'Kareem it's Shelly. I just wanna see my daughter. I'm going to call you back in an hour, please answer the phone. Let's not make this complicated.'* She closed her phone and shut down her computer. She straightened off her desk before she closed the office for the night.

An hour later...

Shelly sat at the bar and sipped on her apple martini. She looked at her watch and opened her cell phone again. She dialed the number and waited for an answer. Kareem answered on the first ring.

'Who dis? Please, you know exactly who this is. I'm really trying to be nice. All I wanna do is see Sabrina. Can you meet me face to face so we can work out some details? I'm in the

50

bar of the Sheraton at the airport. It'll be in your best interest to meet me here within the hour.' Click.

Shelly hung up her phone. She ordered another apple martini and waited. She'd drank four drinks when she looked at her watch and saw that it was two hours later. Shelly smiled and opened her cell phone. She sent a text message to Kareem:

OK. THIS HOW U WANNA DO IT? NO PROB!

Shelly knew that she would have to deal with Connie when she got home. She shook her head and called Connie's cell phone and waited for her to answer. *"Hey Con, where are you? I've been waiting here for two hours. I'm still at the Sheraton.*

Shelly had to play it off like she told Connie to meet her there. She knew Connie would believe that story. All she had to do was add the finishing touches when Connie arrived at the bar. She gathered her belongings and went to use the restroom. When she came out of the bathroom, she took a seat at one of the tables and waited for Connie to arrive.

As Shelly checked her text message, a waiter brought her a drink. He told her that it was from a gentleman on the other side of the room. Shelly smiled and held the glass towards the man. She sipped her drink and smirked at the message she received from Kareem:

IN THE MIDDLE OF SOMETHING CALL ME TOMORROW.

She knew she'd gotten his attention.

Connie walked inside the bar and Shelly waved her over to the table. Connie removed her jacket and sat across from Shelly. "You didn't tell me that we were meeting for drinks, Shell."

"I know. I was getting ready to call you at one point during the day but we got busy and it slipped my mind. I totally forgot. It wasn't until after we were off the phone that I realized that I must've forgotten to call. I'm so sorry." She kissed Connie's hand. "What are you drinking?" Shelly asked as she stood to walk to the bar.

"Just get me a Long Island Iced Tea," Connie said.

"Ohh, looks like someone wants to get freaky tonight. I know how you get when you're drunk," Shelly smiled. She walked over to the bar and ordered the drinks. The gentleman who'd sent her a drink approached her and made small talk. Shelly quickly told the man that she was involved and thanked him again for the drink. Shelly made eye contact with Connie while she waited for the drinks. Connie licked her lips and winked at her. She crossed her legs to reveal a little thigh. Shelly shook her head and smiled. She looked forward to going home tonight.

Chapter 15

K areem looked at his phone and sent the call to voicemail. He didn't feel like being bothered with Shelly. She'd been texting him for the past three days when he stood her up at the bar. He was on his way home and he didn't want to bring any drama. He and Simone were still working through their problems. Kareem parked his car in back of the building's parking lot and sat staring in space. He was pissed that Shelly told him about her and Simone. Ever since she told him, he wondered if Simone was really into women or if she was just involved with Shelly to get back at him. And when Simone told him about her and Trish, his mind began racing again.

Kareem leaned his head against the headrest and closed his eyes. He thought about Shelly's messages and sighed. He knew how spiteful Shelly could be so he knew he had to deal with her before Simone found out. He was all prepared to tell Simone about the call when she came home that night but his jealousy wouldn't allow him to give Simone a reason to have any contact with Shelly.

Kareem shook his head again because he couldn't figure out why he was so mad. He and Simone were married and he knew he loved her with all his heart. He just felt bad because he wasn't sure if he was more upset that Simone had an affair with a woman or that she had an affair with his woman.

Kareem rolled up his window and turned off the car. He got out of the car and walked to the front of the building. He unlocked the door and walked up the flight of steps that led to their apartment. When he walked through the door, the lights were out so he called out for Simone. As he searched the apartment, his phone vibrated. He saw a note on the bed. Simone had taken Sabrina to the mall. Kareem read the text message:

IM GONNA CALL U IN TEN MIN PIK UP THE PHONE!

Kareem grabbed a can of beer from the fridge and turned on the T.V. He watched Sports Center until his phone rang. He saw the blocked number and answered his phone, *"Yo, what you want?*

"I wanna talk about my daughter," Shelly said.

"I ain't gonna talk about dis ova the phone."

"Well meet me, then."

"Where you at?" he asked

"I'm at the bar of the Sheraton by the airport."

"Aiight gimme 'bout half an hour I'll meet you there." Kareem closed his phone, grabbed his car keys and headed back out the door.

* * *

Kareem pulled into the Sheraton and found a parking space in the front of the hotel parking lot. He walked inside and asked to be directed to the bar. Shelly spotted him as soon as he walked in and waved him to her table.

"Hey," Kareem said.

"Hi Kareem," Shelly smiled and gestured for him to have a seat. Kareem pulled out the chair and sat down across from her.

"Look, I'm not here to play games with you! What you want? And why you keep calling my phone this many times?" Kareem looked at Shelly.

"Well it's nice to see you too," Shelly said, "I tried to be nice Kareem, I only wanted to see my daughter. You act like I'm asking for something I'm not entitled to."

"Shelly, do you really think that I'm gonna let you come anywhere near her? You just dropped her off on our doorstep and left. You didn't leave a number or anything. You wasn't ready to be a mother and now you think you can just pop up anytime you want? Nah, I don't think so!" Kareem shouted. He looked around as people were staring at him because of his tone. Shelly looked at him and rolled her eyes. She sipped her Martini and looked up at Kareem.

"Kareem, I know how I left was fucked up. It's not like I'm coming back to get her. I only want to see her and spend a little bit of time with her. I want her to know her mother."

"She knows her mother!" Kareem stated.

"I know you didn't just say that. Simone is not Sabrina's mother! I am! I gave birth to her. We made that baby and Simone had nothing to do with it. No, I wasn't ready to be a mother when I dropped her off but I left her with her father and a woman that I knew would take good care of her. Don't make me take this to another level!" She exploded.

"Am I supposed to be scared?" Kareem asked.

"Kareem, I didn't ask you here to argue with you." Shelly softened her tone before she spoke again. She grabbed his hand and rubbed the back of it. "Kareem, we used to be friends…I"

"Yeah and my friends wouldn't fuck with my wife," Kareem growled.

"She wasn't your wife at the time. Is that what this is about? That why you're being so mean?" Shelly asked.

Kareem held up his hand to a waitress and ordered a shot of Hennesy and a Corona. He slid his hand over his face. He looked at Shelly and shook his head. He was always weak in her presence. She was still the beauty he fell in love with. He closed his eyes for a minute to shake the image of him bending her over and fucking her doggy style.

"Why would you fuck with Simone? Of all the females in the world, why her?" Kareem asked. He'd tried to convince himself not to mention it but once again, his male ego prevailed.

"Why are you bringing up old shit? When I told you about me and Simone, you said you didn't give a fuck and now almost a year later you trippin'? Why?"

"I just need to know what the fuck y'all call y'allselves doing." The waitress brought Kareem his drinks. Kareem touched her arm while he downed the shot and placed the glass back on her tray.

"What difference does it make now? Simone is your wife. I don't mean anything to you anymore. You made that perfectly clear the last time we were together," Shelly flirted. Kareem had that look in his eyes and she wanted to see just how far she could go with him.

"That was because you was getting too serious, Shelly. You knew about Simone from the get go. All of a sudden, you got brand new on me," he said.

"What was I supposed to do? We spent a lot of time together. You damn near spent more time with me than you did with her. And we both know the sex was the bomb! We never had a problem in that department." She licked her lips. She saw the lust in Kareem's eyes as she spoke. "But, like I said, you made it clear that you didn't want to have anything to do with me."

"So that's why you got with Simone? Because I wouldn't leave her for you?" Kareem asked as he slid his hand in between his legs to try and control his erection.

"No, Simone and I just happened. I did befriend her so that I could tell her all about us. I wanted to hurt her just like you hurt me. But she was too nice for that. Look, Kareem, I don't wanna talk about Simone. I want to see my daughter." Shelly knew she had Kareem lusting. She rubbed her fingertips up and down his arm. When he didn't pull away, she slid her chair closer to him and kicked off her shoe. Shelly slid her foot up his leg and found his soldier at attention. "Wow, glad to know I still have that affect on you." Kareem pushed her foot away and pulled back from the table. He looked at Shelly and shook his head.

"I see some things never change, huh? You think you slick," he said.

"I'm not trying to be slick. I'm willing to do anything to see my daughter," she said as she slid her tongue across her top lip. Kareem smiled. He wanted to take Shelly into the bathroom and fuck her right on the spot but he thought about his wife and daughter and ignored the throbbing between his legs. He was going home to make love to his wife.

"I gotta go, yo." He stood to leave.

"Kareem, just think about it. Simone doesn't even have to know. We could meet somewhere…just so I could see Sabrina."

"Nah, I don't want Sabrina all confused and shit."

"Confused? Ok, you really think you can just stop me from seeing her? How about I just see you in court?" She stood to leave. Kareem didn't want Simone to know anything about him meeting Shelly or that she wanted to see the baby. He thought about how much drama Shelly would bring and called her back.

"Wait Shelly, I'll think about it. Call me in about a week."

"A week? I'll be calling you in two days!" She walked up to Kareem and whispered in his ear, "I hope you not trying to play games because I'm serious about going to court." She gently bit his earlobe and walked away.

Kareem stood there with his hands in his pockets. He went into the bathroom and washed his hands. Kareem loved Simone and wanted to be faithful. But he didn't know how long he'd be able to be around Shelly and resist temptation. He knew he could not go home with a hard dick so he sat back at the table and had a few more drinks. Simone would think nothing of his erection as long as she smelled the alcohol on his breath.

Chapter 16

Simone made sure Sabrina was strapped in her stroller and began walking towards Baby Gap. She went into the store and picked up three outfits that she liked. After she paid for the items, she went to The Limited Too and grabbed a few more outfits and then she headed towards the food court. She went to Blimpies and ordered a sandwich. Simone gathered her belongings and found a table on the outer part of the food court. She sat down and reached into the baby bag to get Sabrina's food. Simone poured the jars of food into a bowl and fed Sabrina as she attempted to take bites of her sandwich in between feeding the baby. She gave Sabrina a bottle of juice and ate the rest of her sandwich.

When Simone finished eating, she reached inside the bags and looked at the clothes she'd just purchased. She reached into the bottom of the bags and took out the receipts and stuck them in her purse. Then she put all of the clothes in one bag so she would have less to carry.

Simone wanted to get Sabrina a pair of shoes before she left the store. She gathered her things and pushed Sabrina to the next store. Sabrina was crying to get out of the stroller. She was sleepy and wanted her mother to carry her. Simone took Sabrina out of the stroller and put all the bags inside while she carried her daughter. Sabrina lay on Simone's chest and played with her hair. Simone almost regretted letting her hair grow out. It now hung down to her shoulders and Sabrina uses it as a way to put herself to sleep.

Simone walked past ladies footlocker and spotted the Pastry sign and went into the store. She bought a pair of Pastry's

Women Fab Cookie (precious style) sneakers for herself. As she was leaving the store, she saw a toddler cake runner strawberry sprinkles by Pastry and asked if she could get Sabrina's foot measured. Sabrina's foot was an inch shorter than the smallest size. Simone loved the sneaker so much that she brought it and told herself that Sabrina would be able to fit them in a few months.

Sabrina had fallen asleep on Simone's shoulder. Simone removed the bags from the stroller and placed her daughter inside. She was tired so she decided to get Sabrina's walking shoes next time. She just wanted to get home and put Sabrina to bed. On her way to the exit door, she dropped a bag. Her hands were full so she kicked the bag to the wall so she could bend down to pick it up. Just as she was putting the brakes on the stroller, a woman bent in front of her and picked up the bag.

"Thank you so much," Simone smiled.

"You're welcome." The stranger replied. Just as she handed Simone the bag, a man called out her name. The woman smiled at Simone and turned around and waved at the man, "I'm over here, baby."

Simone's eyes followed the woman's and landed on the man she was waving over. She was speechless as the man walked towards her and smiled.

"Well hello Simone. How are you?" Tarik smiled.

"Tarik?" Simone asked as she looked around expecting to see Trish walking towards them. "Hey," she paused, "how are you?" She hesitated.

"I'm good," he said as he held his arms out for a hug. "Is that Sabrina? Wow, she's getting big," he smiled. Simone turned and looked at the woman standing next to him.

"I'm sorry. Simone, this is Tashi Gray, Tash, this is Simone. Simone's an old friend. And this is her sleeping beauty, Sabrina," he smiled. "Simone, she is beautiful. I can't believe she's so big. How old is she now?" he asked.

"She's nine months. Hello Tashi, nice to meet you. How have you been, Tarik?" She asked as she sneakily nodded her head towards Tashi.

"I've been good, how is Kareem?" Tarik asked.

"He's been working like a slave but he's good," Simone said.

"Tell him to call me. We can still kick it every now and then, right?" he smiled.

"I will definitely pass the message." She stood staring at him awkwardly.

"Well, we need to get going. It was great seeing you, Simone. Kiss Sabrina for me," He said as he kissed Simone on the cheek.

"It was good to see you too. Take care, Tarik." She returned the hug and kiss. "Nice meeting you Tashi," Simone said as she avoided eye contact by busying herself with Sabrina.

"Do you need some help getting to the car?" Tarik asked.

"No, we'll be fine. I'm right out front. But thanks." She said as she watched Tashi grab Tarik's hand and pull him towards Victoria's Secret.

Simone went to her car and packed Sabrina and the bags and then headed home. She thought about how she was going to tell Tricia that her husband has moved on.

Chapter 17

Connie tossed and turned until she heard Shelly come into the apartment. She turned on the light as Shelly walked into the bedroom.

"Shelly, it's after midnight, where have you been?" Connie asked.

"I know how to tell time, Con. I was out having a drink. I had a long day at work and I just wanted to unwind and relax a little. Damn!"

"On a weekday? Would it have killed you to at least call and let me know that you're ok? Especially if you were going to turn off your phone."

"I'm sorry Connie. I just wanted to spend a little time alone. I didn't mean to make you worry." Shelly didn't want to argue. She removed her clothes and went into the bathroom to take a shower. "You comin?" She yelled back at Connie.

"No, I took my shower three hours ago! Goodnight!" Shelly went over to the nightstand and grabbed a dildo out of their goodie bag. She turned on the vibrator to make sure the batteries were good. Once she heard the strong vibrations, she turned towards Connie, "Goodnight to you, too."

* * *

Connie was awake and was dressed bright and early. She couldn't sleep a bit. She wanted to talk to Shelly but she knew that it would only lead to an argument. She prepared breakfast for herself and sat at the table to eat. Shelly walked in the kitchen and lifted the lid to the frying pan. "Where's mine?"

Connie looked up at Shelly and wrinkled her forehead.

"I only made enough for me. You should still be full from last night. I'm sure the least you got was dinner."

"Whatever Connie, I ain't got time for this shit. I'll pick up something on my way to work." Shelly rolled her eyes and walked out of the apartment. Connie finished eating and cleaned up her mess. She walked out of the apartment half an hour after Shelly.

Chapter 18

S imone reached for the phone as she assisted Sabrina to walk across the living room. Sabrina was trying to walk on her own and Simone was trying to keep her from falling. Simone dialed Tricia's number and waited for her to answer.

"Hey Simone, what's up girl?" Trish asked.

"How you doin' Trish? Are you busy?"

"Nah, just finishing up a load of laundry. Why? What's up?"

"Umm...you feel like coming over? Sabrina is getting ready to take a nap and I don't wanna bring her out right now," Simone said.

"I gotta work in the morning. You need something?" Tricia asked.

"I just wanted to catch up and I have something to tell you...Sabrina no!" Simone dropped the phone in time to catch Sabrina from pulling down the glass coffee table. Simone carried Sabrina to the phone and sat on the sofa. "I'm sorry Trish, this girl is so busy. She thinks she can walk now and she won't sit still," Simone said.

"Is she ok?" Trish asked.

"She's ok. I'm getting ready to feed her and put her butt to sleep. Will you be able to drop by?" Simone asked.

"Simone, I really don't feel like coming out today. Can we do this tomorrow when I get off?" Tricia asked.

"Trish, I know it's short notice but you really want to hear what I have to tell you," she paused, "I guess it could wait until tomorrow. I gotta put this girl to sleep. Call me tomorrow."

"Ok now you have my attention. I'll be there in half an hour." Tricia said before she hung up the phone.

Simone hung up the phone and carried her daughter to the kitchen and sat her in her high chair. She grabbed the jars of food while Sabrina banged on her chair.

Simone had just fed Sabrina the last spoonful of food when Tricia called and asked her to open the door. Simone carried her daughter to the door and let Trish into the apartment. Sabrina began to whine to get down. She tried to slide out of her mother's arms.

"Ooh, look at my big girl. What's wrong Brina?" Tricia cooed.

"Here, go to your Godmother." Simone handed the baby to Trish and walked to the sofa.

"Hi Boo-Boo, hey little mama." Trish cooed. Sabrina smiled and got excited as Trish stroked her ego. She grabbed Tricia's ponytail and laid her head on her shoulder.

"Be careful, she'll pull your hair until she goes to sleep," Simone said.

"That's ok, my Boo-Boo can do whatever she wants. Gimme a kiss Mama." Sabrina popped her head up and smiled as she kissed Tricia on the lips. "Oh, that's a big girl. Thank you," Tricia sang. Tricia positioned herself on the sofa so she could face Simone. "Hey girl, how you been?"

"I've been okay," Simone dragged the last word.

"What's up? Why did I have to get over here on a weeknight?" Tricia asked as she rocked Sabrina to sleep.

Simone exhaled and looked at her friend. "Trish, what's up with you and Tarik?"

"I know you didn't get me over here to talk about me and Tarik? I told you before that me and Tarik are done! He still hasn't signed the divorce papers but he has stopped bothering me. So I'll take that any day," Tricia said.

"Are you sure you don't wanna try and work it out? A divorce is so final," Simone added.

"Well that's the point. To finalize our marriage! I just don't trust him," Tricia said.

"You think you'll ever be able to trust him again? I mean, would you want to keep the lines of communication open for reconciliation?" Simone asked.

"Simone, why are you still pushing the issue with me and Tarik? What's up for real?" Tricia was clearly agitated.

"Well, I took Sabrina to the mall last night and I saw Tarik."

"And what? He asked you to talk to me about getting back together?" Tricia assumed.

"No, not exactly," Simone paused, "he kinda introduced me to his girlfriend," she hesitated.

"His what?!" Tricia yelled.

"Well, he didn't really say she was his girlfriend but the way this chic was hugged up all over him, it was obvious that she was something to him."

Tricia stared at Simone. She couldn't believe what she'd just heard. She held her head down and tried to digest what Simone just told her. She was speechless for a few minutes. It seemed like hours before she was able to speak.

"Well, I'm glad he's moved on. He...I...I told...him that...we were...ov...over." Her lips trembled.

Simone stood and took the sleeping Sabrina to her playpen. She laid her on her back and walked over to Trish.

"I'm so sorry Trish. I didn't know how to tell you so I wanted to make sure that you were sure about ending your marriage."

"It ain't even been a year yet! Just a few months ago, he was all in my face trying to get back together and now he's fucking somebody else! That bastard!" Tricia exploded. Simone rubbed her back and let her vent. Tricia cried and cried and continued to call Tarik every name under the sun. Simone got up and grabbed two bottles of water from the fridge and passed one to Trish.

"Trish, it's ok if you want him back. He's still your husband. How long are you gonna make him suffer? Don't you think it's been long enough?" Simone asked.

"I'm not trying to make Tarik suffer. He's the one who fucked up! I'm trying to put my life back together without him!" Tricia sniffled.

"Tricia, I thought you said that you've taken responsibility for your part in the break-up. You just sat here and blamed everything on him. If you're ever gonna get your husband back, you need to re-evaluate yourself and start there." Simone added. She didn't want to say anything but she was getting tired of Trish acting like she didn't do anything wrong.

"Simone, here you go acting like you know everything just because Kareem finally married you! You know, I'm happy that you finally got the husband and family that you've always wanted but don't forget what you had to go through to get it. I'm not like you, I can't put up with my man sleeping with other women every chance he get and keep on forgiving him! I can't be with someone I can't trust!" Tricia exploded.

Simone didn't say anything because she knew Tricia was hurting. She sat there and took everything her friend dished out. She bit down on her tongue as hard as she could to keep from saying anything. Tricia put her head in her hands and cried her tears. She sniffed and sobbed until she heard Kareem's key turn the doorknob. She looked up as Simone walked to the door.

"Hey." Kareem said and looked at Tricia.

"Hi Kareem, I was just on my way out," Tricia sniffed.

"Trish, you don't have to go. Stay a little longer, at least until you feel better," Simone urged.

"Everything ok?" Kareem asked suspiciously.

"Yeah, we're fine, babe. Just give us a minute?" Simone asked.

"Simone, I really have to go. I have to work in the morning and it's getting late. I'll call you later." Tricia walked to the door. She smiled at Simone and waved goodbye to Kareem before she left the apartment.

"What was that all about?" Kareem asked as he headed to the kitchen.

"I told her that I saw Tarik in the mall with his new girlfriend. And she's jealous but trying to act like she's over him," Simone said.

"Wow, Tarik got a girl?" Kareem smiled.

"It's not funny, Kareem. He still loves Trish."

"Well, it's her fault! How long did she expect him to wait? A brutha got needs." He said as he rubbed between his legs.

"Yeah, I know a brutha got needs and I wanted to tell Trish so bad that it's her own fault but she ain't trying to hear none of that. I don't know what her problem is but she gonna mess around and lose Tarik to the next woman. And this chic looks like she's playing for keeps." Simone stretched her arms over her head.

"Word? What's she like?" Kareem asked.

"She looks about ten years younger than us. She's skinny with a long weave," she paused, "Oh yeah Tarik told me to tell you to call him. He said he wanted to hang out or something. I think he's feeling like we all turned our backs on him just because he and Trish broke up."

"Yeah, I'll give him a call one day this week." Kareem went to the playpen and looked at Sabrina. He turned to Simone before he headed to the bedroom, "Did Poopy walk today?"

"No but she almost pulled the coffee table down. She tried to pull herself up and I caught the table just in time. Kareem, this girl is too much. I think she's been here before."

They looked at each other with raised eyebrows.

"I'm tired as hell. You want me to take her to the crib now or are you gonna bring her?" he asked.

"You can take her, that girl is getting heavy. I'll be in there in a few," Simone said. As soon as Kareem was out of eyesight, she called Tricia's cell. She got the voicemail and hung up. Simone joined her husband and daughter in the bedroom.

Chapter 19

Connie walked into the lobby of the Sheraton Hotel. She took a seat at the bar and ordered a frozen margarita. She looked around and saw how empty the bar was. The waitress stopped at a few gentlemen on the end before she sashayed over and slid the drink in front of Connie. Connie handed her a ten dollar bill and smiled.

"That's ok sweetie, this one's on the gentleman." The waitress said as she slid the money back and looked in the direction of the man. Connie followed her eyes and nodded at the man as she raised her glass and sipped her drink. She reached into her purse and handed the waitress two single dollar bills. The waitress smiled and walked towards another customer.

"Excuse me, mind if I join you?" The man asked.

"Sure, have a seat," Connie said.

"I'm Joseph." He extended his hand for a shake.

"I'm Constance McMillan, but everyone calls me Connie, nice to meet you," she said as she reached and shook his hand. Connie began fidgeting with her napkin. She felt an instant attraction to this stranger. She was nervous because she doesn't remember ever feeling anything for any man. She took another sip from her drink and twirled the straw around the glass for lack of anything better to do. She reached for her cell phone and checked to see if she received any text messages. She sighed and put the phone in her purse.

"Waiting on someone?" Joseph asked.

"No, I'm alone tonight; just came out to clear my head," Connie responded.

"So you're not meeting your sister tonight?"

"Excuse me?" She was confused and a little startled.
"I remember seeing you here with your sister a while ago." Joseph said. He remembered sending a drink to the other woman before Connie arrived that night.
"Ok, Joseph, you're scaring me." She grabbed her drink and attempted to leave the bar."
"No, I'm sorry. I'm the hotel's day manager and I sometimes sit in the back over there and finish my paperwork before I go home. I'm not a stalker," he smiled and adjusted his jacket so that she could see his name tag.
Connie relaxed a little and smiled, "I didn't mean to offend you but you can't be too sure these days."
"No don't apologize. I understand completely. I should have properly introduced myself. My apologies to you." He said with his right hand on his chest. Connie could tell that he was trying to impress her. Little did he know, he didn't have to do or say anything else because she was already impressed. He could tell that Connie was still a little nervous but he decided to continue the conversation and see where it went. "So, no sister tonight?" He asked again.
"No, just me. And she's not my sister, she's my friend." Connie knew he was talking about Shelly because that was the only time she'd ever been in that bar.
"Oh, wow, you two resemble a lot. You look like you could be related," he smiled.
Connie sipped her drink and smiled as well. She peeked over her glass and did a quick scan of Joseph to put in her mental rolodex. He looked to be in his early forty's. He was about five ten and medium built. His hair was balding on top but he had speckles of gray on the sides. That, combined with his chocolate skin, made him extremely sexy to her. She closed her eyes as she memorized all of his features. He wore expensive suit and shoes. Connie assumed he was old school when she got a whiff of his cool water cologne.
"So Constance, what brings you out alone on a Wednesday night?" Joseph asked.
"I'm having a rough week and I really needed a drink," she smiled.

"I hear that. So... can I buy you another?" he offered.

"Don't get yourself in trouble by spending all of your money tonight," she flirted, "I'll buy the next round."

Joseph grinned and flashed all of his teeth. "I'm the manager, remember? I have a little bit of pull around here."

"Well in that case, I'd love another one of these margaritas. I was just looking out for you. I don't want you to go home broke and have to explain why," she winked.

"No, I'm not married nor am I seeing anyone special," he winked back.

Connie didn't realize that her flirts were so obvious. She didn't know what she was doing. This was way out of character for her. She was strictly into women but there was something about this man that made her feel bold and beautiful. She figured nothing would come of it and she'd tell him she was gay before she left the bar. She missed the attention of someone wanting her and Joseph looked at her like he wanted to eat her whole. She felt sexy and alive again. "Ok, well I was just looking out for you," she said as the waitress brought over a round of drinks.

"So, what about you? Are you married?" Joseph asked.

"I'm not married. But I'm not single either," she answered.

"Seeing someone? Dating? In love? Care to elaborate?" he chuckled.

"I'm in the middle of something," she paused, "I just don't know what to call it today." She looked down and stirred her new drink. Joseph contemplated how to proceed after her last comment. Connie was in a situation but obviously she was having problems and she was flirting like she was single. He decided to keep it simple and engage in small talk. If she wanted to volunteer information, that was fine with him. She interrupted his thoughts by clearing her throat.

"So why haven't anyone snatched you up yet? Are you gay?" Connie asked.

"Why do most women assume men are gay if they aren't in a relationship? I could ask if you're gay because you're not married either," he smiled.

"And my answer would be yes," she said with a raised eyebrow. She learned a long time ago that that was a good way to inform men that she was gay and most of the time, it played out just as it did with Joseph.

"I never would've guessed." On the outside, Joseph acted like he wasn't phased at Connie's comment but inside he was ecstatic. Like most men, he was sure that he had a shot with her since he didn't have to compete with another man. Just then, he knew how he was going to proceed with Connie. He looked at her skeptical before he spoke, "Is this your way of telling me that you don't want to be bothered?" he smiled.

"No, I am gay. I've been gay for as long as I can remember," Connie said.

"Well that can't be too long. What are you about twenty four?"

"Nice! But no, I'm thirty five," Connie laughed.

Joseph was taken aback. He really thought Connie was in her mid-twenty's. She was a beauty. He adored her eyes. They were a deep blue which complimented her peanut butter complexion to a tee. She had a luscious body with an incredible ass. She wore a skirt that showed the sexist thighs that he'd ever seen. He noticed her when she was there the last time. He was in a meeting when she arrived. He'd just sent a drink to the woman she met so he didn't approach her. He promised himself that if he ever saw her again, he'd introduce himself. She was a bit sexier than her friend.

"Wow, you go girl! You look amazing," Joseph said.

"Thanks," Connie blushed, "So did my confession make you not want to continue our conversation?" she asked.

"No, why would it?"

"Well, most men begin to talk about how much of a waste I am and that if I had the right man, I'd be strictly dickly," her eyes popped out, "oops, excuse my language," she laughed. She was clearly tipsy.

"I guess you meet a lot of boys, huh?" Joseph asked.

"I guess so." She looked at him and smiled.

"So, your friend that I saw you with? Is she…?"

"She's my lover and we were serious until recently. Well we are serious but just having a rough patch."

Joseph frowned. He's been seeing Connie's friend in the bar the past two Thursday nights with a man. If Connie wouldn't have told him that the woman was gay, he'd swear that the two were a couple. He gathered his composure and sipped his rum and coke. "Well, you've got good taste. She's beautiful as well."

Connie shook her head and smiled. She pulled out her phone and sent a call to voice mail. She and Joseph sat and talked for another hour. She felt more relaxed after their conversation.

"Joseph, it was a pleasure meeting you. And thanks for the drinks. You really helped a sista out tonight. I feel much better." She pushed the empty coffee cup aside.

"I'm glad I could help. Feel free to use me again if you just want to chill and get your buzz on," he smiled.

"I wasn't using you. I really had a nice time."

"We should keep in touch in case you're having another night like this. I'm a very good listener-as you can see." Connie tilted her head to the side and was getting ready to object. "Take my number just in case?" Joseph pleaded.

Connie pulled out her cell phone and asked him to recite his number. She dialed the number as he recited and made sure that he locked her number into his phone as well. It had been years since she exchanged numbers with a man. She leaned over and kissed Joseph on the cheek. Connie wasn't sure what she was doing but she did it anyway.

"Let me walk you to your car," Joseph insisted. They walked into the lot and Connie led him to her car. He closed the door as she got behind the wheel. "Have a good night. And remember, call me if you need me," he winked.

Connie smiled and sped out of the parking lot. She somehow thought that Joseph would be able to see her wet panties.

Chapter 20

Simone was preparing Sabrina's bag. She was returning to work in the morning so Moms suggested that Sabrina come to her house for a few hours to get used to being around new faces. Simone reached for Sabrina's food and packed it in the bag. She also grabbed a bottle of apple juice and Sabrina's cup from the fridge. She went into the living room to pack diapers and saw that Sabrina was trying to climb out of the playpen.

"Kareem, would you come in here and get her! I'm trying to pack her bag so I can take her to Moms before I start dinner."

"What you yelling for? I didn't know she was up. She was just sleep a few minutes ago." He walked in and took her out of the playpen.

"Why didn't you take her in there with you? You know she don't stay sleep long. If she would've fell and bust her face you would have been pissed!" Simone frowned.

"Simone, why you gotta yell? It's not that serious! I got her."

"I need a little help, Kareem. I'm busting my ass trying to get everything together so I can get back here and start dinner and go back to pick her up before it gets late."

"If you needed help you should've just said something. I have somewhere to go anyway. I can drop her off and pick her up from Moms' house. That way, we don't have to go back out after dinner."

"I didn't know you were going out. I was trying to get a little alone time in while she was gone. I thought maybe we could officially celebrate my going back to work." Simone licked his neck.

73

"Well I'm not going to work in the morning. I got my man to cover my shift but I gotta do him a favor tonight," he said.

"Why are you taking off tomorrow?" Simone asked.

"Because you're going back to work and this will be Sabrina's first day away from both of us and I wanted to be here in case Moms needed help. I'll take her over in the morning, too. That way I can spend a little time with her before I drop her off. You almost done with her bag?"

Simone nodded her head yes so Kareem started putting on Sabrina's coat. He packed her in the car seat and grabbed the bag from Simone. He kissed his wife on the lips before he headed out the door. "We'll be back in a few hours."

"Tell Moms to call me if she needs anything," Simone yelled.

"And I thought I was going to have the problem letting go. Moms will be fine. She has both our numbers," Kareem said.

* * *

Kareem dropped Sabrina off at Moms' house and sat for about fifteen minutes until Sabrina warmed up to Moms. He felt his phone vibrate and told Moms that he had to leave. He told her that he'd be back in a few hours but she could call him if she needed him before then.

Kareem pulled into the Sheraton and met Shelly at their usual table. She greeted him with a smile. "I already ordered your drink."

"Cool," he replied. "So, what's up?"

"You tell me? Are you gonna let me see my baby or not?" Shelly asked.

"I don't know, Shelly. I didn't get a chance to talk to Simone about it yet. We've been busy wit' something else."

"I'll be honest with you, Kareem. I've already seen a lawyer and he told me my rights. We could do this in front of a judge or we can do this my way," Shelly said.

Kareem swallowed his drink and shook his head. He was stuck between a rock and a hard place. He talked to his lawyer as well and he knew that Shelly did have rights to Sabrina. The last thing he wanted was to get into a custody battle or court ordered visitations. He took a deep breath and looked at Shelly. "I don't wanna proceed but I do have rights, Kareem."

Kareem didn't know what to say. Shelly had him right where she wanted him. He thought about telling Simone when he got home but he didn't want to ruin her first day back at work. He knew she'd think he was trying to get her to stay home by springing this on her the night before she was to report to her office. He sighed again and against his better judgment he looked Shelly in the eyes. "Shelly, let me see what I can do."

"Stop stalling, Kareem. I want to see Sabrina one day this week."

"I ain't stalling. I'm just thinking about what's best for my daughter and my wife. You like running ya mouth and you already tried to fuck up my shit before."

"Kareem please, ain't nobody thinking about you. The only way your shit will get fucked up is if you cross me." She looked at him seductively. "I ain't got nothing but love for you baby."

"Yeah right. I'm out, I got shit to do." He pushed his chair from the table.

Shelly leaned forward and exposed her 38 D's. She tilted her head to the side and smiled. "What? You like what you see?"

"That's that bullshit!" Kareem said as his eyes never left her breasts.

"Can't you just stay until I finish my drink so that you could walk me to my car?"

Kareem seemed to be mesmerized by her breasts. He agreed and sat back in his chair. He didn't want Shelly to see his soldier trying to bust a hole in his pants. He signaled the waitress to bring him another round.

Shelly continued to entice Kareem. She made sure her breasts stayed on the table so he couldn't help but stare at them. Every now and then, she would rub her hand across her nipple to make it erect.

Once she had his undivided attention, she changed the conversation to her daughter. She asked Kareem all kinds of questions about how Sabrina reacted when she first came to live with him and Simone. She asked him how old Sabrina was when she started teething, if she could walk and if she was talking. Kareem answered her questions without revealing too much personal information. Every time Shelly asked about the kind of mother Simone is, he avoided the question and kept it on Sabrina.

"Kareem, do you have a picture of her?" Shelly asked. Kareem dug into his wallet and pulled out two photos of Sabrina.

"Wow, she looks just like us. She has my complexion and nose. But she has your everything else," Shelly beamed as she passed the photos back to Kareem.

"Here, you can have this one." Kareem gave her the photo of Sabrina at three months old.

"Thanks, this means a lot to me," she smiled.

"Look I really gotta go. Are you ready?" he asked.

"Yep, just let me finish this." She took the shot glass and turned it up to her mouth. She put her lips around the entire glass as she looked directly in Kareem's eyes. Once the glass was empty, she licked the rim of the glass and then she licked her lips. "All ready," she teased.

Shelly walked ahead of Kareem. She stopped at the bar and paid her tab. Shelly winked at the man who'd brought her a drink a few weeks ago. He smiled and shook his head. Kareem followed her out the door.

Once they were in front of her car, Shelly turned around and hugged Kareem. She made sure her breasts were touching his chest. She slid her hand between his legs after his dick tapped her on the thigh. She kissed his neck and licked his earlobe.

"Looks like someone wants to come out and play," she smiled, "let me drive you to your car."

"I'm right over there," he pointed to his left.

"No problem, get in." Shelly let go of his hand and opened her car doors. Kareem reluctantly got in the car and Shelly drove to the back of the hotel by the garbage dumpsters. She put her car in park and turned the lights off.

"How about I help you out for helping me out?" She reached over and massaged his dick. Kareem was helpless. The throbbing between his legs was unbearable. He wanted to get out of the car but he couldn't move. Shelly turned the radio up just in time to hear R. Kelly's voice, '*My mind's telling me no. But my body's telling me yes.*'

Before Kareem could protest, Shelly had unzipped his pants and found the opening of his boxers. She bobbed her head up and down and expertly blew his mind. Kareem let himself enjoy the blowjob. He grabbed the back of her head and helped her help him forget that he was a married man.

Chapter 21

A few hours later…

Connie smiled as she read the text message. She heard Shelly enter the apartment then put her phone on silent. She sat on the edge of the bed and looked through an essence magazine.

"Hey," Shelly said as she sat her purse on the dresser.

"What's up?" Connie responded.

"I had to run a few errands. Did you eat yet?" Shelly asked.

"No, I just got out the shower. I was getting ready to call you and ask you to bring something. But since you're here, you wanna order something?" Connie asked.

"Yeah, how about Chinese?" Shelly suggested as she searched the drawer for a T-shirt.

"I don't care," Connie said.

"You wanna order while I jump in the shower real quick?" Shelly said.

"What you want? Chicken and Broccoli?"

"Yep and don't forget my egg roll." Shelly walked out of the bedroom.

Connie called and ordered the food while Shelly was in the bathroom. She received another text message from Joseph and smiled. She sent a text him back and told him that she'd speak with him tomorrow and that she was turning her phone off.

Shelly entered the bedroom wearing nothing but her T-shirt. She sat next to Connie and kissed her on the neck. She wanted to finish what she started with Kareem. She really wanted to be fucked.

"I see you're in a good mood tonight," Connie said.

"I wanna make it better. How long we got before the food gets here?" Shelly grinned. Before Connie could respond, the phone rang. It was the delivery man asking that someone come to the front door and get the food.

Connie hung up the phone, "he's here now. I guess I'm going down to get the food unless you plan on paying him with tits and ass," she smiled.

"No boo, I'm saving all this for you," Shelly said as she smacked her ass and went to get her purse. "You have money? All I have is a ten."

"I'll put in the rest. He gonna get a healthy tip tonight cause all I have is a ten too." She proceeded out the door.

After they were done eating, they began their night of kinky sex. Shelly asked Connie to strap on a dildo and begged to be fucked doggy style. Connie was excited. She usually didn't let Shelly use the strap-on on her but tonight would be the first time. Ever since she'd met Joseph, she was feeling some type of way. She didn't want to give Shelly any reason to suspect anything, but she really wanted to experience a dick between her legs. This was the perfect opening. She could get what she wanted without bringing it up.

Connie was the first to strap on. Shelly reached two orgasms before she'd had enough. She thought about Kareem the entire time. She was biting her lip to keep from calling out his name. After her second release, she couldn't take anymore. Connie had her begging to stop. Shelly grabbed the sheets and pulled herself away from Connie. Connie followed and made sure the tip of the dildo continuously vibrated on Shelly's clitoris. Shelly finally pulled herself down on the floor and collapsed.

"Damn! You made me wanna try some of this tonight. Baby, I wanna feel like that." Connie removed the strap-on and went to their bag and attached a clean vibrator and handed the equipment to Shelly and joined her on the floor.

"You sure you want some of this? You never wanted it like this before," she whispered in Connie ear while she lie on top of her and caressed her nipples.

"Um um, I wanna feel what you felt, baby. Just be easy, ok?" Connie said in between kissing Shelly's neck.

"Ok, don't say I didn't warn you," Shelly smiled. She put on the equipment and spread open Connie's legs. She used her fingers to relax her clit before she began to sex her. Connie moaned in pleasure as Shelly slowly switched from her fingers to the dildo. Connie arched her back and enjoyed the ride. Shelly rode her to ecstasy and ten minutes after Shelly began, Connie was experiencing the same pleasures that Shelly had moments before.

Connie squirmed and inched away just like Shelly had. Shelly bent down and kissed Connie's neck. Connie tried to kiss Shelly, but Shelly was too quick and kept moving lower and so Connie couldn't reach her lips. Connie was so into her orgasms that she didn't realize that Shelly was trying to avoid kissing her.

Once they were done, Shelly went to the bathroom and washed up. She grabbed her phone out of her purse before she went into the bathroom. She opened her phone and checked her voicemail. She had a message from Kareem. He told her that she could see Sabrina in the morning and it would be the only time so she needed to be available. Shelly deleted the message and smiled. She was going to see her daughter in the morning. She wanted to share the news with Connie but she didn't feel like being nagged. She shook her head no and turned off her phone.

Chapter 22

Simone met Kareem at the door once she heard him outside the apartment. She grabbed Sabrina out of the car seat and removed her clothing. Sabrina had just gone to sleep and Simone wanted to give her a bath before Sabrina was too far gone.

"Can you wait a few minutes before we eat? I just wanna give her a bath real quick." Simone asked Kareem.

"Yeah that's cool. I can take a quick shower while you're doing that." Simone went into the bedroom and grabbed the things she'd placed on the bed for Sabrina's bath. She went into the kitchen and filled Sabrina's bathtub. She took it in the bedroom and proceeded to give Sabrina her bath while Kareem disappeared into the bathroom.

Simone was finished half an hour later. She fed Sabrina and put her to sleep. She went into the living room and found Kareem in his pajama pants asleep on the sofa. She gently tapped his arm, "Kareem get up so we can eat."

"I'm up. You already fixed the plates?"

"No, I'm on my way in the kitchen now. Sabrina is sleeping in the crib. You wanna eat in here or the kitchen?"

"In the kitchen, if you want me to stay woke." Kareem followed Simone and took a seat at the table.

"Kareem, can you pour us something to drink?" She said a little louder than she meant.

"What's with the attitude?"

"It's not an attitude; it's just that you're not helping out around here. I just gave the baby a bath, I cooked dinner, I'm making the plates, the least you could do is get the drinks. You're laying up sleep while I'm doing all the work."

81

"Simone please don't start. I told you before that all you have to do is ask if you need help," Kareem said.

"Some things I shouldn't have to ask. You see me doing all the work and you just sit right here and wait until I have time to cater to you. You know you're gonna have to help out a little more now that I'm back to work," Simone said.

"Cater to me? What you talking about? Just because I dozed off on the couch you wanna start something? Look, I'm way too tired for this shit tonight. Can we eat? We both gotta get up in the morning."

Simone continued fixing the plates and sat down across from her husband. She bowed her head and blessed the food before they began eating. She looked up at Kareem as he ate his food in silence. "I'm sorry. I didn't mean to snap on you. I'm just worried about going back to work. I'm a little nervous," she admitted.

"Nervous about what? You are ready to go back, right?" Kareem asked.

"Yeah but I'm going to be a supervisor now. I'm just a little worried about how my co-workers are going to respond to me. I haven't seen them in over a year. Now I'm going to be their boss. I know some of them are going to hate," Simone admitted.

"Don't worry about it. You know what you're doing and before you left, you were the best accountant in your department. If you wouldn't have left you'd been a supervisor. Relax, they'll get over it," Kareem said.

"I guess you're right. I'm also excited. You don't know how much I miss working. Don't get me wrong, I love staying home with Sabrina but I'm ready to go back to work."

"You done?" Kareem asked. He took his plate and placed it in the sink. Simone said she was done so he grabbed hers also. He ran dish water in the sink and went to the table and grabbed their glasses. "Why don't you make sure Sabrina is still sleep while I clean up in here," Kareem suggested.

"Kareem you don't have to do this. I told you I didn't mean to snap. I'll get it," Simone said.

"But you was right, I do need to help out a little more. Sabrina is getting older and she is a handful. I don't mind baby."

Simone suspiciously looked at her husband. She couldn't remember the last time Kareem volunteered to clean up. But she wasn't going to ask any questions, she enjoyed the night off.

"Ok then, I'll go get my shower and meet you in the bedroom," she smiled.

"Cool." Kareem was glad that Simone didn't ask questions. He was really trying to stall. He felt bad about what he did with Shelly and he didn't want to have sex with Simone but he knew she wasn't taking no for an answer. He washed the dishes and sighed. He knew he'd fucked up. And he also knew that he couldn't change what he did.

Kareem went into the bedroom and saw Simone applying lotion to her legs. He lay across the bed and closed his eyes. Simone rolled over on top of her husband and whispered in his ear. "Congratulations to me." She slid her tongue across Kareem's top lip and he opened his mouth and made Simone's lips disappear in his. She moaned and put her hand in her husband's pajamas, "I miss you baby." Kareem kept his eyes closed the entire time. His body wasn't responding to his wife's touch and he wanted her to think it was because he was tired. He also couldn't look at her after letting Shelly give him a blowjob.

Simone gently massaged his balls to try and get a reaction. Kareem moaned in an attempt to make her think he was becoming aroused. He caressed her back as they continued to lock lips.

"Uhmmm," she moaned, "I got something for you." She began to move towards his waist. She pulled his pj's off and licked his chest. Simone massaged his dick as her tongue slowly explored his body. When the tip of her tongue was about to touch his shaft, Kareem got nervous.

"Hold up baby, I'm supposed to be congratulating you, remember?" He flipped her on her back and began sucking different body parts. He started with her nipples and sucked every inch of her upper body until he reached her middle. Kareem gently spread her legs slightly apart and sucked her thighs. He teased and kissed her in places she didn't know had reactions. She grabbed the back of his head and forced him between her legs. She wrapped her legs around his neck and arched her back. Kareem licked her clit and sucked until it was two sizes bigger. Simone moaned and lifted her ass off the bed. The higher she lifted, the further she tried to push Kareem's head into her pussy.

Kareem removed Simone's legs from around his neck and spread them widely apart. He licked her hips and used his hands to spread her pussy lips apart. He stuck his tongue inside her canal and fucked his wife to another orgasm. Simone was on cloud nine. She closed her eyes and enjoyed the ride. Kareem didn't stop until she couldn't take anymore. She tried to escape from his grasp but he grabbed her hips and pulled her back down to him. Simone began to tremble from a third orgasm. Kareem sucked her clit while she trembled to make it more pleasurable. Simone rubbed his head and moaned. "Baby, I can't take no more." She pulled him up to her and kissed his lips.

"Have a nice first day, baby," Kareem smiled.

"How could I not after this?" She said just before she dozed off.

Chapter 23

Simone reached over and turned off the alarm clock. Although she was excited about her first day of work, she was tired. Kareem really wore her out during their 'celebration'. She wasn't complaining because it had been a while since their last session. She tiptoed into the bathroom and took a shower. She didn't want to wake Kareem until she was just about ready to leave. Simone finished her shower and put on a t-shirt. She went into the living room and checked on Sabrina. Sabrina was sitting up playing with a stuffed animal. Simone bent down and took her out of the playpen.

"Hey Poopy, how long have you been woke?" She cooed. Sabrina laughed and tugged on Simone's hair. Simone took her into the kitchen and opened a box of cheerios and poured some in a bowl. She placed Sabrina in her high chair and put the bowl in front of her. Sabrina ate the cheerios while Simone made an omelet. She sat at the table and ate her breakfast. Sabrina pointed and tried to reach for her mother's food. Simone gave her pieces of the egg and then handed her the sippy cup with orange juice.

Simone took Sabrina with her into the living room to double check her baby bag. She was a little nervous about leaving Sabrina but she knew she would be in good hands with Moms. Simone did Sabrina's hair and laid an outfit on the sofa for Kareem to get her dressed. She took Sabrina into the bedroom and placed her in the crib. Sabrina cried and tried to climb out of the crib while Simone sat at the vanity and curled her hair. Sabrina screamed until Kareem woke up. He turned and saw Simone at the vanity.

"Don't you hear her crying, Simone?"

"Kareem, I'm doing my hair. She'll be alright for a few more minutes." Kareem pulled the blankets back and sat on the side of the bed to stretch. He got up and took Sabrina out of the crib. He sat her in the middle of their bed while he walked to the bathroom. Sabrina crawled to the edge of the bed and climbed down. She crawled over to Simone and reached to be picked up.

"Wait a minute baby, I'm almost done." Sabrina was ten months and almost walking. She could grab onto things to pull herself up but she was still scared to let go. She crawled out of the bedroom and found Kareem brushing his teeth in the bathroom. "Da...dy," she cried, "da...dy." Kareem turned around and saw Sabrina on the floor crying. He hurried with his teeth and picked her up off the floor. "It's ok, daddy's got you now." He grabbed a wash cloth and wiped her face. "Simone did she eat yet?" Kareem yelled into the bedroom.

"She had some cheerios but she doesn't eat until another hour." Simone said as she entered the kitchen fully dressed.

"Look at mommy, she's going to work. You look good baby." Kareem kissed his wife.

"I'm a little tired but it's all good. I'm ready to do this. Baby, all of her things are packed. All you have to do is get her dressed. Make sure you bring her stroller in case Moms wants to take her out."

"Simone, I got it. I'll make sure she has everything she needs," Kareem said.

"Go ahead and get her dressed, her clothes are on the couch." Simone said as she scrambled throughout the house making sure she had everything she needed on her way out.

"We're not leaving yet."

"Why not?" Simone stopped in her tracks.

"Because I wanna spend a little time with her before I drop her off at Moms. That's why I took off, remember? I'll drop her off in a few hours. I told Moms last night that we'd be a little late," Kareem explained.

"Ok, I gotta go baby. Love you." She kissed Sabrina on the lips and waved, "Bye bye Poopy...bye bye." Sabrina waved bye and smiled. She said bye bye as soon as Simone closed the door.

Chapter 24

K areem got dressed after he'd put Sabrina back to sleep. Once she ate her breakfast, she just needed a little rocking and she was out cold. He put his boots on and grabbed the things that Simone packed for Sabrina and placed them next to the door. He reached into his pocket and turned on his cell phone. He sent a text message to Shelly asking her to call him. Kareem's phone rang five minutes later. He told Shelly that he had about an hour to spare and asked her to meet him at Short Hills Mall. He told her that he'd be there in half an hour.

Kareem pushed Sabrina into the food court. He went to order an orange juice and sat at a table to wait for Shelly. Sabrina was woke and trying to climb out of the stroller. She cried for Kareem to pick her up as an attempt to get out. Kareem un-strapped her and removed her jacket. Sabrina jumped on his lap and reached towards the floor. She wanted to get down and crawl. Kareem didn't want her to crawl on the floor but he knew she would fall out crying if she didn't get down. He stood up and let her walk around the tables. He held her hands while she tried to run free. Sabrina struggled to get free from his grip and managed to hold onto a chair and walk her way around the table alone. Kareem followed closely so that she wouldn't fall. He felt his phone vibrate and checked the text message:

I AM HERE, WHERE R U?

Kareem responded:

IN THE FOOD COURT, U CAN'T MISS US.

Kareem lifted Sabrina from the floor and sat her in her stroller as he sat in a chair. He looked around nervously. He knew he had no business allowing Shelly to see Sabrina behind Simone's back. He sipped his juice and Sabrina reached out and tried to grab the juice. Kareem unzipped the baby bag and handed her the sippy cup. Sabrina turned the cup to her head and drank.

Shelly approached Kareem from behind, "Hey Kareem."

Kareem turned around and greeted Shelly. He was impressed with her outfit. Shelly wore a hunter green pant suit which accentuated her curvaceous ass. She had on a yellow shirt under her suit jacket and sported a pair of three inch stiletto boots. She smiled as she looked at Sabrina.

"Hey Shelly, you look nice" He gestured for her to have a seat. Shelly pulled a chair and sat opposite Kareem so that she could get a good look at Sabrina.

"She seems healthy and happy. You're doing a wonderful job with her." She wanted to hold her but she didn't want to ask for too much too soon.

"Shell, we only have a few minutes before we gotta go." He ignored her last comment. He took Sabrina out of the stroller and held her in his lap. She reached for his carton of juice and knocked it over. Kareem was able to get the juice before it spilled onto the table. "Poopy, don't do that." He pushed the juice away from his daughter.

"Kareem, I'm not trying to keep you. I have to get to work shortly," she smiled, "Oh my goodness, look at my baby." Shelly put her hand over her mouth. "She is big. How many teeth does she have?"

"Shelly, don't do that," Kareem said.

"Do what? She is my baby." Shelly retorted.

"She doesn't know that. As far as she's concerned, me and Simone are her parents!" Kareem was getting agitated.

Sabrina played with the stuffed animal that hung on her stroller. She was clueless as to what was going on around her. She looked up at Kareem and called his name, *da...dy* she tugged on his arm. He turned her around to face him.

"So you and Simone are really trying to raise my baby like she's your own? When do you plan on telling her about me?" Shelly studied Sabrina's face. She was the spitting image of Kareem.

"Shelly, what did you expect me to do? You left her with us. Simone is the only mother that she knows. She doesn't remember you! And what do you expect us to tell her about you?"

"She needs to know that I am her biological mother! Simone is her stepmother!" Shelly said. Kareem began putting on Sabrina's jacket.

"What are you doing, Kareem? I just got here."

"I told you we couldn't stay. I knew you couldn't handle this."

"I can handle it. Kareem, I'm sorry. Please stay for a few more minutes. I just wanna spend a little time with her. I won't mention anything about being her mother again." Shelly's heart stung as she spoke those words. She had to tell Kareem what he wanted to hear in order to spend time with her daughter.

Kareem hesitated a little as he put Sabrina back in her stroller. Shelly slid her hand on top of his and gently massaged the back of his hand. She rubbed his hand until the expression on his face returned to normal. She bent down towards Sabrina and began talking and playing with her. Kareem watched Shelly interact with Sabrina and stayed on point just in case Shelly tried something slick.

Sabrina reached for Shelly to pick her up. She didn't want to be strapped in the stroller. "Oh, she wants me, Kareem. Can I pick her up?" Shelly asked.

"She just wanna get out. That girl hates to be in one place for too long. She thinks she can walk." Kareem lifted Sabrina out of the stroller and stood her on the floor. Shelly moved closer to Kareem and kissed his neck.

"Shelly, stop! It ain't even that type of party."

"It could be," she smirked, "I had a good time last night. And there's plenty more where that came from." She said as she rubbed her breast up against his arm.

Shelly looked enticing. Kareem turned his head to keep from gawking at her breasts. He couldn't believe that Shelly still had this affect on him after all the time that had passed.

"It's time for us to get outta here." He began putting on Sabrina's jacket.

"We'll have to do this again, Kareem."

"No, this ain't gonna to be a regular thing, I..."

"Ok, just promise me one thing. You'll talk to Simone and try to work out me seeing her once a month?" Shelly begged.

"Are you crazy? Simone can't know that I let you see Sabrina!"

"She doesn't have to know. Just talk to her and act like I just contacted you. I need to have a relationship with my baby, Kareem. Or, maybe I can talk to Simone." Shelly said as she ran her hand down his hip and felt his soldier stand at attention.

"No! You crazy as hell! You remember what we talked about last night. If you're trying to fuck up my shit, you better be ready for the outcome. I mean it this time Shelly!" he paused and looked at her, "You know what? We ain't doing this shit again," he strapped Sabrina in the stroller.

"Kareem I told you before that I'm not gonna tell her. I don't want her to find out either. Today and last night will be our little secret," she winked, "we still have a lot to discuss so I'll text you so we can meet at the spot." She walked over to Sabrina and waved bye. Sabrina said bye and smiled as Shelly walked away from them.

Kareem exited the mall and checked to make sure Shelly wasn't following him. He didn't want her to see him drop Sabrina off at Moms' house. He called Moms to let her know that he was on his way. He drove around aimlessly for half an hour before he pulled into her driveway. He went inside and helped Sabrina get settled. He told Moms that Simone would pick her up later and he left. Kareem drove around Moms' block a few times before he went home.

Chapter 25

Two weeks later…

Connie pulled into the parking space a block from her building. She sat in the car until she finished her phone conversation with Joseph. She smiled as Joseph asked her to meet him for dinner at the Hotel. This was his third attempt to get her out. Joseph tried to make it seem like it was on a platonic level but Connie knew that her attraction to him placed it on another level. She enjoyed flirting with him. He was an attractive man and she was having fun. She found that it was just like flirting with a woman.

Connie got out of the car and walked into her apartment building. She flicked on the light and walked through the apartment searching for Shelly. Once she was satisfied that she was alone, she kicked off her shoes and prepared for a shower. She sat on the bed and thought about Joseph's proposal and then she thought about Shelly. She and Shelly were only passing each other by lately. They rarely communicated. They got together for sex on occasions. Connie tried to make things better between them and Shelly half-heartedly attempted to be cordial. She seemed to be preoccupied these days. Every Thursday Shelly would make up an excuse as to why she wouldn't be home for dinner.

Connie still had Joseph on her mind. She'd finally agreed to meet him at the hotel's bar for drinks. She figured she'd only be sitting at home alone anyway. Joseph stepped right into her life and showered her with the attention she missed at home. She even looked forward to seeing him. Just before she went into the bathroom, she grabbed a personal vibrator from her purse. She turned on the shower and adjusted the temperature of the water.

She stood in front of the mirror and removed her polo shirt. She looked at her reflection and smiled. She slid her hand across her nipples and they became erect. Seconds later, she felt that tingling sensation between her legs. Connie slid down her pants and underwear together. She placed her forefinger and thumb on her clitoris and squeezed. She moaned as she felt the pulse beating on her fingers. Connie closed her eyes and imagined Joseph's hands massaging between her legs. She tilted her head back and closed her eyes.

She made her way to the toilet and sat down on the closed seat. The cold porcelain added a sensation between her legs. She reached on the sink and grabbed her new vibrator. She slid it on her finger and turned it on. She spread her legs as wide as she could and placed the vibrator directly on her clit. The pulsing sensation seemed to beat faster. Connie moaned in pleasure as she leaned back on the toilet bowl and lifted her feet in the air. She continued to rub the vibrator against her clit.

She felt as if she'd lost control of her body. She moved back and forth as she rubbed her spot. She moaned and arched her back as far as she could until she reached the most electrifying orgasm she's had in months. As she regained control of her body, she turned down the speed on the vibrator. Connie was shaking as she put her feet on the floor. She got herself together and took her shower.

As she stood under the water, she smiled at the thought of Joseph being the one to make her clitoris beat the way it did. Connie lathered her washcloth and began to wash her body. When she got to her middle, she still felt tingling. She took the washcloth and vigorously rubbed until she reached another orgasm. Constance took a deep breath and exhaled. She washed up and stepped out of the shower.

When she entered the bedroom, Shelly was searching through the closet to find an outfit. Shelly didn't usually come straight home on Thursday nights. She came home today to change her clothes. She was wearing pants and she wanted to put on a skirt. She turned around and looked at Connie.

"Hey Shells." Connie said. She was a little nervous about seeing Shelly at home on a Thursday. "You finally get to stay home with me tonight?

"Unfortunately, I can't. I have plans." Shelly looked away from Connie.

"What plans?" Connie asked. She continued to play it off like she wanted Shelly to stay at home with her. She didn't want anything to seem out of the ordinary.

"My boss is taking us out for dinner to discuss a new client. And you know I'm his right hand, so I need to be there." She walked towards the bathroom. Connie was glad she hadn't taken out an outfit for the night. She didn't want to explain anything to Shelly about her whereabouts. Although she didn't have to sneak and go out, it just seemed more sinful to creep. And she was only looking to have a little harmless fun.

"Ok, but tomorrow we're going out so don't make any plans," Connie said, "and if you have any, cancel them. We haven't spent any time together in weeks." She raised her voice so Shelly could hear her in the bathroom.

Connie began to put lotion on her body. She couldn't wait for Shelly to leave. She tried to act like everything was normal. She put on a tank top and a pair of shorts and lay across the sofa with the TV. remote. She kept peeking over her shoulder to see if Shelly was out of the bathroom. She jumped up and hurried into the bedroom to get her cell phone before Shelly got out of the bathroom. She wanted to have the phone next to her in case Joseph sent her a text message.

Shelly finished her shower and went into the bedroom to get dressed. After applying lotion to her arms and legs, she slipped on thong underwear. She sprayed a little Perry Ellis 360 perfume under her breasts and between her legs. She knew that scent drove Kareem crazy. Shelly bent down and slid on a black mini skirt. She made sure her top would exploit her breasts. She knew Kareem wouldn't resist her in this outfit. It wouldn't take much since he already gave in and let her suck him off. She tried her best to suck the skin off in that parking lot. She wanted him to see what he'd been missing.

"Damn, who you looking all sexy for? What's with the thong for a work meeting?" Connie asked as she stood in the bedroom doorway.

"Con, it goes with the outfit. You know it wouldn't be tasteful to put on regular underwear with this skirt." Shelly said over her shoulder.

"And why are you changing into a mini skirt, again?" Connie asked as she made her way to the bed. She smacked Shelly's ass and let her hand linger a little longer than necessary.

"Con, please don't start." She sat on the bed and put on her shoes.

"I'm not starting anything. I'm just remembering the days when you used to wear stuff like that for me. Now you don't even pretend it's for me."

Shelly exhaled and shook her head. She thought about what Connie said and agreed with her. "You know, you're right. I think we have lost it a little bit. We're not very intimate anymore. We need to fix that."

"And we can start right now." Connie said as she slid on top of Shelly."

"No Con, I have to go. I'm gonna be late." Shelly wined but didn't try to fight it. She enjoyed sex with Connie and wasn't about to let anything keep her from being fulfilled. Hell, if she was lucky, she'd get the something else she'd been missing from Kareem.

After they had sex, Shelly went into the bathroom and took another quick shower. Once she got out of the shower, she checked her phone and responded to Kareem's text. She walked into the living room where Connie was sprawled on the sofa and kissed her on the cheek. "I'll see you later."

"What time are you coming in?" Connie asked.

"I'm not sure. It could be late so don't wait up." She winked and walked out the door.

Connie picked up her phone and called Joseph. She let him know that she would be about an hour late.

Chapter 26

S imone pulled into Moms' driveway. She got out of the car
and rang the bell. Moms let her in and went back to the
kitchen. Simone followed and saw Sabrina sitting on Tricia's lap.

"Hey Trish, I've been trying to call you forever." Simone
said as she reached for Sabrina.

"Hey girl, I know and I'm sorry. I've been busy with
work. Speaking of which, how are you adjusting to going back to
work?"

"Oh girl, it feels like I never left. Last week, a few of the
people were looking at me funny and doing a little whispering
behind my back. But after I had my first department meeting and
introduced myself properly, we're kinda getting to know each
other and it eased the tension a little. So I'm good." Simone said
as Sabrina pointed to the floor and tried to get off her mother's
lap.

"So Moms, is Sabrina adjusting ok? Or is she driving you
crazy?" Simone asked.

"Chile hush, she just as sweet as she wanna be," Moms
smiled.

"Yeah right. Every time I see her, she pulls my hair and
tries to snatch my earrings out my ear," Trish laughed.

"Leave my baby alone. She's just being friendly,"
Simone smiled.

"Oh I'm just playing, come here Lil' Mama." Trish
reached for Sabrina. Sabrina nearly jumped into her arms. Trish
kissed her on the cheek and hugged her tight. Sabrina was such a
happy baby. She was spoiled but she adjusted extremely fast to

Moms and Marvin. Simone didn't expect her to adjust so quickly but she was glad she did.

"So Trish, what's really going on? I know you've been busy but please, you could've at least returned my phone calls," Simone smirked. Moms looked on with raised eyebrows.

"What's going on between you two?" By the look on her face, they could tell that she thought they may have had another episode.

"Trish, you didn't tell her?" Simone asked.

"Tell me what?" Moms asked as she placed her hand on her heart.

"Relax Moms, it's about Tarik," Tricia began.

"What about him?" She looked between the two women. Simone looked at Trish and nodded for her to tell the news.

"Simone saw him at the mall a few weeks ago."

"And?" Moms was getting irritated.

"He was with his new girlfriend," Simone added.

"I thought you said he didn't say she was his girlfriend. Did you lie Simone?" Tricia was clearly pissed.

"Look at you," Moms said, "why does it matter to you? Trish you can't have it both ways. You don't want the man so how come he can't move on with his life?"

Simone watched Tricia interact with Sabrina. Tricia was paying Moms no attention as she spoke. She bounced Sabrina up and down on her lap and played with her.

"Trish, did you hear me?" Moms yelled.

"Momma, how could I not hear you? But I'm not about to sit here and let you and Simone gang up on me again. I already know how both of you feel and I'm tired of hearing it!" Sabrina sat down on Tricia's lap. "It looks like someone needs a diaper change." Trish walked in the living room and Simone followed.

"Trish, I'll change her," Simone offered.

"Simone I got it. She only peed." Simone sat on the sofa and watched Tricia change the baby's diaper.

"Trish, I'm not gonna lecture you about anything. I know that you're hurting and I'm just trying to be here for you. If you wanna have a *'Tarik ain't shit'* party, I'm here." They both laughed. Tricia wrapped the dirty diaper and then pulled Sabrina to her feet.

"Ma...mi ma...mi." Sabrina smiled and got down on the floor. She held onto the coffee table and walked to Simone. "Hey Poopy...hey there," Simone sang. Sabrina climbed on her mother's lap and kissed her on the lips. "Thank you, Poopy. You giving mommy a kiss?" Simone asked. Sabrina smiled and touched Simone's lips before kissing her again.

"Simone, you staying for dinner?" Moms asked.

"I guess so. This is Kareem's night to hang out."

"How is he doing, anyway? You two ok?" Moms asked.

"We're better. We're just taking it one day at a time. We're communicating better," Simone smiled.

"Well that's good. Sabrina come go wit' Nana to the kitchen." Moms took Sabrina's hand and led her to the kitchen.

"What was that about? What's up with you and Kareem?" Trish asked.

"Nothing much, we hit a rough patch a few weeks ago but we're working it out," Simone said.

"You sure? You wanna talk about it?" Trish pushed.

"Kareem just had issues with me going back to work. But as you can see, we've worked it out," Simone smiled. Trish smiled and leaned back in her chair. She exhaled and closed her eyes.

"What's up Trish? What's on your mind?" Simone asked.

"It's Moms, she's getting on my nerves. All she talks about is me and Tarik. I'm getting sick of her trying to force me and him together. It's obvious that I still love my husband. But for reasons no one understands, including me, I can't be with him. I know it seems selfish but this is my choice," Tricia explained.

"I understand. I think Moms is just trying to keep you from making a huge mistake. That's what parents do, Trish. And I didn't understand that until I got Sabrina."

"But it's my mistake to make! It's nobody's place to tell me what I should do or what I can accept in my relationship!"

"You're absolutely right about that. I can't speak for Moms but I just think that you and Tarik are perfect for each other. You two had the perfect relationship and I wanna make sure you know what you're doing. I saw your reaction when I told you about Tashi. And I know you still love him, Trish." Simone looked sympathetic.

"Simone, this is getting old. I love Tarik. There's no question about that. But what kind of person would I be if I stay in a marriage and have to wonder what he's doing every second he's not with me? It's not fair to him or me. This isn't an easy decision but it's the right decision," she sniffed and wiped tears from her eyes, "I hope I helped you to understand because I don't wanna hear anything else about Tarik from you or anyone else!"

Simone sympathized with her friend. She wished there were something she could do to make Trish feel better. After hearing Tricia's explanation, she knew that the best thing for her to do was to stay out of it.

"Well on a brighter note, I'm planning a birthday party for Sabrina," Simone beamed.

"Oh my goodness! Her first birthday. Simone, I hope you don't plan on going all out and having some extravagant gala," Trish said.

"It's her first birthday. I'm doing it up!"

"Simone, she's not even going to remember anything about that day. Save your money and keep it simple," Trish pleaded.

"I want her to have it all. I'm going for a princess theme," Simone said ignoring Tricia's last comment. She was a little agitated that Trish would tell her how to spend her daughter's first birthday. "I'll get a clown and we'll have games."

"She's turning one, Simone. What games could she possibly play?" Tricia frowned.

"Don't do that. Don't try to talk me out of this. I really want this for her," Simone said.

"Moms, could you come here for a second?" Tricia yelled. Moms walked through the door with Sabrina crawling behind her.

"What is it?" she asked.

"Would you tell Simone that it's a waste of money to give Sabrina a big birthday bash," Trish said.

"Now Trish leave her alone. Every mother overdoes it on the first party. We don't learn until it's over and we see that the party is for the adults," Moms laughed.

"Thank you Moms," Simone turned to Tricia, "I hope you realize that as her Godmother, you will be helping with the party."

"I'm not gonna have time," Tricia whined.

"Well you better make time. It's her first birthday, Trish," Simone pleaded. Sabrina crawled to her mother and stood in front of her. "What's up Poopy?" Simone asked as she picked her up and sat her in her lap. "Ma...mi doosh," Sabrina pointed towards the kitchen.

"Oh, she wants her juice," Moms said, "She was drinking it before we came in here. Let's go, I'll get ya juice." Moms grabbed Sabrina's hand and let her back into the kitchen.

"Seriously Simone, you know I would love to help out, but I'm scheduled to be away for a week next month so I need these next few weeks to prepare. And I didn't know you were gonna throw a bash." Trish saw Simone's facial expression and felt horrible. "But I will be there for the party even if I have to take off. Simone, you know this is my busiest time of the year." Trish said with sincerity. "And besides, you don't need me hanging around trying to convince you not to go all out for your daughter's first birthday," Trish smiled, "But you can still send me my half of the bill. You know I got you." Trish smiled and rubbed Simone's shoulder. Simone was a little upset but she understood.

"Trish, you better be at the party!" Simone poked out her lips to emphasize that she was upset.

"I'll be there. Besides, we'll have plenty of birthdays to plan," Trish smiled. Moms yelled that the food was ready so they headed into the kitchen.

"Well, now all I have to do is convince Kareem that we should have this party."

"Girl, y'all ain't discussed it yet?" Trish was clearly surprised.

"Not yet, but I'm sure he'll see things my way," Simone smiled.

"Moms, we're not waiting for Marvin?" Trish asked.

"Naw, he's working late. I'll feed him later," she winked. They all bowed their heads for prayer and then ate their meal while Sabrina made a mess in her high chair.

Chapter 27

Kareem turned off the shower and stepped out of the tub. He wrapped a towel around his waist and walked into the bedroom. He reached for his cell phone and called Simone.

"Hey baby, what's up?" Simone asked.

"You know I'm going out tonight and I just wanted to make sure that my girls didn't need anything before I go," he said.

"Not that I could think of," Simone frowned trying to make sure they didn't need anything.

"You sure? Sabrina ok?" he asked.

"Yeah, we're good. Go 'head out and have fun. I love you."

"Aiight, I love you, too. I'll see you later." He hung up the phone after hearing Simone disconnect the call. Kareem went to the closet and pulled out a sweat suit. He got dressed and put on his sneakers. After sitting in front of the TV. for another half hour, he sent a text message to Shelly. He'd thought about her in a sexual way ever since she sucked him off. He knew he had no business thinking about her but the old feelings were beginning to resurface.

[YO WHAT TIME U COMIN?] He sent the message and waited for her reply. Kareem contemplated staying home. He knew the kind of drama Shelly would bring if she didn't get her way. He was trying to protect Simone from getting hurt. He knew he could prevent the situation from going any further by admitting everything to his wife. He felt like a hypocrite. Just a few weeks ago he was dogging her out because she kept Shelly a secret and here he was not only keeping her a secret, but creating more secrets. He sat there a little longer and convinced himself that he was doing the right thing by meeting Shelly. He felt his phone vibrate and checked the message:

[GOING 2 B A LIL LATE SUMTHING CAME UP]

He replied: [HOW LATE]

She replied: [HALF HOUR]

Kareem had a little time to kill so he sat back and watched ESPN until he was ready to leave. As he leaned back and watched the highlights of the sports, he had to ask himself if Shelly was worth losing his family. He thought about it and then got up and left.

* * *

Joseph sat at the end of the bar and sipped his drink while he looked over some paperwork. He checked his watch a few times and prayed his plan worked. He really liked Connie and wanted to show her that she was being played. He'd been observing long enough to know that Connie's lover would be in the bar with the mystery man tonight. He'd watched them meet for weeks. He checked his watch again and shook his head. They usually met earlier so Joseph looked at the door every time someone entered the bar. He looked at his phone before he answered. He smiled at the thought of hearing Connie's voice.

"Hey sweetness," Joseph flirted.

"Hey yourself, I'm just calling to let you know that I'll be about an hour late. Something came up that I couldn't control," she said.

"It's ok, I'm still finishing up some paperwork so no rush."

"Ok, I'll be there as soon as I can," Connie said.

Joseph closed his phone and looked up in time to see Kareem walking through the door. Kareem took a seat in the back of the bar where the lights were dimmed. After fifteen minutes, Shelly walked in and joined him at the table. She removed her jacket and revealed her oversized breasts.

* * *

Connie sat in her car and called Joseph to let him know that she was outside. He told her that he would meet her in the front. Joseph didn't want Connie to walk in and see her lover just yet. He needed to run a little interference before the secret was out.

Joseph met Connie at the front door and escorted her to his office on the opposite side of the hotel. Once they were inside, he hugged her and kissed her on the cheek.

"It's nice to see you too," Connie smiled.

"I've been waiting to see you all day. Now, I'll sleep well tonight," Joseph smiled.

"Oh please, stop beating me in the head." Connie smiled at Joseph's corny remark but was flattered at the same time. She removed her jacket before she sat down. She was wearing a pair of Apple Bottom jeans with a red tank top that exposed her 36 c's. Her breasts were not nearly as luscious as her lover's but they were voluptuous in their own right.

"So how was your day?" Joseph asked after he licked his lips.

"My day went well, how was yours?"

"About the same as usual, mostly paperwork. But I wanna talk about you," he smiled.

"What about me?" Connie asked.

"I'm trying to get to know you a little better."

"Joseph, you know I'm in a relationship," Connie fidgeted.

"Yeah and how's that going, again? The last time we talked, you were having problems." He sarcastically reminded her.

"Not problems, more like we were going through something," she admitted.

"Well is it better?" Connie diverted her eyes downward and Joseph knew that was an indication that she was getting ready to lie.

"We're ok," she lied. Joseph was beginning to feel bad about what he was getting ready to do. He saw that Connie really cared about her lover and he also saw that she was hurt. He wasn't going to tell her anything that would add to that. He'd just let her see for herself. His original plan was to talk bad about Shelly and create hypothetical scenarios and see Connie's reactions. But after seeing the hurt in her eyes, he knew that he had to go about it another way. He figured he could just walk her through the bar area and let her 'accidentally' spot Shelly with her friend.

Chapter 28

S helly reached over and grabbed Kareem's hand. She smiled and flirted by caressing Kareem's hand more than necessary.

"Whatchu doin' Shells?" He snatched his hand away.

"I just wanted to thank you for allowing me to see my daughter. I really appreciate you going out on a limb for me," she smiled.

"It's all good, but that's a done deal."

"What you mean?" She asked as a waitress brought their drinks and sat them on the table. The waitress looked at Kareem and winked, "You running a tab?"

"Yes, I will be running a tab, as usual," Shelly interrupted. The waitress smirked and walked away from the table. "Now what's a done deal?" Shelly asked as she turned her attention back to Kareem.

"Shells, you know we can't do this. I don't want Sabrina to get confused. And I don't want Simone to find out," Kareem said sounding rational.

"But Kareem, we agreed that we would work something out. I want to spend time with my baby."

"Maybe when she gets a little older and can understand the situation...I..."

"A little older? Then she'll forget about me and won't know who I am," Shelly slammed her hand on the table.

"Newsflash, she already don't know who you are. Yo, why don't you stop being so selfish for a change and think about Sabrina," Kareem suggested.

"I am thinking about her!" Shelly yelled.

105

"No you not, Shelly. I thought the most selfish thing you could do was to leave her but now I see I was wrong." Kareem shook his head hoping to get through to her.

"Kareem, I was really hoping we could work this out and come to some type of agreement. But I see that you're not going to be happy until you get papers in the mail," she sipped her drink, "I'll do this my way and I will get to see my daughter!" Shelly was livid. She wanted Kareem to agree to her terms but he wouldn't even hear her out.

"Here you go again threatening me with court. Am I supposed to be scared? Is this the part where I beg you not to do that? You think I'ma fuck you and it'll be all better? I told you before that I'm happy with my wife and I'm not letting you near my daughter. Why would you want to confuse her anyway?" he asked. Kareem was upset but he didn't raise his voice. He knew it would piss Shelly off if he showed little emotions.

"It's not a threat, Kareem. You're leaving me no choice!" Kareem shook his head and smiled. He drank the last of his beer and signaled for the bartender to send him another round. "And we both know this ain't about sex. You've already proved how much you love Simone. You married her and then you came in my mouth," Shelly said with a smirk.

"You think because I let you do what you do best that it means something? You need to move on Shelly. It ain't even that type of party between us. You won't get a chance to taste this again!" Kareem said as he stroked between his legs.

"Kareem please," she licked her lips, "you may have Simone fooled with that bullshit, but I know better. If I wanted to fuck you again, you'd be fucked! If it wasn't that type of party, you wouldn't be here," she smiled. She was still pissed with Kareem but she didn't want to mess up her chances of getting some dick. She missed him so much and she'd already set in her head that she would be fucking him when they left the bar.

The waitress sashayed over to their table and placed a bottle of beer and a double shot of Hennesy in front of Kareem. Shelly exhaled and sucked her teeth. "Oh I'm sorry, did you want something as well?" she asked Shelly. Kareem shook his head and exposed his perfectly white teeth with a smile.

"I want the same thing you want, so kick rocks bitch!"
Shelly shook her head and looked at Kareem, "My goodness,
why don't she just offer you a lap dance?"

* * *

Joseph asked Connie where she wanted to sit. Connie
suggested that they sit at the bar. Joseph signaled for bartender
while she took a seat at the end of the bar and sat her purse next
to her.

"We can put your bag in my office so you won't have to
worry about it," Joseph offered.

"No, it'll be fine right here. But thanks for asking,"
Shelly smiled.

"What are you drinking?" Joseph asked.

"Hmmm, I think I'll have an apple martini."

"Coming right up." Joseph turned towards the bartender,
"you heard the lady. And I'll have my usual."

He turned to Connie and smiled, "Did I tell you how sexy
you look tonight?"

"No you didn't but thank you," she replied. The bartender
placed their drinks in front of them. Connie dug in her purse and
pulled out her last four singles.

"Put your money away, I'll take care of everything,"
Joseph said.

"No, the least I can do is leave the tip," Connie insisted
and slid the singles to the edge of the bar for the bartender. "You
know, I'm glad I came out tonight. I would have only been
sitting around doing nothing. Although I was a little skeptical
about hanging out with you…I…"

"Why is that?" Joseph cut her off.

"Well I just don't want to give you the wrong impression.
I think that you're a great guy and we get along well. But I'm
only available for friendship." She stirred her drink.

"Connie, I like you as well and if I've given you any
reason to think that your friendship isn't enough, then I
apologize. And if I've disrespected you or your relationship, I'm
sorry," Joseph said.

"No, Joseph, I didn't mean it like that," she shook her head, "I just wanted to be perfectly clear about us so that there won't be any misunderstandings," she said.

"Well I hope you feel better now that you've gotten that off your chest, maybe you can loosen up a bit," he chuckled.

"Very funny, actually I do feel better." She raised her glass and thanked him for the drink before she took a sip.

"Anytime Constance." He raised his glass as well. Joseph stood and looked across the room to see if Shelly and her friend were still there. As he stretched to play it off, he noticed Shelly walking towards the bar.

"Are you tired?" Connie asked.

"No, not at all, I just needed to stretch my legs." He sat on the left of Connie when he saw Shelly stand up. He made sure he blocked her view.

As soon as Shelly approached the bar, Joseph turned to face Connie, "Would you mind if I excused myself just for a second? I need to get some papers from my office."

"Oh sure, I'll be ok," Connie smiled. She did all she could to keep her feelings for Joseph under control. She was very attracted to him and it was a struggle being so close to him and not reacting the way her body wanted.

"Ok then, I'll be right back." Joseph got up from the bar and sipped the last of his drink. Just to the left of him, about three bar stools down, Shelly was ordering a drink. Connie looked past Joseph and squinted. She thought she was wrong. She grabbed Joseph as he was about to walk away.

"Wait a minute," she said.

"You ok?" he asked and took a step towards her.

"Just stand here for a second, please." Connie eased to the side so that she'd be completely covered by Joseph.

Joseph faced her and knew that she'd saw Shelly. "What the hell is Shelly doing here?" she said more to herself than to Joseph.

"What's going on, Connie?" he asked. Connie strained to hear Shelly order a corona and a shot of hennesy.

108

"Oh, she must be having her meeting here," she whispered, "just stay here until she leaves. I don't want her to see me," Connie pleaded.

"Are you in trouble?" Joseph teased.

"No, I'm not in trouble. I just didn't mention to her that I was going out and I don't want her to think I followed her here. She's having a meeting with her boss," Connie said.

Shelly grabbed her drinks from the bar and walked back to the table and placed the hennesy in front of the man with whom she shared the table.

Joseph took a seat back on the bar stool and asked Connie if she were ok.

"I'm fine," she said as she watched Shelly. The longer she stared, the more familiar the man looked. Joseph watched Connie as she watched her lover. He was trying to see a reaction but Connie was doing a good job hiding her emotions. Just when Joseph thought his plan backfired, Connie covered her mouth with her hands. She looked surprised as Shelly blatantly flirted with the man. She shook her head and spoke softly, "Kareem." She recognized him from some of Shelly's old photos. "Wow," she smiled.

"What's wrong, Connie?" Joseph asked. For a brief second, she looked like she'd seen a ghost. Connie looked at him still wearing her smile. She sipped her drink and looked over at Shelly, who was staring at Kareem like she wanted to eat him up.

"Well, it seems that I'm gonna have to leave." Joseph knew Connie was trying to act like it was no big deal but the expression on her face told it all when she said Kareem's name. However, Joseph still played it off like he was clueless.

"Connie, please tell me what's going on," he urged.

"Can we go and get my jacket please?"

"Sure." Joseph said as he glanced at Shelly and Kareem. He escorted Connie back to his office.

"Joseph, I'm so sorry I have to leave so suddenly but, I really need to get home before Shelly. I don't want her to know that I was here and I definitely don't want her to know that I was having drinks with you," she put on her jacket, "I know it's a little complicated but I really have to go. I'll call you," Connie said.

Joseph was at a loss for words. He didn't know what to make of the situation. He thought Connie would go to the table and create a scene and come running into his arms for comfort.

"Ok well I'll just walk you to your car." He grabbed his suit jacket off the back of his chair and let Connie out of the hotel. Once she was in view of Shelly, she stopped for a minute and stared at the two of them. Although Shelly was practically sitting in Kareem's lap, it was obvious that they were in a heated discussion. Connie recognized the way Shelly rolled her head. She knew that's what Shelly did when she was debating or arguing a point.

Connie followed Joseph as he squeezed her arm to tug her along. When they got to her car, she kissed Joseph on the cheek as she inhaled his cologne. She had just made her decision that he would indeed be her first piece of dick.

"Be careful, Connie, please call to let me know that you made it home safely. Or just call me if you need anything," he smiled.

"Thanks for inviting me out tonight. I think this is just what I needed. I'll call you," she smiled as she got into her car.

Chapter 29

Connie walked into the apartment with tears in her eyes. Although she really shouldn't have been, she was surprised to see Shelly in the bar with Kareem. From what she observed, Shelly was quite comfortable and very flirty. Connie pulled out her cell phone and sent a text message to Joseph to let him know that she was home and ok. Joseph responded and said that he was glad to hear. He also told Connie that she could call him anytime if she needed.

Connie took a shower and cleaned her face. She didn't want Shelly to walk in and see her crying. Although she was hurt, she somewhat blamed herself. She knew getting involved with Shelly was a bad idea from the start. After hearing Shelly's story on that first day outside the restaurant, Connie should have ran far away. Not only was Shelly younger, she was confused. She wasn't sure if she wanted to be with men or women and that alone should have sent Connie packing.

She sat on the side of the bed and applied lotion to her body. "How could I have not seen this coming? All the signs were there," she paused, "that's ok, we'll see who'll be laughing in the end." When she finished, Connie went into the living room to watch TV.

Shelly walked into the apartment almost two hours later. She was surprised to see Connie lying across the sofa. "Hey Con, what are you still doing up?" she asked as she kicked off her shoes.

"I was waiting for you so we can talk," Connie sat up and turned off the TV.

111

"Okay," Shelly sang the word, "let me just take a shower first." She headed to the bathroom but Connie was on her heels.

"This can't wait Shelly, we need to talk now!" Connie insisted.

"Is the issue gonna be solved before I get out of the shower?" Shelly asked.

"What is the big rush about you taking a fucking shower!?" Connie yelled.

Shelly paused, "why am I getting the third degree cause I wanna wash my ass?"

"Shelly please, I've smelled your ass after we've had sex. I've smelled you after you've come from the gym. Hell, I've even smelled your ass when you're on your period. What smell are you trying to wash?"

"Girl, what the fuck is you talking about?"

"You are such a liar, Shelly."

"Lying about taking a shower?" Shelly was both confused and irritated.

"Where were you tonight?" Connie asked.

"I told you I had a meeting with my boss." She looked away nervously.

"Oh so you work for Kareem, now?"

"What!?"

"You trying to wash off the smell of his dick so I won't know you fucked him?" Connie blurted.

"You trippin', Con." Shelly didn't know exactly what, but she knew Connie knew something.

"Did you fuck him?" Connie stepped in Shelly's face.

"Back the fuck up Connie!" Shelly stepped back just in case Connie would try something.

"You know what, this is some bullshit! How long you been fucking your ex?" Connie asked.

"First of all, you don't know what you're talking about." Shelly was desperate so she decided to tell Connie about Sabrina.

She sat on the bed, "I've been meeting with Kareem about Sabrina."

"I though we agreed that we would wait on that. We only talked about you wanting to see her." Connie calmed down a little and sat next to Shelly.

"Let me finish Con. I talked to Kareem and he let me see my baby," she said excitedly.

"I'm happy for you, but that's not an excuse to sneak around Shelly. You could have told me what was going on. We're supposed to be in this together. But instead, you steady sneaking around seeing him, wearing shit like this," she pointed to Shelly's outfit, "lying about it and flirting all up in his face. Now that doesn't sound like it was about no baby!"

"Wait a minute, how do you know all of this? Did you follow me?" Shelly asked.

"Don't flatter yourself. I didn't follow you," Connie rolled her eyes.

"Well how you know?" Shelly yelled.

"Don't try and flip the script. This is not about me, it's about your creeping ass! Don't worry about how I know. Your biggest concern should be *that* I know." Connie began to pace.

Shelly knew Connie was pissed. She never intended for her to know that she'd been sneaking to be with Kareem. She really cared for Connie but she was in need of some dick. And she had to use Sabrina as an excuse or Kareem wouldn't give her the time of day.

"I know this looks bad but it's not what you think," Shelly said.

"Oh really? Is that why you haven't answered my question? Did you fuck Kareem?" Connie wanted to know.

"Con, we just made love a few hours ago. Do you really think I could go out and fuck someone else right after that?"

"It seems I don't know you at all lately. I'm not sure what you're capable of. But I do know that I'm tired of your confused ass!" Connie shouted.

"Confused? Connie, you're jumping to conclusions. I am not sleeping with Kareem. We were only talking about me seeing Sabrina. It ain't nothing more than that." Shelly needed Connie to believe her. She didn't want their relationship to end. Connie was a good woman and was committed to their relationship. Shelly was too busy pushing her away to realize it.

"Con, I'm sorry you had to find out this way. I was going to tell you as soon as we came to some kind of agreement. I didn't tell you sooner because the last time we talked about it, we ended up arguing and I didn't want to go through that again." Shelly pulled Connie down on the bed and put her arms around her shoulder.

"Shells, don't play games with me," she shrugged her off, "tell me if I'm not enough for you. I thought by now that you'd be completely secure with your sexuality, but..."

"Con, I've never tried to hide the fact that I'm bi-sexual. But since we got together, I've been committed to you. I'm not thinking about no one else." Connie wanted to believe Shelly because she loved her. She felt like an idiot. She knew deep in her heart that Shelly was up to something with Kareem.

"So how long you been seeing him?" she asked.

"This was only my third time meeting with him," Shelly lied.

"So what's going on with you seeing your daughter?" Connie asked.

Shelly smiled, "well I saw her once and I am trying to get Kareem to let me see her on a regular. He's trippin' but he knows that he can't keep me away."

"Shelly, why won't you just go to court and seek visitation? There's no way a judge won't grant you visitation," Connie suggested.

Shelly wanted Connie to believe her story so she told her about the lawyer she met. She didn't want Connie to continue to have any suspicions about Kareem.

Connie listened intently to Shelly's story. She found it very funny that Shelly all of a sudden felt the urge to blurt everything out. They talked and argued for another two hours. Connie finally got tired. "I'm going to bed, Shelly. I have to go to work in the morning and I need some sleep," she grabbed a pillow off the bed, "I'm sleeping on the couch."

"You don't have to sleep on the couch. I'll stay to myself," Shelly said.

"It's not about that, I just wanna be alone right now." Connie walked past her and went into the living room.

Chapter 30

K areem tried not to wake Simone as he took a shower. He stayed out later than he planned and didn't want her to know what time he crept into the apartment. He removed his boots outside the door so that she wouldn't hear him enter. He felt his way through the living room to get to the bathroom. He stumbled over Sabrina's walker and banged his foot on the coffee table.

After rummaging through the fridge to find something to eat, Kareem joined his wife in bed. He silently prayed that he washed off all traces of Shelly.

The next morning…

Simone tapped Kareem on the shoulder, "babe, wake up," she said excitedly.

"What's up?" he wiped his eyes.

"Look, Sabrina is walking," she pointed towards the door. Kareem sat up on the side of the bed as Sabrina carried her sippy cup and headed in the bedroom.

"Look at daddy's big girl," he cooed. Sabrina laughed and held out her arms towards Kareem and tried to run. She dropped her cup and stopped to pick it up. As she bent down, she fell on her backside. Simone walked over to make sure she was ok.

"What happened? When did she start walking?" He asked.

"I put her in the bed with you so I could get ready for work. I walked back and forth and she kept reaching out and calling for me. When I was in the bathroom curling my hair, I heard her calling me. I turned around and she was standing in the doorway smiling. I couldn't believe she walked so I went into the living room and she followed me," Simone explained.

"Damn, she ain't even a year yet and she's already walking." Kareem smiled and picked up his daughter.

"Well, she'll be one in a few weeks." Simone bent down to put on her shoes. "Speaking of which, I was thinking of inviting Tarik and Melissa to the birthday party."

"What party?" Kareem asked.

"Sabrina's first birthday. I was thinking we could do a little something right here. I really want Melissa to bring Christopher. I would love to see them." Simone continued to get ready for work.

"Hold up hold up, we didn't even discuss a birthday party," he raised his hands to protest. "How come you didn't talk to me about it? I know you probably already over did it." Kareem said.

"Well what was there to talk about? It's her first birthday. I know you want her to have a nice party. And I know you would have left it all up to me anyway, so I cut the middle man and took care of it. All you have to do is show up, babe." She kissed him on the cheek and grabbed Sabrina from his arms.

Kareem felt stupid after Simone finished talking. He knew that she was telling the truth but the way Simone said it made it seem like he didn't care enough to even mention the party to him. He went to the bathroom to brush his teeth so he could get ready for work as well. He wanted to say something to Simone about going behind his back and planning a party but what was he going to say when he was out being unfaithful. He shrugged his shoulders and let it go.

"Babe, do me a favor and drop her off at Moms. I need to make a stop before I go to work. Her things are packed and she's already dressed. All you have to do is put on her coat." After kissing Sabrina on the lips, Simone placed her on the floor next to Kareem in the bathroom. She told them both she loved them then walked out the door.

* * *

Simone sat at her desk and flipped through her rolodex. She stopped when she got to Tarik's number. She picked up the phone and dialed his office number. His assistant put the call through and she smiled when she heard his voice.

"Hey girl," he beamed.

"What's up?" she asked.

"I was just about to go to lunch, what's up? Everything ok?" Tarik asked.

"Yeah, everything is fine. I just called to invite you to Sabrina's birthday party." There was a pause. "Tarik, are you there?" she asked.

"Yeah I'm here, when is it?"

"It's two weeks from tomorrow." Simone could hear him flipping through papers.

"Mmm, I should be able to make it," he said.

"Tarik, you have to be at the party. It's your Goddaughter's first birthday," Simone said.

"I know I know, I'll be there."

"Great, I gotta go now, but I'll call you with the details."

"Ok."

"Oh wait, I almost forgot. Can you give me Melissa's number please?" Simone asked.

"Yeah, let me look through my phone and find it." He retrieved the number and called it out to her.

"Thanks Tarik, I'll see you in a couple weeks." Simone ended the call and called Melissa. She was all prepared to leave a message when Melissa picked up the phone.

"Melissa?" Simone asked.

"Yes, who's this?" she asked.

"It's Simone, is this a bad time?"

"No, hey Simone, how are you?"

"I'm well, how are you?"

"I'm good," Melissa said.

"Melissa, I'm at work right now and I was expecting to leave a message. But I just called to see how you and the baby are doing. I also wanted to invite you and Christopher to my daughter's first birthday party."

"Daughter? When did you have a baby?" Melissa was surprised.

"Girl it's a long story. We'll have to discuss that another time. But I really would like you to bring Christopher. I would love to see y'all," Simone said.

"I don't know Simone," Melissa hesitated.

"Lissa, please just think about it. The party is going to be at my place in two weeks. Can I give you a call in a few days with more details?"

"Sure call me whenever it's convenient for you. I'm not working right now. So I'm available," Melissa said.

"Ok girl, I'll call you. Melissa please think about it," Simone begged.

"I'll, talk to you later." They ended the call and Simone went to lunch.

Chapter 31

Shelly sat in Mrs. Sylvan's office and discussed her case against Kareem and Simone. She decided to go ahead and seek legal visitation rights. Ever since Connie confronted her about Kareem, their relationship had been shady. The relationship was shady before the confrontation but this time Shelly didn't have the upper hand. She'd been walking on egg shells for weeks. Connie was taking her time trying to reconcile the relationship and Shelly was concerned that she didn't want to try and work it out. Shelly felt like her world was coming to an end.

"Are you sure you'd like to go forward with the legal proceedings, Ms. Swift? We can start the paperwork now." Shelly thought about Kareem and how he wasn't returning her phone calls or text messages. She was not going to end up losing her lover and her baby. So she decided to go for the one thing she was sure she'd get in the end, her daughter.

"I'm sure. I just wanna be able to see my baby. Can you estimate about how long this process will take?" Shelly asked. She was nervous. She really didn't want to take Kareem to court but she had to do what she had to do.

"Well, first we'll petition the court for visitation rights and then they'll send a letter to Mr. and Mrs. Brown informing them that we are seeking legal visitation. We should have a court date in about a month. Judges usually make custody and visitation cases a priority," she paused, "I need you to be sure that you're ready for this. This can get really ugly. They are going to try and make you out to be a heartless monster for leaving your child," Mrs. Sylvan said.

"I know, but do you think I have a chance of getting visitation?"

"If I didn't believe we had a shot, I would have told you so. I won't have a problem making a case and winning it. But I just need to let you know that it can get a lot worse before it gets better. Be prepared to be called everything but the child of GOD." Shelly thought about it and sighed. She knew Kareem; even though he said he wasn't worried about going to court, she knew he'd flip when he got papers in the mail.

"I'm ready. I have nothing to lose. They already won't let me see her and a judge can't do no worse than that," Shelly said. She sat in the office for another hour discussing her case with her lawyer.

*   *   *

Shelly walked into her apartment and called out for Connie.

"I'm in the kitchen."

"I went to see my lawyer today. I decided to seek legal visits with Sabrina," she smiled.

"That's great. What did the lawyer say?" Connie asked. Shelly sat opposite her and explained to her what Mrs. Sylvan said and the estimated time frame.

"Congratulations and good luck. I hope this is what you really want, Shell."

"What do you mean by that?" Shelly asked.

"I just mean that I hope you'll be happy seeing your daughter," Connie said in a non-chalant manner.

"This is what I want," she hesitated, "I also want you, Con." She reached for Connie's hand. Connie looked at Shelly and melted inside. She didn't want to continue to be a hard ass but she needed to show Shelly that she meant business.

"I think it's time for us to talk." Connie said as she pulled her hand from Shelly's grip. "Let's go in the living room." Shelly followed Connie to the sofa.

"Shells, I had plenty of time to think about us and I really want us to work but I have to be able to trust you."

"Con, you can trust me. My heart belongs to you."

"Just let me finish, Shelly. I am willing to do my part in making this relationship work but you have to be willing to do the same thing."

"Whatever I need to do to gain your trust again, I'll do it," Shelly added.

"You have to be honest with me. I hate the fact that you felt you had to sneak behind my back."

"I'm sorry, Connie."

"It's not just that, Shelly...I...I... want us...well."

"What? What do you want?"

"I think we should have a threesome. I really think that will bring us closer." Connie said hoping Shelly would agree to it. Shelly was speechless for a few minutes. She was so excited but she didn't dare let Connie know how she felt about the situation. She tried to play it cool.

"Why would you wanna bring another woman into our relationship?"

"I don't. I was thinking of a man." Shelly's mouth dropped to her chest. She didn't want Connie to see the excitement in her eyes. She wrinkled her forehead and looked at Connie, who was waiting for a response.

"What are you talking about, Con?" She asked.

"I know you want to as well. Shelly I'll never forget the look in your eyes when you looked at Kareem. You were all over him like you wanted to fuck him right in that chair." Shelly wasn't aware how much Connie had seen but she knew she wasn't lying. She'd always had a weak spot for Kareem.

Shelly looked defeated. She didn't know what to say. She didn't want to deny Connie's allegations because she knew it was true. "Are you sure about this Connie?"

"I think if we do it together, we'll be able to move past our issues. I really think that will help us. And besides, I never had sex with a man before and I want to experience that with you," Connie pleaded. She knew Shelly would go for it; she just prayed that she wouldn't be stupid enough to suggest Kareem.

"I don't know Con that could be dangerous."

"Why? Do you think you'll change your mind about being with me and want to be with men again?" Connie asked.

"No, it's not that. Have you thought about how we may feel watching each other have sex with someone else?" Shelly asked.

"I've been thinking about this for a while now. If you say that you don't want Kareem then this is the perfect way to prove it," Connie said.

"Even though my word should be enough, how is us having a threesome proving that I don't want Kareem?" Shelly looked at Connie like she was crazy.

"Trust me, it will," Connie winked. She didn't want Shelly to know what she was thinking. She thought that if she saw Shelly fuck another man then she could see if she looked at him the same way she did Kareem. If she saw the lust in her eyes with another man, then she was sure Shelly wanted to be with men. But if she didn't, she was positive that this lust was only for Kareem.

Either way, she would get to fuck Joseph. And hopefully, she'd get to keep Shelly. But she'd already made up her mind to let go of Shelly if she couldn't trust that she didn't want to be with Kareem.

"Did you have someone in mind?" Shelly asked.

"Not really, I was thinking that we could go out and meet someone that we both agreed on."

Shelly hesitated. She sighed before she looked up at Connie. "Ok, if you're really sure you want to do this then let's go for it. It may not be a bad idea to bring something different to our sex life. Although we have fun, it won't hurt to step it up a little," she paused for a minute, "Connie lets promise that we won't get carried away with this man thing. I've heard stories where it backfired. I know one couple that broke up cause one of them started creeping with the man on a regular. Let's just make sure we don't go there. If one of us feels like we want to do it again, we should talk about it."

"I've thought about that, too. I think we'll be alright. Our love is strong enough to withstand that." Connie kissed Shelly on the cheek and stood, "I have to make a run sweetie, but I'll be back in a bit."

"Where are you going?" Shelly asked.

"I forgot to turn in a few receipts at work and they need them tonight. I'm going to stop by that sandwich spot, do you want anything?" Connie asked.

"How long are you gonna be? Because I'm not hungry right now but I may want something in a few."

"How about I just call you when I get there and see if you want anything? I should only be about an hour." Connie walked towards the door.

"That'll work. I'll see you when you get back, be careful," Shelly said.

Chapter 32

Connie sat in her car and dialed a number on her cell phone. "Joseph, how are you?" she smiled.

"Connie? I'm good how are you?" he asked.

"I've been better but I'll survive. I need to talk to you about something. I know it's short notice but can you get away for a few minutes?" Connie asked.

"Sure, you can come here," he suggested.

"No, I don't wanna meet there. I have to go to the sandwich shop down the road from your job. Can you meet me there in fifteen minutes?"

"Is everything ok, Connie?" Joseph was concerned.

"It's all good. I just don't have much time and I really wanna discuss something with you."

"I'm leaving now. I'll see you in a few," Joseph said.

Connie sat in her car for a few minutes before she went into the shop. She thought about what she was getting ready to do. She already got Shelly on board and now it was time to reel in Joseph. She was sure that he wouldn't be a problem with the way he lusted after her every chance he got. Connie exited her car as she watched Joseph pull into a parking space. She walked over to his car and waited for him to get out.

"It's good to see you," Joseph said and gave her a hug.

"It's nice to see you, too," she returned his affection.

"You sounded urgent on the phone, are you ok?" he asked.

"Yeah, I'm ok, lets go inside and sit for a minute?" She suggested. They walked into the sandwich shop and took a seat at a booth. Connie sat there for a few moments and stared at Joseph.

It was obvious that she wanted to say something but she seemed to be getting her thoughts together.

"Would you like to order something to eat?" he asked.

"No, I can't stay. I'm getting food to go. Joseph, I wanted to talk to you about what happened a few weeks ago…I"

"Connie you don't have to explain anything to me. I'm just happy that you're ok."

"No, I need to tell you something because it'll explain what I have to ask you," Connie said.

"What is it?" he asked.

"That night I saw Shelly in the bar, I thought she was cheating on me. She lied and told me that she had a meeting with her boss and I found her there with her ex. And I know you saw what I saw and it didn't look innocent."

"I'm sorry Connie, I wish there were something I could do to ease your pain," Joseph said. Connie's eyes lit up and she smiled inside. Joseph walked right into her trap.

"Well, like I said, I don't have much time so I'll get right to the point. I…I need a…f favor from you," she stuttered.

"What do you need?" He leaned in close to her.

"I don't know how else to say this but straight up. I know that you want me. And I've been having a hard time controlling my emotions for you." Joseph was stunned to hear Connie admit that. "But because of my relationship, I can't pursue our emotions."

"What do you need, Connie?" Joseph was getting impatient.

"Ok, I want to make love to you. But I want you to make love to me and Shelly," she confessed.

"Excuse me?" He was confused.

"I know it's not the typical favor but it's the only way we'll get to have each other," Connie said.

"What makes you think I want to make love to your lover?" Joseph asked.

"Humph, Joseph please, Shelly told me that you had a drink sent over to her way before I met you, so I already know you find her attractive. I'm giving you the chance to have us both." Connie was beginning to worry that Joseph wasn't going

126

to go with her plan. "Look Joseph, I know what I'm asking, and I know it's a lot to consider. I can't prove it but I know Shelly cheated on me. Why should she get to have her cake and eat it too? I love cake." She licked her lips to try and seal the deal.

"I don't even know what to say. You're handling being cheated on very well."

"Just say that you'll think about it," Connie said. Joseph smiled and shook his head side to side.

"Excuse me for a minute." Connie walked over to the counter and called Shelly. After she hung up, she placed the order and went back and joined Joseph at the table. "Joseph, I know I'm being a little forward and that's only because I'm pressed for time." She looked away from him before she spoke again. "I'm not sure if this will mean anything to you but I want you to know this. I've never been with a man before. For as long as I can remember, I've been attracted to women. For the first time in my life, I'm attracted to a man and I really want you to be the first man to make love to me." Joseph looked at her and raised his eyes. "And please don't think that I'm saying all of this to make you say yes. You already know how attracted to you I am," she blushed.

"Constance, I don't doubt what you're saying. I'm shocked that you are telling me this at all," Joseph admitted.

"I'm sorry I sprung this on you like this." The cashier called Constance's number and she went up to the counter to get her food. Joseph was standing behind her when she turned around.

"I'm not going to keep you because I don't want your food to get cold. But I do need to confess something to you as well." He stopped and thought about telling her about his motive but decided against it when he realized that he could get what he wanted and more in the end. "When I first saw Shelly I did find her attractive but your beauty is way more attractive to me. And the text messages, phone calls and what little time we spent together, has drawn me closer to you. So I will think about your offer and I'll be in touch."

"Oh thank you so much, Joseph." Connie hugged him and kissed him on the cheek. She inhaled deeply before she let go to keep his scent in her nostrils on her ride home.

"Be careful and take care," Joseph added.

"You too," Connie said as they walked outside.

Chapter 33

S imone was on her way to the kitchen but stopped in the living room. "Kareem, can you ride with me to the store to pick up some last minute things for the party?"

"Why do I have to go?" he asked.

"Because I can't handle Sabrina and everything else. And, I would like your input on some things," she explained.

"You don't need my input, Simone. The party is in two days and you didn't ask for my opinion about anything. Sabrina can stay here with me. I'm not going anywhere," Kareem said.

"Why can't you just go with me?"

"Cause I don't wanna go. You'll get in the store and have me walking around while you picking up shit we don't need. And Sabrina will want to get down and run around knocking things down. Nah, we'll stay here." He flicked through the TV. channels while Simone stood there with her hands on her hips staring a hole in his head.

"Kareem…"

"Simone I'm not going. Go and get what you need. I'll even cook dinner while you're out." Simone knew there was no point continuing the conversation because once Kareem made up his mind, more conversation would only lead to an argument. She grabbed her things and walked out the door.

Kareem heard Sabrina on the baby monitor and went in the room to check on her. Sabrina had climbed off the bed and had opened the nightstand drawer. She was tearing all kinds of papers and letters. She even had paper in her mouth.

"Poopy, what are you doing?" he asked as he ran to his daughter and took the papers out of her mouth. Sabrina was laughing and spitting as Kareem grabbed her hands to keep her from fighting him. Once he was satisfied that he had all of the paper out of her mouth, he sat her on the bed and cleaned the mess she made. He sorted through the paper and tried to salvage what he could. Some papers were wet so he sat them on the dresser to dry.

Kareem grabbed Sabrina and carried her into the living room. He closed the door as they left the bedroom. Sabrina struggled to get down but Kareem didn't put her down until they got to the sofa. "You are so bad, girl." He said as he stood her on the floor. Sabrina smiled and reached up to kiss her father. Kareem reached on the coffee table and grabbed the remote. As he flicked through the channels, Sabrina tried to open the front door. "Sabrina come over here to daddy," Kareem called.

She didn't come to him but she cried as she continued to try and open the door. Kareem got up and went to his daughter. "Come on Poopy, we not going outside." He picked her up and walked to the living room. Sabrina cried and pointed to the door.

"Ma…mi" she screamed and pointed to the door. She fell out on Kareem's lap and almost hit the floor.

"Mommy be right back." Sabrina kept crying and pointing. "Ok Poopy, let's go out and check the mail." Kareem put Sabrina's jacket on and grabbed his keys. They went outside of the apartment building and walked up and down the block a couple of times. Sabrina tried to run and fell twice. She kept getting up and pulled away from Kareem when he tried to help her and hold her hand.

After another five minutes, Kareem picked Sabrina up and carried her into the building. To his surprise, she didn't kick and cry. He went straight to the mailboxes and checked the mail. There was a stack of papers in the box. "When is the last time mommy checked the mail?" He locked the box and they went back to the apartment.

Kareem put the stack of mail on the sofa so he could sort it out. He removed Sabrina's jacket and took her into the kitchen. Kareem sat her in the highchair and began to warm a can of spaghetti and meatballs for her to eat. He quickly went into the living room and retrieved the stack of mail. He sat opposite

Sabrina and began sorting the papers. He came across an envelope from family court. He squinted his eyes as if that would make the envelope read something different. He got up from the table to check on Sabrina's food. He turned off the pot and put the food in a bowl. He let it sit on the countertop to cool off. He went back to the table and picked up the envelope. *"No that bitch didn't"!* Kareem tore open the letter and read it. He saw that he and Simone had to appear in court in two weeks for visitation visits for Shelly. He was livid. He looked at Sabrina and shook his head. "She ain't getting you back, Poopy!" Kareem snapped out of his zone when Sabrina started banging on her chair. He looked up at her and went to get her food.

"Da...di eat eat," she pointed to the bowl.

"Come on Poopy, let's get you something to eat so you can take your nap." Kareem fed his daughter and put her to sleep. He took her into the bedroom and turned on the baby monitor then he went back to the living room.

He sat on the sofa and pulled out his cell phone to send Shelly a text message. He waited a few minutes but didn't get a response. After a half hour he tried to call Shelly's phone but he still didn't get an answer. Kareem paced the living room trying to figure out what to do. He knew that telling Simone wasn't an option especially before the birthday party. He cursed and sat down on the sofa. He wished he could go back in time and not answer Shelly's call. He wished he would have told Simone the truth in the beginning. He was too busy trying to make Shelly see that he was a better lover than his wife. He was too busy trying to get the last laugh. Like Simone said, all he had to do was take it or leave it. Now all he could do was hope he could get in contact with Shelly and try to convince her not to go through with the visitation.

Kareem walked into the kitchen and took out a family sized frozen lasagna and placed it in the oven. He made something for dinner because he didn't want to give Simone any reason to go off on him, especially not now. Kareem grabbed two bottles of beer and went back into the living room and tried to call Shelly again. He sat on the sofa and thought about the two times they'd had sex. He knew he was drawn to Shelly but she wasn't worth his family. He stuck the envelope in his back pants pocket and closed his eyes, deep in thought.

Chapter 34

Connie hadn't heard from Joseph since she made the offer a week ago. She wanted to call him but she didn't want to seem desperate. But she finally received a text message from him last night. She eased out of the bed and took her phone into the bathroom to check the message:

> [I WILL DO IT 4 U!]
> [THANK U, CAN U TALK NOW?"] She replied.
> [CALL ME.] Joseph sent.

Connie went back into the bedroom to make sure that Shelly was asleep. She slipped on a pair of pants and grabbed her jacket and car keys. She was not going to take the chance talking in the apartment so she went out to her car. She told Joseph the entire plan. She also apologized for the fact that she wanted to do it ASAP. She and Connie would go out for drinks tomorrow night at a neighborhood bar and he would pop in and make a play for Shelly. Connie explained everything to Joseph until she was certain that he knew exactly what he was supposed to do. They ended the call and she went back up to the apartment.

* * *

Shelly rolled over and inched closer to Connie. She snuggled up against her and put her hand on Connie's breast. Connie tossed and turned to face Shelly.

"Did I wake you?" Shelly asked.

"No, I was up. I couldn't sleep," Connie answered.

"What's on your mind?"

"I was actually thinking about us. Well about me. I never had sex with a man and I'm just a little nervous about what to expect," Connie explained.

"It'll be just like the time I strapped on for you, except he'll be sexing you." Shelly propped up on a pillow. "Con, it seems like you're having doubts about this, we don't have to do this."

"I want to do it. I just don't know what to expect." Truth be told, Connie was so attracted to Joseph that she was scared that her feelings would surface while she and Shelly were with him.

"Well, if it'll make you feel better, we can practice before we get with…our victim," she smiled.

"Our victim?" Connie asked.

"Yeah, I mean look at us. The two of us together will be like an unexpected birthday gift. We got it going on so let's not get the poor man sprung," Shelly laughed.

Connie didn't say anything, she only chuckled.

"I just had another thought. What if all of us enjoy it so much that we want to get together on a regular to have a little fun?" Connie was trying to make future arrangements with Joseph. There was no doubt in her mind that she would enjoy the escapade.

"Con, I thought this was like a one time thing," Shelly said.

"It is, I'm just saying…what if."

"What if …what?" Shelly asked.

"What if we wanted to make it a regular thing, like every few months or something?"

"We haven't even found someone to do it with and you already have plans to do this again and again?" Shelly asked.

"I'm not making plans. I'm just asking a hypothetical question. But since you're so sensitive about it, lets change the subject!" Connie got out of the bed and put on her robe. "You want some coffee?" She asked as she headed towards the kitchen. She knew she'd gone too far too soon so she had to get away from Shelly to avoid any drama.

"Yeah, I'll have some," Shelly responded. After Connie left the room, she got out of the bed and followed her into the kitchen. She didn't want Connie to be upset with her. She stood in the doorway and watched Connie prepare the coffee.

"Let's go out tonight," Shelly suggested.

"I could use a drink. Where did you wanna go?"

"I don't know. We could go anywhere."

"Let's go someplace different. We should be looking for potential victims and I don't want to run into the same men we see all the time. We're looking for someone we don't know."

"Ok, sounds good to me," Shelly agreed. "But in the meantime, we can get you all prepared for the ride," she walked over to Connie and licked her neck. They walked back to the bedroom and made up for lost time.

Chapter 35

Simone dialed Tricia's cell number and waited for an answer.
"Hey Simone, let me call you back, girl."

"No I just wanted to remind you about the party tomorrow." Simone said.

I'll be there but I'll call you later, I'm in the middle of something right now," Tricia said.

"Ok." Simone said and ended the call. She began to clean the apartment. She started in the kitchen and didn't stop until she finished the bathroom. She double checked her things and made sure she had everything for the party. Once she was satisfied she had everything, she went and took a shower.

An hour later, Simone was in the kitchen preparing food for the party. She looked at the clock and noticed that Kareem and Sabrina were still out. He insisted on taking her to the mall to get her a birthday outfit. They'd been gone for three hours and Kareem hadn't called. Simone was beginning to worry. She called his cell.

"Hey baby," he answered.

"Hey, I just called to check on you two. Is everything ok?" she asked.

"Yeah, we're fine. We just chillin'."

"Oh ok. Did y'all eat?" Simone asked.

"I was going to stop and bring something back. You want something? Or did you eat?"

"No, I didn't eat. I've been too busy. I'm cooking for tomorrow right now. We're going to have plenty of food so don't eat anything too heavy. I just want a salad."

"Ok, we'll be there in about an hour," Kareem said.

Simone clicked over as soon as she hung up with Kareem, "Hey Trish,"

"What's up girl I was busy with one of the staff members in New York. Her manager wants to fire her and I'm trying to be the voice of reason and give the girl another chance. I just hate to have to let someone go in this recession. Poor girl will never find another job. Girl, it's a mess. But what's up?"

"Nothing, I'm cooking food for tomorrow. I want to try and get most of this done tonight. You should come over here and help me," Simone suggested.

"Girl, you know I would but I'm swamped. I have to finish two reports tonight in order to make it to the party tomorrow. I'm so sorry that I haven't been much help with the party and everything," Tricia said.

"Don't worry about it, it's ok. I know this is your busy time, I'll just see you tomorrow. And you'll be happy to know that I didn't overdue it," Simone said.

"Yeah right," Tricia laughed.

"I didn't, you'll see. I gotta go girl, these potatoes are done. See you tomorrow," Simone said.

"You need me to bring anything?" Tricia asked.

"No, I think I have everything but I'll call you in the morning in case I forgot something."

"Ok, see you later."

"Bye bye," Simone said.

Simone had just finished making the potato salad when Kareem and Sabrina came home. She walked into the living room when she heard his key. He put Sabrina down and she ran to Simone and gave her a hug.

"Hey Poopy, where you been?" Simone said as she picked up her daughter.

"Ma...mi ma...mi see," Sabrina said as she held up her arm and showed Simone her bracelet.

"Ooh let mommy see, daddy bought you a bracelet? It's so pretty." Simone removed Sabrina's jacket and sneakers.

"Hey baby," Kareem said and bent down to kiss his wife.

137

"Hey, what took you so long? I'm starving. I almost ate some of this food that I cooked," Simone said.

"I'm sorry, baby. We were having fun. Sabrina ran around the mall until she got tired. But I got your salad just before we came home so it's fresh."

"Thank you baby, did y'all eat?" Simone asked.

"No we were waiting until we got home. I got Sabrina a happy meal. She stood in front of McDonald's and wouldn't leave until I let her carry her box. She finally let me have it when we got in the car."

"You know how she is when she wants something. Go get her chair from the kitchen and we'll eat in here," Simone suggested.

"Why can't she just eat on the floor?" Kareem asked.

"Because I just cleaned up in here and I don't want to have to clean up a mess again. I would feed her but I don't feel like dealing with her falling out trying to do it herself, so just put her in the highchair and give her the food."

"She'll still make a mess, Simone."

"I know but it won't be as big of a mess. Where's the food?" She asked as she looked around at the bags.

"Yo, I found some cute outfits. I wound up getting three cause I couldn't decide which one I liked better."

"What sizes did you get?"

"The sales lady helped me with the size. She told me that we could return them if they didn't fit." Kareem gave Simone the bag and she looked through them. She was impressed with the clothes that Kareem picked out. "These are nice. I didn't think you had it in you." Simone smiled as she put the clothes back in the bag.

Kareem picked up the ringing phone while Simone set up their food on the food trays. He passed the phone to Simone.

"Who is it?" she asked.

"It's Melissa," Kareem said and took over setting up the food.

"Hello?" Simone asked.

"Hey Melissa, what's going on?" Simone asked. Melissa told Simone that she'd just settled into her hotel room. She asked Simone what time the party was going to start.

"It's going to start at about 1pm. But I wanted you to come by earlier so we can catch up," Simone said. Melissa told her that she was going to meet with Belinda in the morning. But she did say that she'd try.

"Ok sweetie, I'm feeding the baby. I'll see you tomorrow." She hung up the phone and ate her salad. She thought it was nice that Melissa kept in touch with Phil's daughter. In spite of everything that happened.

Chapter 36

Shelly sat on the bed and double checked the outfit that she'd laid out earlier. She and Connie were going out to meet a potential victim and they wanted to look nice. She decided on a pair of House of Dereon jeans and a button up shirt. Without trying, her breasts were spilling out of the shirt.

Connie walked into the bedroom naked. She went to her drawer and pulled out a pink g-string. She slipped it on and pulled out a pair of white sweatpants from the closet. It was sexy but she didn't have to try to impress because she knew she'd already had Joseph's attention. She pulled out a spaghetti strap shirt that went with the pants. She purposely didn't wear a bra so that her nipples would be standing at attention all night.

"So, are we ready?" Connie asked as she switched to her black coach bag.

"I have everything. Let's do this," Shelly said. "We can take my car. But you have to drive, you know I'm gonna get my drink on," Shelly said.

"Fine with me." Connie said as they walked out of the apartment.

* * *

Shelly and Connie sat at the bar and drank their drinks. A few men offered to buy them drinks but they refused. Shelly noticed a guy in the corner staring at them. She whispered to Connie and smiled. "That dude over there is looking good. What you think?"

"I don't know Shells, I'm not feeling the way he's looking at us. He looks like a serial killer or something." Connie laughed and shook her head no.

Shelly turned around in time to see a man walking towards them. She stared at the man like he was familiar. He stopped in front of her and smiled.

"I've been watching you ladies from across the room. I saw you reject a few offers but you can't blame a man for trying. Can I buy you ladies a drink?" he offered." Shelly looked at Connie for approval. Connie raised her eyes and nodded her head.

"You sure can. I'm Shelly and this is my friend, Connie."

"I'm Joseph, nice to meet you ladies. Do you mind if I sit?" He sat on the stool next Connie. He waved the bartender their way. "Another round for the ladies, please. And I'll have a rum and coke."

"So Joseph, are you from around here?" Shelly asked. She still wondered where she'd seen him before.

"No, I'm not from around here. I was out taking a drive and decided to pop in here for a drink."

"Well, I'm glad you did," Shelly flirted. Connie sat back and let Shelly take control of the situation. She was too busy trying to control the urge to throw her tongue down Joseph's mouth. The bartender brought their drinks and the women tipped their glasses to Joseph. "Joseph, you look so familiar to me. Have we met before?" Shelly asked.

Joseph looked at Connie and she discreetly nodded at him. "Well I'm a manager at the Sheraton Hotel. We have happy hour on Thursdays, maybe you've come by and saw me there?" He made the statement into a question.

"That's possible. I've been there before," Shelly said.

"So, Connie is it?" She shook her head yes. "Why are you so quiet?" Joseph asked.

"I'm always quiet. I'm just enjoying the scenery and music."

"Would you ladies be more comfortable at a table? I can barely hear you," Joseph suggested.

"I don't mind," Connie said.

"Let's go." Shelly got off the stool. Joseph led them to the only available table in the back. He slid out their chairs so they could sit. "Would you ladies like another drink?"

"Sure," they answered. Joseph walked back over to the bar.

"What about him, Con?"

"He seems nice, he's handsome and he's not stingy. He'll do," Connie said.

"You remember I told you about the guy that sent me a drink at the Sheraton, that's him."

"Well he's cute. I think he may be our victim," Connie smiled. Joseph came back to the table and sat their drinks in front of them. The three of them began talking and getting to know each other. They stayed in the bar until closing. Connie had stopped drinking over an hour ago but Shelly wanted to drink up everything in the bar. And Joseph had no problems buying her whatever she wanted. He even winked at Connie a few times when Shelly wasn't looking.

"Do you mind if we exchange numbers, Shelly?"

"We're a package deal, Joseph. You can't have her without having me," Connie interrupted.

"What does that mean?" he asked.

"It means exactly what it sounds like. We're a package deal." Shelly licked her lips and kissed Connie on the mouth.

"Oh really?" Joseph smiled.

"Still interested?" Connie asked.

"Definitely! How do we keep in touch?"

"How about we make you dinner tomorrow night?" Connie asked.

"I love to eat," he flirted.

"Good, so do we," Shelly added. She winked at Joseph and stood. "I need to use the ladies room before we go. I'll be right back, baby."

"I'll be here," Connie smiled.

"So how about you give me some of what Shelly just gave you?" He winked.

"In due time. And you won't be disappointed. I promise," Connie flirted.

Shelly returned from the ladies room and grabbed her jacket. "Are we ready?" she asked.

"Yep. Joseph, we'll see you tomorrow. Give me your number and I'll call you with the details," Connie said and followed Shelly out of the door.

Chapter 37

Kareem tossed and turned as Simone got out of the bed. He squinted and glanced at the clock.

"I'm sorry baby, did I wake you?" she asked.

"What you doin' up so early?" he asked.

"I wanted to get started cooking the rest of the food before Sabrina got up. I still need to straighten out a few things." She slipped on her pajamas.

"You need me to help with something?"

"I'm gonna need you to help put up the decorations a little later," she said. "And I'ma need you to get Sabrina when she wakes up. I'll be too busy getting ready for the party."

"Ok, I got her." He lay back under the covers.

Simone went into the kitchen and began cooking food. She took a break an hour later and went to check on Sabrina. Sabrina was trying to climb out of her crib. She was almost over the side when Simone came into the room.

"Poopy," she called as she lifted her out of the crib. "Kareem, get her! She almost fell on the floor face first and you laying here sleep!" Simone put Sabrina in the bed with her father.

"I ain't even hear her. Why are you yelling?" He asked as he sat up.

"Because I left the monitor in here with you and you didn't hear her making noise?" Simone was upset.

"No Simone, I didn't hear her. I was sleeping! You think I was ignoring her or something?"

"I think she almost fell face first on the floor and it pisses me off that you were right in here with her and didn't hear a thing! What if I wouldn't have come in here to check on her?" Simone shifted her body to one side with her hands on her hips.

"Simone, she didn't fall, so why are you trippin? Just calm down and go finish doing what you were doing. I got her, I'm up now," he said. Simone shook her head and went into the kitchen.

Kareem came into the kitchen with Sabrina on his hip.

"Ma...mi," she reached out to Simone.

"Happy birthday, Poopy," Simone said and kissed her daughter on the cheek.

"Ma...mi." Sabrina whined and continued to reach for her mother.

"Mommy can't take you now, Poopy. I'm cooking. Kareem can you give her a bath and get her dressed?"

"You want me to do it now?" he asked.

"No, I need the decorations to go up now. People will start showing up soon. I'll feed her while you do that. Just give me five minutes to finish this," she said.

"Aiight, what you want her to eat?" he asked.

"You can give her some cereal. That'll hold her until we eat at the party. Kareem sat at the table and waited for Simone to finish. "Oh, I meant to tell you that Tarik is coming. And Melissa, too."

"What you think this is Soul Food or something? Why you trying to get everybody together at the baby's party?" he asked.

"Calm down, it'll be ok. Everyone is civilized." Simone shook her head.

"They better be, cause if any drama jump off, I'ma set it the fuck off!" he replied.

"Stop cussing, Kareem. She's sitting right on your lap."

Kareem turned Sabrina towards him and kissed her. "Happy birthday, Poopy," he said as he bounced her up and down.

"Ok Kareem, go ahead with the decorations. I got her." Simone took the baby from his lap. "You can go ahead and take your shower when you're done. I'll give her a bath after she eats."

145

"Aiight." Kareem went to the living room and started putting up the decorations.

* * *

Melissa arrived at the party a little after noon. "Hey Simone." Melissa reached for a hug as Simone opened the door.

"Hey girl, long time no see. Oh my goodness, look at Christopher, he's so big," Simone said as she took him from Melissa's arms.

"Belinda and I had to cancel brunch so I came a little early. I hope you don't mind that I didn't call first," Melissa said.

"No girl, I'm glad you're here. We can get a chance to catch up before the guests arrive," Simone said, "Kareem," she yelled, "bring Sabrina out here."

Kareem walked into the living room holding Sabrina's hand. "How you doing, Melissa?" He kissed her on the cheek.

"I'm well, thank you. How are you?" She looked at Sabrina who ran straight to Simone. She reached to be picked up because Simone was holding Christopher.

"Got our hands full with this one, you know how it is," he smiled.

Simone removed Christopher's jacket and sat him on her lap. He looked up and saw his mother and reached out to her. Simone handed Christopher to Melissa and picked up Sabrina. Kareem went back into the bedroom while the two ladies talked and reminisced.

"She is beautiful, Simone. She looks just like Kareem," Melissa said.

"Thanks girl, Christopher is as handsome as ever. How is Mike?"

"He's good. He had to work so he couldn't make the trip with us."

A few of Simone's co-workers arrived next. She turned on the music and let the kids dance. Kareem came and took all of the jackets into the den. The doorbell rang and Kareem went to answer. It was Tarik and Tashi. Kareem stepped aside and let them into the apartment.

"What up man?" Kareem asked.

"I'm good." He stepped aside and introduced Kareem and Tashi. "Hey listen, I hope you don't mind that I brought Tashi with me. We have plans afterwards and it was convenient to just bring her along."

"No problem man." He pulled Kareem aside. "Tricia will be here in a little while so please don't cause a scene."

"Come on man, you know me better than that."

"Yeah I do, but Tashi is a dime piece and once Tricia sees that, all hell is gonna break loose. Just try to be cool," Kareem said.

"I got you. We won't ruin the party," Tarik chuckled. Tarik walked into the living room and saw Melissa and Christopher. "Hey baby, why didn't you tell me you were coming?" He gave her a hug.

"Um um," Tashi cleared her throat and swung her long weave out of her face.

Simone looked at Melissa and smiled.

"Oh, I'm sorry. Tashi this is Melissa, my lil sister and Lissa, this is Tashi."

"His girlfriend," Tashi finished.

"Nice to meet you, Tashi." Melissa shook her hand.

"And you remember Simone right?" Tarik said.

"Yes I do, how are you Simone?"

"I'm well and you?"

"Just fine. We brought Sabrina a gift. Where would you like it?" Tashi asked. Simone pointed to the pile of gifts on the other side of the room. "Oh, I didn't see that," she walked away towards the table of gifts. Tashi was brown skinned. She wore a pair of jeans that looked like they were painted on. Her apple-shaped ass switched with every step she took. She knew they were staring so she turned around and blew a kiss at Tarik.

Tarik took Christopher from Melissa's arms and took a look at him. He complimented him and sat down next to Melissa. Tashi walked around and mingled with some of the other guests.

She kept a close watch on Melissa. She wasn't too happy with how long Tarik hugged her. It just didn't seem like a sisterly hug.

Simone and Kareem entertained their guests and made sure everyone had drinks. She went to the table that held the food and started putting utensils in the pans so people could serve themselves and eat. She heard the doorbell and went to the door.

"Hey Trish." She kissed her on the cheek.

"Hey girl, I'm sorry I'm late." She took off her coat at the door.

"That's ok, you didn't miss much. But I need to warn you that Tar..."

"Tarik is here?" Tricia asked with surprise as she saw him sitting on the sofa holding a baby boy. She didn't know who the baby belonged to until she saw Melissa coming out of the bathroom taking the baby in her arms. "Is that Melissa? What are they doing here?" she asked.

"Come on Trish, Tarik is Sabrina's Godfather, you know he was going to be here. And I invited Melissa to bring Christopher," Simone said.

Tarik walked over to Tricia and Simone and smiled. "Hi Tricia, it's nice to see you."

"It's nice to see you, too." She leaned in for a hug. "How've you been?" she asked.

"I've been ok, and you?"

"I'm good," Tricia smiled in a flirtatious way. Tarik still held her hand as they walked towards the sofa.

"Tarik, what time are the reservations?" Tashi interrupted. Simone glanced over at Melissa, who was watching the entire scenario play out.

"Trisha, this is my friend, Tashi. Tashi this is Tricia, my..."

"His *wife*," Tricia answered.

Tashi smiled to keep from showing her embarrassment. She gently pulled Tarik's arm, "Can I see you for a minute?"

"She's a piece of work," Simone said, "I didn't know he was going to bring her. He told Kareem that they had plans afterwards and that's why he brought her," Simone said. "Are you ok?"

"Girl, I'm fine. And so is Tarik. Now where's my lil' mama?" She searched for Sabrina. Simone stood there for a minute. She was on a delayed reaction. When it finally registered what Tricia had said, she smiled and went back over to the table.

"Hi Tricia," Melissa said.

"How are you, Melissa?" Tricia was cordial. She wasn't going to disrupt her Goddaughter's first birthday party. She still felt a little chill up her spine when she looked at Melissa.

"Tricia, can I talk to you for a minute?" Melissa asked.

"Melissa, I really don't think now is the time." Tricia said.

"I know it's a birthday party but I really want to say something to you. Can you give me five minutes?" Melissa pleaded while she carried Christopher on her hip.

Tricia looked around the room and spotted Tarik and Tashi in what seemed like a heated discussion. "Come on, we can talk in the hall." They headed into the hallway and bumped dead into Mr. and Mrs. Woodsby.

"Hey Moms, hi Marvin," Tricia greeted.

"Hey Trish, nice to see you," Marvin responded.

"Mi Moms," Melissa said.

"Melissa?" Moms was surprised. "Hey baby, how are you?" She gave her a hug. "Is this that big boy of yours?" She kissed Christopher on the cheek. He smiled and laid his head on his mother's shoulder.

"Well, where y'all going?" Moms asked.

"We're just standing here talking for a minute. We'll be inside in a few," Tricia said.

"Na...na...na...na," Sabrina sang.

"Hi baby, how is Nana's birthday girl doing?" Sabrina smiled and kissed Moms on the lips. "You wanna go wit' Nana?" Marvin took Sabrina from Trish and lifted her over his head. Sabrina laughed and tried to reach his face from upside down. Moms and Marvin headed inside of the apartment but Sabrina reached for Tricia. "We'll see y'all inside," Moms said and closed the door behind her.

149

Tricia stood in front of Melissa and played with Christopher. He was all smiles and trying to get down. Melissa held him tight so he wouldn't climb out of her arms.

"Can he walk, yet?" Tricia asked.

"Yeah he can walk, but I'm not putting him down in this hallway. He'll be all over the place." Sabrina reached out and touched Christopher's hand. They looked at each other and smiled.

"So what did you wanna say, Lissa?" Tricia asked.

"Tricia I want to tell you how sorry I am for everything that I put you through. I'm not going to stand here and try to justify anything that happened because none of it should have happened at all. I love you, Trish and I would never do anything to intentionally hurt you. What happened between Tarik and me was a mistake. I know you can't understand that but it's the truth. And that's the only way I know how to describe it." She paused and looked Tricia in her eyes. "I'm asking for your forgiveness, Tricia. You didn't deserve to lose your family because of this and I'm so sorry."

"Melissa, I've thought about this day over and over again. I knew we would be standing face to face one day but I never knew how I would handle it. I know what happened between you and Tarik was a mistake but this is about me and you. Not Tarik. I trusted you like a sister. That was the ultimate betrayal and woman to woman, it still hurts. We became friends because my husband asked me to get to know his friend. He said that I would like you. And in all honesty, I wasn't trying to like you; I just wanted to keep you close to make sure that you and Tarik's relationship was platonic. But through everything, we became friends. I stood up for you. I even lied to my husband to protect you and your husband when I knew Phil was dead wrong. And you sleep with my husband? You didn't even have the decency to tell me to my face what happened. I had to find out in a hospital room full of people- my family and friends," Tricia sobbed. She had tears in her eyes but she controlled them in front of the kids.

"I know. Tricia, I'm sorry," Melissa said.

150

"Melissa, I know you're sorry. You don't have to keep saying it cause that doesn't make me feel any better. I want to know how to get past this! I want to know how to trust my husband again! I want to know how I trust women again."

Melissa stared at Tricia and silently cried. "I wish I had answers for you, Trish. But I don't. I can only assure you that I would never do anything to hurt you again."

"I know, Melissa. I honestly believe you but I still don't know how to look at my husband and not see what you and he did. I'm trying though," Tricia smiled.

"Please figure something out because Ms. Thang in there is a hot mess!" She laughed.

"I know. She's not his type." They laughed and Tricia walked over to Melissa and gave her a hug. "I'm not going to hold onto this for the rest of my life. I am working on forgiving you, Melissa. And I have love for you," Tricia said.

"Thank you, Trish," Melissa said.

"Hey you two," Simone opened the door, "the party is inside, lets go." She grabbed Sabrina who reached for her. "And I just wanna warn y'all, Tashi got ya boy hemmed up in a corner. She won't let him out of her sight." They all laughed as they waked back inside the apartment.

Chapter 38

K areem was cleaning up when Tarik joined him in the kitchen.

"You were right, man," he laughed.

"Ya think?" Kareem smirked.

"Yeah, but it was the other way around. Tashi started trippin' when she met Melissa and Tricia."

"You better talk to her. You know she don't wanna see Tricia. Especially with all her girls around," Kareem laughed.

"I know. I tried to tell her to calm her ass down. She has no idea." Tarik shook his head. "I came in here to get the ladies some wine. Simone said there were some in the fridge," Tarik said.

Kareem went to the fridge and handed Tarik two bottles of wine and went back to the dishes. "Man, I just wanna finish these dishes up real quick. Now that it's only family here, I can get away to straighten up a little. Give me five minutes and I'll be out there to have your back," he smiled.

"Hurry up, man." Tarik said and walked back into the living room.

Simone had opened most of the gifts while the guests were still there. She waited until they left to open the rest. She let Sabrina stand at the table and tear the wrapping off a gift box. Sabrina finally got the paper off and put it in her mouth.

"No Poopy, you don't eat that." Simone grabbed her and removed the paper from her mouth. She opened the box and removed three of the cutest outfits she'd saw in a while. "Poopy, look what auntie Lissa bought you. Go say thank you," Simone urged.

Sabrina went to Tricia and kissed her on the lips. "Not me lil' Mama, go kiss Lissa," she turned Sabrina towards Melissa. Sabrina went to Melissa and tapped her legs. She reached up and kissed her on the cheek.

"Thank you for that kiss, Sabrina," Melissa smiled.

"Ok, now let's see what auntie Trish got you," Trish said. She went to the gift bag she put on the table and handed it to Sabrina. Sabrina laughed and tore into the bag. She pulled out a jewelry box. Tricia reached for the box and opened it up. She pulled out a pair of gold birthstone earrings and a matching necklace and then passed it to Simone.

"Ohh look, Poopy. You got more jewelry." Simone pulled Sabrina towards her and put the earrings in Sabrina's ear. Sabrina pulled at her ear and tried to take them off. "She's not used to wearing earrings. Once she gets used to them, they'll be fine," Simone smiled. "Ok Poopy you have to give Auntie Trish a big hug and kiss." The smiling Sabrina went to Tricia and did as she was told.

Kareem went to Sabrina and picked her up and tossed her in the air. "Now let's open Daddy's gift."

"You brought her something else, Kareem? I thought the bracelet was her gift," Simone said.

"Of course I got my baby something else. We were at the mall and I couldn't resist these." He sat Sabrina on the sofa next to Simone and put a large bag on the floor in her reach. She reached into the bag and tried to pull out the items. Kareem saw her struggling and helped her take out the items. He pulled out two pairs of sneakers, two outfits, and a leather jacket.

"Wow, Kareem, a leather jacket? That's a lot," Tricia said, "she ain't but knee high," she laughed.

"I know, but I just couldn't resist. This jacket is nice," he smiled. "Poopy, happy birthday!" He kissed her on the cheek and then sat her back on Simone's lap.

"Ok it's time for my gift," Tarik said.

"Don't you mean our gift?" Tashi asked as she grabbed Tarik's arm. Tarik looked at her and shook his head. Everyone else in the room raised their eyes and grunted. "Like I was saying," Tarik continued, "I knew you all would buy clothes and jewelry so I got her something she could use in her future. I opened up a college account for her. And I've already deposited one thousand dollars. I have it set up where she'll automatically get one hundred dollars a month direct deposited. And of course, you all will be able to make deposits whenever you'd like." He turned and faced Melissa. "I know this is Sabrina's party but I just wanted to tell Lissa that I did the same thing for Christopher when he turned a year a few months ago."

"Why didn't you tell me?" Melissa asked.

"You would have only objected."

"Thanks Tarik," Melissa smiled.

"And Tricia, I hope you don't mind that I added your name to both of the accounts. The gifts are from both of us," Tarik said. Tricia smiled.

"Tarik, I don't know what to say. Thank you so much," Simone said.

"You put her name on the accounts?" Tashi asked with a slight hint of attitude.

"Of course I did. Tricia and I are the Godparents of both kids." He said matter-of-factly. Tashi looked around the room before she excused herself and went to the ladies room.

"Wow!" Melissa said. Everyone burst into laughter. "Where'd you find her?" she whispered?"

"Don't start. She was just a distraction until my *wife* came to her senses," he said as looked at Tricia sideways.

"Well Marvin and I gave her money. So Simone, you all can just deposit it into her account," Moms said.

"Kareem and I just want to thank everyone for the gifts. We appreciate everything and we are so glad that all of you made it." Simone said as she stood next to Kareem. Sabrina and Christopher were busy playing with all of the wrapping paper. They were in a world of their own, having the time of their lives.

Tashi returned from the ladies room and whispered something in Tarik's ear. Tarik turned to everyone as he stood.

"Looks like we're gonna have to be leaving," he said.

"Leaving so soon?" Tricia asked.

"Yes, we have plans," Tashi smiled.

"Uhm Tarik, can you call me this week? There's a few details we need to work out and some paperwork we need to go over," Tricia said.

"Sure, I'll give you a call. It was great seeing all of you." He went and picked up both of the kids. "Melissa, how long are you staying?"

"I'm leaving tomorrow. But I may be back in the next few weeks. I think Mike mentioned that he has a medical seminar out this way," she answered.

"Tarik, we really must go. We have reservations," Tashi urged. Tarik kissed Christopher on the forehead and kissed Sabrina on her cheek. He stood them both on the floor and headed towards the door. Tashi led the way out of the apartment. Just before she walked out of the door, she turned to everyone and told them that it was nice meeting them and thanked Simone for her hospitality.

"Tarik, we might be playing spades next week. You should stop by. Of course, Tashi you're welcome too," Kareem said after he saw the look in her eyes.

"Call me. See y'all later," he said and followed Tashi out the door.

"Well Marv and I have got to get going, too." They stood and kissed everyone before they left.

"Simone, I'm gonna give her a bath while you do the girl thing," Kareem said.

"Thanks baby." The women sat around for a few more hours and got to know each other all over again. Christopher went to sleep shortly after Kareem took Sabrina in the room. By midnight they said their goodbyes and called it a night.

Chapter 39

Connie made sure the apartment was spotless as Shelly prepared the food. They were excited and nervous about Joseph coming to dinner. She went to the mirror to make sure she looked good enough to eat. Shelly noticed her fidgeting and grabbed her by the waist.

"Connie, just relax. It'll be fine. Let me start it off and then you do whatever you feel. And you don't have to do anything you don't want." Shelly kissed her on the neck. "But this can be an amazing experience. You can get the best of both worlds."

When the doorbell rang, Connie began to feel nervous between her legs. She couldn't understand the strong urge to be with this man. She wanted Joseph badly and the time had finally come.

Shelly escorted Joseph to the living room as she thanked him for the fresh roses he gave her. He walked over to Connie and also gave her a dozen of roses.

"Joseph, you shouldn't have," Connie said and smelled the roses.

"It's the least I could do since you ladies prepared the meal. By the way, what's on the menu this evening?"

"I can't take credit for anything. Shelly did all of the cooking. I hope you like southern food because she fried some chicken, made some greens and potato salad," Connie said.

"I also made some cornbread so I hope you're hungry," Shelly smiled.

"Wow, be careful, with a meal like that, I may not want to go home. At least I may not want to leave tonight," he winked.

"Now you're talking," Shelly licked her lips, "dinner will be ready in about fifteen minutes."

"Let's sit and have a drink while we wait," Connie suggested. They all went into the kitchen, where the table was immaculate, and sat down. Connie went to the ice bucket and pulled out a bottle of Verdi. She grabbed the strawberries out the fridge and dropped a few in the glasses before she filled them with champagne. She passed each of them a glass and then raised hers. "What shall we toast to?" she asked.

"How about to great company?" Joseph said. They all smiled and clinked their glasses. "I must say that you ladies look wonderful tonight."

"Thank you," they said in unison.

"Well dinner is ready. I'll make the plates. Connie would you get the salad, please?"

"What can I do to help?" Joseph asked.

"Just sit back and relax. We'll take care of you," Connie said. Shelly looked at her and gave her an approving nod.

They sat at the table, ate their meal and enjoyed stimulating conversation. Joseph flirted with Connie while Shelly flirted with him. The evening was going well. They sat at the table and talked a while longer before Shelly offered dessert.

"This meal was delicious. I'm not sure if I can handle dessert, but what do you have?" he asked.

"I'm sure you'll be able to have a little dessert. Once you see what it is, you'll have some," Shelly teased. "Why don't we all go into the living room and get more comfortable." The three of them went to the living room and got comfortable on the sofa. "Joseph, anybody ever tell you how sexy you are?" Shelly asked.

"I think I've heard that before. But it sounds a lot better coming from someone as beautiful as you."

"Connie, you ok?" Shelly asked.

"I'm fine." She slid her hand up Joseph's arm to get his attention. She sensed that he was more attracted to Shelly. But what she didn't know was that Joseph was playing it off so Shelly wouldn't suspect anything. Although Connie didn't want to expose herself, she wasn't going to sit there like she was invisible. She turned around and swung her legs on Joseph's lap.

Shelly smiled at the fact that Connie seemed to be ready to get the party started. "You do this a lot Joseph?" Connie asked.

"What do you mean?" He looked at Connie and frowned.

"Have threesomes with women you just met?" Connie asked.

"No, actually this is my first time," he confessed.

"So why now? Why with us?" Connie asked.

"I'd be a fool to turn down two women this gorgeous. Besides, you only live once, right?" He responded.

Connie smiled and lifted her feet so that Joseph could remove her shoes. After he removed her shoes, he turned to Shelly and removed hers as well. He turned back to Connie and leaned in and kissed her on the lips. "I've wanted to do that ever since we met." Only the two of them knew the real meaning behind that statement.

"Hey be easy with her, she's never been with a man," Shelly said.

"Well I'll just make sure she won't forget her first time with a man." Joseph pulled her closer to him and gave her a more passionate kiss. Connie returned the same passion and longed for more.

Shelly stood and walked over to Connie. She pulled her up from the sofa and removed her shirt. Once her breasts popped out, Joseph was mesmerized. He couldn't believe his luck with two perfect sets of breasts at his disposal. Joseph got up and stood behind Shelly. He rubbed against her as he kissed the back of her neck. While he seduced her, Shelly was getting Connie in the mood. She gently pushed Connie on the sofa once her jeans were off. "Joseph, are you ready for dessert?" Shelly asked as she spread Connie's legs apart and invited him to eat.

"Definitely." Joseph got on his knees and rubbed up and down Connie's legs. He took his time and licked her thighs and massaged her clit with his tongue. While he was on his knees, Shelly stood on the sofa in front of Connie to receive the same treatment. Connie leaned her head against the sofa and pulled Shelly closer to her face. Shelly rested her knees on the back of the sofa for support. Connie moaned as she gave head to her lover. Joseph was doing a number on her. She moved and squirmed to match his licks. She didn't leave Shelly out because the better he made her feel, the better she made Shelly feel. Joseph paused and looked up at Connie and Shelly. He was pleased at what he saw. Although he enjoyed tasting Connie, he wanted to be inside her. He continued his task and decided to let the girls take charge.

Shelly got down from the sofa and sat down while she watched Connie being pleased. She was happy that Connie seemed to be enjoying herself. Joseph stopped after a few more minutes and got between Shelly's legs and licked her breasts. He played with her nipples until they felt like they were going to fall off. She moaned in pleasure and grabbed the back of his head. She reached for Connie and stuck her finger inside Connie's pussy. Connie moaned and played with her own nipples. Shelly then pushed Joseph back on the floor and stood over him. She grabbed Connie's hand and led her down to the floor. "Just do what feels right." She told Connie.

Shelly stood over Joseph and sat on his chest. She opened her legs and let him eat her goodies. Connie got on her knees and rubbed Joseph's dick. She felt how hard it was and got aroused. She slowly bent down and licked his shaft. She took her time and sucked the tip of his dick. After a few minutes, Joseph began to hump and make his dick go farther in her mouth. She sucked as he pumped. She enjoyed the feeling of his shaft in her throat. She moaned and grabbed the base of his dick. She held his hips to make him stop pumping. She began to suck him faster without his help. She found it easier and more pleasurable to use only her head as she bobbed up and down. By the sound of things, Joseph enjoyed her services.

Shelly gyrated her hips as Joseph lifted his head slightly off the floor and sucked Shelly's clit so hard that she yelled in excitement. The orgasm she was having was incredible. She held his head a little longer so that he wouldn't move until she was done with her orgasm. When she was done, Joseph gently pushed her aside and he headed straight for Connie.

Joseph lay Connie on her back and lifted her legs around his waist. She shook from the anticipation of what was about to happen. "Don't worry baby, I won't hurt you." He slid his shaft into her slit and eased in and out. He continued with this position for a while until Shelly saw that Connie was having all of the fun. Shelly stood over Connie and grabbed her legs. She held them up above her head so that Joseph could go deep. Connie moaned and enjoyed every minute of it. Shelly sucked on Connie's legs as she massaged them. Then she bent down and sucked Connie's nipples. This sent Connie over the edge. She was feeling all kinds of sensations throughout her body. She didn't want that feeling to end. Shelly kissed her on the lips and stuck her tongue in her mouth. Connie felt like she was in heaven. She even began to match Joseph's strokes. Connie grabbed Shelly's legs and felt her way to her clit and began to massage it. She stuck a finger inside of her and let her ride. Shelly seemed to be enjoying herself as much as Connie.

Joseph moaned and groaned as he reached an orgasm. He pumped until everything in him was in his condom. He slowly got up and removed the condom. Shelly took it from him and placed it a plastic bag that was on the coffee table. She sat Joseph on the sofa and got in between his legs to make him rise again.

Joseph was amazed that Shelly was able to get him erect again. Usually, he'd need at least an hour to get it up again after an orgasm like that. Once Shelly succeeded in her goal, she slid another condom on him and jumped on top of him and rode him silly. She bent down and kissed him as she gripped the back of his head for support. Shelly had her feet on the sofa and squatted over Joseph and rode him until she reached her second orgasm. She felt satisfied that both of her partners had given her an orgasm.

Connie went and kissed Joseph as he tried to catch his breath. He was still horny because Shelly didn't wait for him to reach his orgasm; she jumped off after she got hers. He took Connie and bent her over on her knees. He slid down and thrust into her as he spread her ass cheeks apart. Connie was feeling no pain. She matched his strokes as he rode her. He gently guided her on her stomach and closed her legs as he re-entered her. Just looking at Connie's ass was enough to send him to an orgasm. Joseph wanted Connie to have an orgasm too so he slid his hand under her and played with her clit until he felt her body jerking from an orgasm. He lifted her back to her knees and thrust in and out until he reached his final orgasm.

Joseph collapsed on top of Connie and kissed the back of her neck. She moaned as he rubbed her ass. Shelly was on the sofa using her vibrator trying to reach another orgasm. Connie looked up and saw her and decided to help. She took the vibrator from Shelly and stuck it in her pussy and watched Shelly squirm and moan as she ejaculated all over the dildo.

The three of them sat on the sofa and caught their breath. Joseph eased closer to Connie without being noticed. An hour later they were all asleep with Connie resting on Joseph's chest.

Chapter 40

Simone began sorting laundry at 6am. She wanted to get an early start so she could spend the day with her family. She and Kareem were going to take Sabrina to the park. Simone went through the pockets of Kareem's jeans to be sure there would be no surprises in the machines. As she shook a pair of jeans, an envelope fell to the floor. Simone took the envelope and sat it on the coffee table.

Once she put the clothes in the laundry bag, she saw a pair of Sabrina's socks that needed to be soaked. She walked into the kitchen and got the spray. When she went back into the living room, she bumped into the coffee table. Simone bent down to pick up the envelope and saw that it was addressed to Mr. and Mrs. Kareem Brown and proceeded to read the letter. Simone's mouth dropped as she read that she and Kareem had to appear in court in four days due to the fact that Shelly petitioned the courts for visitation.

She put the envelope inside her purse and continued with the laundry. Simone went into the bedroom to check on Sabrina and Kareem to make sure they were still asleep. She reached on Kareem's nightstand and grabbed his cell phone then took it into the living room with her. She closed the bedroom door behind her and went and sat on the sofa.

Simone couldn't believe that she was getting ready to search through her husband's cell phone. She hadn't done that since before she went to prison. But she knew there was a reason Kareem hid the letter from her. Her gut told her that Shelly had contacted Kareem. Simone went through his phone book but didn't see Shelly's name. She then checked the received calls to see if there were any unknown numbers. There were two so she wrote them down on the piece of paper she had in front of her. Just when Simone was about to close the phone, she thought about checking the text messages. She looked through the messages and one caught her attention.

Simone read and re-read the message. Kareem was asking someone to call him back. Simone clicked on the view details button and saw that it was one of the numbers that she'd written down. She was going to send a text message to that number hoping that it was Shelly. She knew she was taking a risk because she didn't know what she'd do if it weren't Shelly. Simone sent a text message to the number:

[meet me @ laundry world on rt. 22. VERY important- about Sabrina. B there in 1 hr.]

Simone waited a few minutes and checked that the message was delivered then deleted the message from Kareem's phone. She turned the phone off and took it back into the bedroom. She went back into the living room and finished packing the laundry and detergent. It took her fifteen minutes to finish up and get dressed.

Simone went back into the bedroom and woke Kareem. She told him that she was leaving and to listen out for Sabrina. Simone turned the volume on the baby monitor all the way up so that Kareem would hear Sabrina when she awoke. She peeked in the crib again before she walked out the door. She hurried before Kareem got up because she didn't want him to ask if she'd found anything in her pockets.

*   *   *

Simone stood by her washing machine and looking by the door to see if anyone came in looking for Kareem. She was almost positive that Shelly would be coming. She was standing in the back of the laundry because she didn't want to be noticed.

Ten minutes later, Shelly walked inside Laundry World. She looked around frantically before she actually walked through the place. Simone saw her coming her way and turned her back to her and reached in her purse to pull out the letter from the court. Shelly looked at her phone again and frowned. She was walking back outside getting ready to dial a number. Simone knew she was getting ready to call Kareem and she couldn't let that happen.

"Shelly?" She called. Shelly turned around and looked at Simone. She squinted her eyes a little until she recognized her.

"Simone?" She asked and looked around.

"Yep, it's me and I came alone." She walked towards Shelly with the envelope in her hand.

"Simone, I really shouldn't be talking to you." Shelly hurried towards the parking lot to go to her car.

"Yeah well, all you have to do is listen. Because I'm only gonna tell you one time. Stay the fuck away from my family! You'll never get your hands on my daughter!" Simone yelled.

"Your daughter?" Shelly stopped in her tracks. She faced Simone. "You and your husband must've lost y'all fucking minds because I don't remember either of you there when I pushed her out. Sabrina is MY daughter!"

"You gave up the right to call her your daughter when you left her on our doorstep," Simone said.

"I really don't care what you say Simone, like I told Kareem, all I want is to spend some time with my baby and get to know her."

By the look on Simone's face, Shelly could tell that she hit a sore spot so she ran with it. "Oh Kareem didn't tell you?" Shelly smirked.

"Don't worry about my husband. Or my daughter for that matter. You're dealing with me now so please don't get it twisted. I will do anything I can to protect my family!" Simone spat.

"That's cute. Kareem said the same thing after he came in my mouth and then again after we fucked in my car. *I'm not gonna let you ruin my family!*" Shelly mimicked. "So sad that he wasn't thinking about his family while he was running up in me," Shelly retorted.

"Oh please Shelly, that shit ain't gonna work with me. I know you, remember? You…"

"Yes, you do know me. And I know you remember?" She licked her lips.

"You are a liar and you'll do anything to make sure no one is happy because your tired ass can't find happiness. But you'll never come between me and my husband again. As far as Sabrina, I strongly suggest you reconsider coming to court asking for anything! You'll never get our baby!"

"You need to be blaming Kareem for all of this. I told him the last time he brought Sabrina to see me that if we couldn't work something out that I was going to court! He slept on me- literally- and now you trying to sleep on me?"

"Kareem would never bring Sabrina to see you. So stop lying!" Simone shouted.

"I know I was there at the mall with Kareem and Sabrina and I don't remember seeing you. Your husband still feeding you them lies and you still eating 'em like it's gravy. You need to get a grip. Sabrina is Kareem's and my daughter. She's not your child and you can't keep me from seeing her!" Shelly teased. "I'll see you in court."

"You miserable bitch!" Simone said just before she ran up to Shelly and pushed her on the ground. She jumped on top of her and began punching her in her face. Shelly covered her face as best as she could. When Simone couldn't get good shots of her face, she punched her arms and chest. "You'll never get near my husband or my daughter you stupid BITCH!"

Simone's foot slipped and Shelly took advantage. She grabbed a handful of Simone's hair and pushed her to the side. Shelly didn't let go when she got up. She pulled Simone to her feet and kicked her in the stomach. Simone fell to the ground holding her stomach. Shelly made the mistake of not rushing her while she was down. Simone ran up to Shelly and pushed her against a car. She balled up her fist and drew her hand back. She was prepared to swing full force but just as she was getting ready to connect, someone grabbed her arm.

"Hey, break it up. That's enough!" Both women looked up at the woman. "Connie?" Shelly was surprised, "what are you doing here?" Connie stood between the two women and gently pushed Simone away from Shelly.

"Remember what I said Shelly. If you come to court and get any visitation rights, we'll take Sabrina and leave. Either way, you'll never get your hands on her!"

"Fuck you, Simone! You can stop playing house with my daughter!" Shelly yelled while Connie remained in front of her to prevent anything from happening.

"I don't have to play house with my family. Thanks to you, I have everything I need. Get a life, bitch!"

"I got yo bitch!" Shelly tried to get around Connie.

"Whateva, just stay away from my husband and my daughter! I promise you that you'll regret it!" There was a crowd in front of Laundry World. People had gathered out once they heard all the commotion. Since the laundromat was on the highway, it wasn't too crowded but enough people were gathered around.

"Let me go, Connie," Shelly urged.

"Shut up, Shelly. It's over," Connie said.

"You better listen to her cause you don't want none." Simone said as she walked back into the laundromat. She began putting her clothes in the dryer like nothing had happened.

Chapter 41

Connie entered the apartment and went straight to the kitchen and grabbed a bottle of water. She couldn't believe all that she'd heard Shelly admit. That morning when Shelly got a text message, she began to act strange. She started to hurry around the apartment and rushed out. Connie wanted to know what was so urgent so she followed her.

When Shelly got to the laundromat and went inside, Connie got out of her car and stayed a few steps behind so she wouldn't be noticed. After Shelly walked out of the laundromat, Connie hid behind a car.

"Connie, where are you?" Shelly yelled. Connie walked into the living room and stood face to face with Shelly. "Con, it's not what you think."

"What do I think, Shelly? I knew you were up to no good when you left outta here all sneaky and shit. That's exactly why I followed you. So there's no need to tell me that it's not what I think. I heard everything you told Simone."

"But I was lying to her. I just wanted to piss her off. It's not true," Shelly cried.

"It all makes sense now. You at the bar with Kareem, the way you were all over him. I knew it was more to it than you said. You fucked him, Shelly," Connie said.

Shelly shook her head no and cried harder. "Connie it was all about Sabrina, I swear." She pulled Connie's arm to get her to sit on the sofa.

"Simone was right, you are a liar. You don't give a damn about Sabrina. All you wanna do is be a part of Kareem's life. You made that perfectly clear when you told Simone that Sabrina is you and Kareem's daughter!" Connie said as she pulled from Shelly's grip. She walked into the bedroom and grabbed a duffel bag out of the closet.

"No, what are you doing, Connie?" Shelly ran to the closet and tried to block her from taking anything.

"I'm done, Shelly. I can't do this with you anymore," Connie said. She went to the dresser and pulled out a few of her belongings and stuffed them inside the bag.

"Connie please, just think about this. We can work this out. We can get past this," Shelly sobbed.

"You know what Shelly? I'm tired of you. You walk around here like your shit don't stink. At any given moment, you treat me like shit. And when you get ready, we make up and act like nothing happened. I deserve better than this. You can't give me what I give you." She continued to put clothes in the bag.

"I can change, Connie. Please don't leave. I love you!"

"Simone had a good point when she said that you can't find happiness. You are..."

"I found happiness with you, Connie." Shelly interrupted.

"You are very selfish, Shelly." Connie walked towards the front door with Shelly in tow.

"I'm begging you Connie. Please don't leave. You're all I have. You and Sabrina."

"You say you love Sabrina and all of this was about her? Well if that's the truth, the best thing you can do for that girl is to stay out of her life!" She twisted the doorknob but Shelly grabbed her arm.

"Why would you say something like that? You know I love my baby," Shelly cried.

"You need to get your shit together. Kareem don't want you! After all I heard, I should've let Simone whoop yo ass!" She began to walk down the stairs. She turned around after she took two steps and looked at Shelly. "You need to ask yourself why every time you break up with a woman she runs to a man. Simone seems very happy with her husband so you can give up that fantasy, too. Take care of yourself, Shelly." Connie walked down the stairs and out of the apartment building.

Shelly stood in the doorway in total shock. First, she never thought Connie would leave. And she was still trying to digest her last comment.

Chapter 42

Connie called Joseph and told him she needed someone to talk to. He gave her directions to his house and she went to get comforted.

"Come on in, Constance." He invited her to his house. Connie walked in and stood at the doorway.

"I'm sorry for bothering you, Joseph. I hope I'm not keeping you from anything."

"No, don't worry about it. I told you that you could call me anytime and I meant it. Now come in and have a seat." He escorted her to his TV. room.

Connie sat on the recliner chair and began so silently cry. Joseph knelt down to her side and laid her head on his shoulder. He was in love with Connie but he didn't want to overstep his boundary by exposing himself; especially after Connie asked him to respect her relationship. "Talk to me Constance, what's wrong?" he asked.

"I can't talk about it right now. You know, I shouldn't have come here. I'm going to leave. I'll call you in a few days." She headed towards the door.

"You don't have to leave. It's ok if you don't feel like talking. I won't force you, just sit and calm down. I'll make you a drink." He rushed over to his bar and fixed her an absolute and cranberry.

"Thank you," she said as she took the drink. "I can't believe my life. If it could go wrong, it has gone wrong." Joseph looked at her and let her vent. He let her get some things off her chest without pressure. "I have to find someplace to live. Shelly and I are over."

"What…what are you talking about?" he asked.

"Oh my goodness, what did I do? I just packed some of my things like an idiot and left. I don't have anywhere to go." She stood and began pacing around the room.

"Slow down, Connie. You're welcomed to stay here for as long as you like," Joseph offered.

"That's really kind, but I can't stay here," she cried.

"Why not? I have plenty of room. And that's what friends are for."

"Not after what happened between us."

"What's that supposed to mean?" he asked.

"I just can't stay here, Joseph. I'll start calling around for a hotel room until I find a place," Connie insisted.

"Well at least let me help you with that. I do have some pull at the Sheraton, remember," he smiled, "I can get you a generous discount," he said.

"I can't let you do that."

"Nonsense, it's done. Are you hungry? Would you like to freshen up or lay down for a minute?" Joseph asked.

"I'm fine, Joseph. Thanks for everything." She sipped her drink and placed it on the table next to her. "I can't believe this. I'm sorry to get you involved with all my drama," She solemnly said.

"Don't worry about it; I'm here for whatever you need. I'll go and make the arrangements for the hotel. Make yourself at home." He left the room and closed the door behind him.

Chapter 42

Kareem sat on the sofa feeding Sabrina a bowl of oatmeal. Sabrina refused to sit on the sofa next to her father so she stood in front of him. He fed her while she ran around the apartment coming to him for spoonfuls when she wanted.

Simone stormed inside the apartment and threw her keys on the end table.

"What's wrong baby? What happened?" He asked as he saw how disheveled she looked.

"Why the fuck would you hide this from me?" She held the court papers in the air, Sabrina jumped on Kareem's lap when she heard Simone's tone.

"Fuck that paper, what happened to you?" He approached her with Sabrina lying on his shoulder.

"I found out about this! That's what happened to me," she yelled. The louder she became, the tighter Sabrina gripped Kareem's neck.

"Simone, you're scaring the baby." He said as an attempt to stall for time. He backed away from Simone.

"Kareem, how could you not tell me?" She never moved from her spot.

"Baby, I was going to tell you. I was trying to protect you."

"Kareem, we're supposed to appear in court in a few days! Exactly when were you going to tell me?" she demanded.

"Simone calm down...I..."

"Don't tell me to calm down! And what the fuck is you doing taking Sabrina to see Shelly?" Kareem closed his eyes hoping he was dreaming. He held Sabrina close to his chest as he rocked her to sleep.

"Let me put her in her crib," Kareem said. Simone went into the bathroom and cleaned her face and combed her hair. Her sweat suit was dirty and there was a hole in the back of her shirt from being thrown to the ground. Kareem stood in the doorway of the bathroom and shook his head. "What happened, Simone?"

"I had to fuck her up!"

"Who? Whatchu talking about?"

"I found this court notice in your pants pocket this morning." She threw the paper in his face. "Then I found her number in your cell phone and sent her a text message asking her to meet you. And like a fool, she came. I told her to stay the fuck away from you and Sabrina! She started talking slick so I put foot to ass!"

"Simone, I was gonna handle it," he said.

"How was you gonna handle it, Kareem?" She stepped in his face. "You were gonna go to court and have them people thinking that I was too busy to make an appearance? Do you realize how that would've looked on our part?" she shouted.

"I'm sorry, Simone. I fucked up! But what are we gonna do about court? Kareem asked.

"We're gonna go to court like we're supposed to. That bitch ain't gonna show." She brushed past him and went to the kitchen. He followed while trying to apologize.

"See, she trying to come between us again," Kareem said.

"She already tried. She tried to convince me that you two are still fucking," Simone said.

"What? What she say?" Kareem wanted to know how much Shelly told.

"Yeah she ran that same bullshit that she did before. She's just trying to throw shit in the game. But I know better this time. I know how she operates. Misery loves company but we ain't miserable." Simone shook her head and stared at her husband. "Now answer my question," she demanded.

"What question?" he asked.

"Why in the hell would you take Sabrina to see her? And don't lie Kareem. Shelly said a lot of stuff but I know she's telling the truth about this. She got too much pleasure knowing something that I didn't know. She made sure she rubbed it in my face, too. So talk!"

"Baby, it was only one time, I swear." Kareem lowered his head and decided to tell the truth about everything-well almost everything. "She reached out to me a few months ago and asked to see Sabrina. I told her no but she kept threatening me with court. I didn't want us to go through that so I finally agreed to let her see the baby." Simone shook her head and sighed. "Simone, I only took her to see Shelly so she wouldn't try and take her from us. I went and talked to a lawyer and he said it was a good chance that Shelly could get the visitation and take her back if she wanted."

"You went and saw a lawyer without me?" She looked confused.

"Yeah, because I got tired of her threatening me with court. I was only trying to protect you, baby. The last thing I wanted was for Shelly to come and take Sabrina away from you."

"But this is not the way you handle it, Kareem! *We* are supposed to figure something out, not *you*. You are supposed to put Sabrina's best interest first, not Shelly's. How was it in Sabrina's best interest to see a stranger that thinks she's her mother? Shelly doesn't want to have anything to do with Sabrina. She only wanted what she's always wanted and that's you!" Simone looked at him suspiciously.

"Well that ain't gonna happen. She's just pissed because we got the family that she wants." Kareem was trying to convince Simone, without saying, that he was innocent of Shelly's allegations.

"I'm sure she's not coming to court so we won't have to worry about her threats. But if she does, like I told her, she'll regret it. Stay away from her, Kareem, or you'll regret it too!" Simone warned.

"Baby, you don't have to worry about me. I'm committed to us. You and Sabrina are my world."

"You better be! I'm going to lie down. Would you please go down to my car and get the laundry? I'm too pissed off to do anything but sleep!"

Chapter 43

Tricia sat in the recliner chair and opened the latest book she was reading. She reached over and grabbed her iced tea. She heard her cell phone ringing and jumped out of the chair. She ran into the bedroom and picked up the phone just as it stopped ringing. She looked at the missed call and called back the number.

"Hey Tarik, you just called?" she asked.

"Yeah, where are you?"

"I'm home. Why?" Tricia asked.

"Because I'm not too far from you and I wanted to know if I could stop by. We can go over that paperwork you mentioned the other day," he suggested.

"Oh, ok. Come on by," Tricia said. Tarik told her that he was on his way and ended the call. Tricia straightened up the house and herself before Tarik arrived. She pulled her hair back into a ponytail and changed into a pair of jeans.

Tarik arrived ten minutes later. He stood on the doorstep and waited for Tricia to open the door.

"Hey," he greeted.

"How are you?" She looked around.

"What's wrong?" Tarik asked.

"Nothing, I was just looking for the hip attachment," she smiled.

"Ha ha ha…very funny. I'm alone. Can I come in?"

"I'm sorry, come on in." She stepped aside and let him inside the house. "Have a seat."

"So how have you been?" Tarik asked.

"Working like crazy. You know how it is this time of year. I'm trying my best to save jobs. The head office wants to start lay offs so I'm in charge of coming up with ways to prevent that. But you know how our people are. No one wants their hours cut. So, I have my hands full."

"Yeah I know what you mean. I've made some investments of my own just in case I get the pink slip. You never know who's gonna get laid off," Tarik said.

"Would you like something to drink?" Trish asked.

"No, I'm good. Trish, I didn't get the chance to apologize about the party," Tarik began.

"Apologize for what?" she asked.

"For bringing Tashi. I didn't plan to bring her but it was easier since we had plans. I wasn't trying to flaunt her in your face."

"It's ok. It wasn't as bad as I imagined," she fidgeted, "is it me? Or is your girlfriend not a people person?" she smiled. Tarik chuckled. "And thank you for adding my name to the gifts for the kids. That was such a great idea to get them college accounts."

"No problem. You know I got your back," he smiled, "yeah, Tashi was tripping just a little bit. And for the record, we're just friends," Tarik added.

"Does she know that? Because she made it perfectly clear that she was your girlfriend when you introduced her."

"Yeah, she was trippin because you were there."

"Oh and I apologize about that little *his wife* thing," Tricia said.

"Yeah, that shocked the hell outta me. I didn't know you still considered yourself my wife," Tarik said. Tricia didn't respond. "Well it's not like it was a lie, you are still my wife- at least for the time being," he chuckled.

"Well that's what I wanted to talk to you about. Since you didn't sign the papers, they expired. We have to get another copy. I already sent for them but I just wanted to ask if you'll sign them this time around?" Tricia said. Tarik looked away for a few minutes. Tricia didn't want to push so she didn't say anything right away.

"I still don't want a divorce, Trish," Tarik said.

"You've moved on. Won't that be easier if you didn't still have a wife?" she asked.

"Trish, I have needs. I was lonely and missing you. Tashi and I aren't serious. She knew my situation from the start. I never lied to her or led her to believe that we were anything but friends. She knows that I'm still in love with you. That's why she acted up at the party. We talked and she knows her role."

"Tarik, I don't know what to say," Tricia said.

"Why don't you just think about it for a minute? Why don't we stop playing games and fix our marriage? I know that the thought crossed your mind or you wouldn't have entertained Tashi, or the rest of us, with that outburst," Tarik said.

"Tarik, I…I…I'll be honest. It's not that I don't want to be with you, my pride won't allow me to…"

"This is about your pride?" He was shocked. "Tricia, I put my pride aside and overlooked you and Simone. I don't care what our friends think-I love you and I want my family back. How could you care what they think?" he shouted.

"I'm sorry, I don't mean to yell. Just think about this: All of the people you're worried about are involved in all of this anyway. And everyone else have forgiven each other and moved on. Why can't you?" Tarik asked.

"I'm not concerned about what everyone else did. I have to be able to move on in my heart. I don't wanna have to wonder for the rest of our lives," she confessed.

"Wonder about what? You think this will ever happen again?"

"No, I'm not worried about Melissa," Tricia said.

"Well what else could it be? You didn't have any problems with trusting me around women before all of this happened. Why now?"

"Because you gave me a reason not to trust you." She looked at Tarik then turned her back to him. Tricia missed her husband dearly. She hated that she had her father's pride. She took a deep breath and turned back to face him. "Melissa and I talked and I told her that I was going to try and forgive her. It's only right that I do the same thing for you."

"Are you saying that we can work on our marriage?" he smiled.

"Tarik, I'm saying that I love you and for as long as I can remember, I've wanted to be with you. And I still do. I just don't know how."

His phone vibrated and he pulled away from her and looked at the phone. "I have to meet Tashi," he said. He closed his phone and squeezed Tricia's hands. "I have to go. Can I call you when I'm done?" he asked.

"Yes you can. I should be here but if something comes up, I'll call you." Tricia said. They walked to the door and hugged before Tarik walked out of the house.

"Listen, just think about it, please." Tarik kissed her cheek and walked to his car. He looked back at her and winked before he opened his door.

Tricia watched him drive away before she closed the door. She couldn't believe what just happened. It was something about seeing him with Tashi that made her realize what she had. She heard her mother's voice in her head telling her that someone else would snatch him up if she didn't want him. Tricia put on a good front but she was heartbroken about seeing Tarik with another woman. She would definitely think about what she and Tarik discussed. One thing that she couldn't deny was that she missed the hell out of her husband.

Chapter 44

Connie parked her car in front of the building she once shared with Shelly. She wanted to get some of her things so she waited until Shelly left for work. Connie ran up the steps two at a time and used her key to unlock the door. She twisted the knob and entered the apartment. Connie looked around the apartment and saw that it was a mess. Shelly hadn't bothered to clean up at all. There were clothes strewn all over the place.

Connie made her way to the bedroom and saw that her clothes were laid out all over the bed. It looked as if Shelly had been sleeping on her clothes. She wished she could just leave everything there but working at IHOP, she needed to salvage everything that she could. She went to the closet and pulled out a suitcase and began packing her clothes and a few pairs of shoes. She ran into the bathroom and grabbed a new bottle of deodorant and some sanitary napkins. She was spending all of her money on the hotel room so she barely had money to eat; let alone buy toiletries. She stuffed as much as she could in her suitcase and then went back into the living room.

She found a notebook next to the phone and scribbled a note for Shelly.

The key is under the mat. Take care of yourself,

Connie-

Connie took one last look around the messy apartment and walked out the door. She locked up and put the key under the mat then left.

* * *

Joseph stared at Connie as she sat across from him in his office. She sipped on her margarita trying to figure out how to ask Joseph for help. She had been refusing his help for the past two weeks but now she was broke and desperate.

"Talk to me, Constance. You said you wanted to discuss something with me. So talk to me," Joseph urged.

"This is hard for me, Joseph." Connie set her drink on his desk and looked at him. "I know I've been refusing your help but I want to take you up on your offer, if it still stands."

"Which offer?" he asked.

"You know I appreciate you getting me the discount room but I can't afford to stay there. I need to start saving so I can get my own apartment but I'm spending all of my money here," she smiled, "and I'm tired of eating IHOP."

Joseph chuckled, "Why didn't you say anything? I told you that I'm here for you for whatever you need."

"Because I'm used to taking care of myself. And we've never discussed what happened and I'm still feeling some kind of way about that."

"I thought you wanted that to happen. You said that you wanted me," Joseph said.

"I did want you. And I don't regret having you but I thought Shelly and I would be together."

"Now I'm confused," Joseph frowned.

"It was all fine and good when it was a one time thing." She sighed. "Let me try to explain this so you'll understand. I feel like you look at me differently because you had me and Shelly. As long as Shelly and I were together, I really didn't care what you thought of me but now..." she paused.

"Now...nothing has changed. I still see you the same way," Joseph said, "You are welcome to stay with me for as long as you need."

"I just need to make it perfectly clear that although we did it, and I'm attracted to you, I'm gay. I don't want you to expect anything from me because I'm not even sure how to deal with what I'm feeling," Connie admitted.

"Constance, I understand. You don't have to worry about me. I'll be on my best behavior." He smiled and crossed his heart.

"Thank you Joseph. I appreciate everything you're doing for me. But I insist on paying you for letting me stay with you."

"That won't be necessary, Constance." He picked up his drink and shook it around in the glass.

"I insist," Connie said.

"Let's be real, Constance, you can't afford to pay me anything if you're planning on saving money. I'm helping you out because I want to, not because I want or expect anything in return."

"Thank you." She sipped her drink and smiled. "Do you know that you're the only person who calls me Constance?"

"Would you prefer me to call you something else?" he smirked.

"No. I love it," she smiled.

Chapter 45

Court day…

S imone gathered Sabrina and took her into the bathroom to give her a bath. She and Kareem were to appear in court in two hours and they had to drop Sabrina off at Moms' on the way.

Sabrina was cranky and fussy. She pulled Simone's hair and splashed water everywhere. Sabrina cried when her mother wouldn't let her play in the water longer. She yelled so loud that Kareem walked into the bathroom to make sure everything was ok.

"Why she crying like that?" he asked.

"Because she's spoiled. She wants to sit down and keep playing but we don't have time for that today." Simone grabbed a towel and took Sabrina out of the tub. "Kareem, can you grab her stuff for me and put it on the bed? I thought I was going to dress her in the bathroom but she's out of control." Kareem followed Simone into the bedroom with the items.

"Poopy, cut it out!" Kareem said. Sabrina looked at him and slid to the floor.

"Kareem, you're making it worse. Just leave her alone. I got her." Simone picked her up off the floor.

"Sabrina stop!" Kareem said more sternly. Sabrina looked at him and began crying. Simone took her in her arms and consoled her. "Stop that, Simone! That's why she's so spoiled now. You need to let her know who's in charge. She don't have no business falling out like that." Sabrina cried harder.

Kareem took her from Simone. "Go get ready, I'll get her dressed," he said.

"Kareem, I got her. Go and fix her something to eat." Simone said.

"No, it'll save some time if I do it. You too busy petting her and letting her act out. I love her too but one of us have got to be the tough one and obviously, it's not gonna be you. " Kareem took Sabrina and began putting lotion on her body. Simone stood there with her hands on her hips.

"Kareem, why do you do that?" she asked.

"Do what?" He looked up at his wife.

"You saw that I was getting her dressed and you just come in and take over like I don't know what I'm doing."

"Simone, you just letting her do whatever. We don't have time for you to fight with a one year old. We have to go. You always let her do that falling out shit. Then when she gets out in public, she do the same thing!"

"You know what? Forget it!" She went into the bathroom and took a shower.

Kareem finished getting Sabrina dressed and took her into the kitchen and made her a bowl of cereal. Sabrina sat in the high chair and began banging on her table.

"Come on Poopy, let's eat." He sat at the table and fed Sabrina the cereal. She usually ate her food by herself but Kareem insisted on feeding her so she wouldn't make a mess. Sabrina fussed but she ate her food as her father fed her. He had to be a little stern with her and he found that she did as he said when he changed to that tone.

"Ok, I'm ready," Simone said.

"You wanna eat something before we go?" Kareem asked.

"Nah, I'm not really hungry. I'm too nervous to eat but I'll have some juice." She walked to the fridge and poured herself a cup of orange juice.

"Don't worry baby, it's gonna be alright. If she shows up, they'll see right through her bullshit," Kareem said. He took Sabrina out of the high chair and went into the living room to put on her jacket. Simone grabbed the baby's bag and they headed out of the apartment.

"We should take your car," Kareem said "we don't have time to put the car seat in my car."

"Ok, but I'm too upset to drive," Simone said. They got into the car and drove to Moms house to drop off Sabrina.

* * *

Kareem spotted their lawyer in the back of the waiting area. He and Simone walked over and greeted Mr. Porter. Kareem introduced the two as Mr. Porter led them to a private room.

"It looks like Ms. Swift isn't here. I spoke with her attorney and she says that she hasn't heard from her in a few days," Mr. Porter said.

"That's good news right?" Simone asked.

"Yes it is. If she doesn't show, the judge will take that as a sign that she's not serious. Then he'll dismiss her petition."

"Good! Shelly don't want to have anything to do with Sabrina anyway. This is just her way of trying to interfere in our family," Simone said.

"What if she does show?" Kareem asked. He was worried that Shelly could win.

"Well, like we discussed before, as her biological mother, she does have rights. But I think we should take it one step at a time. Her own attorney doesn't seem confident that she'll appear today. Depending on what time they hear your case, they're going to prolong it. The judge is going to allow her time to arrive. He'll have you sit and wait until he thinks enough time has elapsed. So prepare to sit here for most, if not all, of the day." Mr. Porter checked his watch. "You guys can go into the courtroom in about five minutes, they're going to begin calling petitioners. I will be in there shortly. I need to meet with another client."

"Thank you so much Mr. Porter. We'll see you inside," Simone said.

Kareem and Simone walked back into the courtroom and took a seat in the third row. Simone began to bounce her leg up and down.

"Baby, you gotta relax. You was so sure she wasn't comin' why you trippin' now?" Kareem laid her head on his shoulder.

"I know but you never know. You know that bitch is crazy. There's no telling what she may do," Simone whispered.

"It's gonna be ok." Kareem rubbed her arm.

They spent the entire morning in the courthouse before the judge dismissed the case. Kareem turned to Mr. Porter and thanked him for his service. Simone and Kareem hugged and marched out of the building smiling.

Shelly met them on the steps as they exited the building.

"We need to talk!" She said.

"We ain't got nothing to talk about!" Simone said and stepped in front of Kareem.

"Simone please, this is something you both need to hear," Shelly begged. She looked sincere. Simone looked at Kareem and he shrugged his shoulders. Simone rolled her eyes at Shelly and shook her head.

"Make it quick, Shelly. And you better not come with the bullshit!" Simone said.

Chapter 46

Simone called Tricia and asked her if she could come by the house. Tricia agreed and Simone told her that she'd be there in twenty minutes. Simone was so excited to share the news about Sabrina. She pulled up to the house and saw Tricia sitting on the sun porch talking on the phone.

"Hey girl." Tricia said as she ended the call.

"What's up? Looks like you're in a good mood, you sitting on the porch having a drink," Simone smiled.

"It's a beautiful Saturday afternoon and I'm not working. That alone is something to celebrate." She raised her glass of wine before she sipped.

"Girl, we need to go inside. I've got something to share." She raised her eyes.

"What happened?" Trish asked as they went inside the house. They sat in the living room and Simone plopped down on a sofa.

"Girl, I think the drama is over," Simone sighed.

"Drama? What drama?" Trish asked.

"Girl, we ain't talked since the party but Shelly was trying to get visitation rights."

"What?" Trish yelled. She sat her drink on a coffee table and moved to the edge of her seat.

"Yeah girl, she contacted Kareem and everything. I just so happened to find the court notice in his pocket a few days before we had to be in court," Simone explained.

"Get outta here!"

"Yes. I tricked her ass into coming to meet me and when I saw her, I tried to beat the shit outta her. I started thinking about all the bullshit she put us through before and I lost it."

"So what happened with court?" Trish asked.

"She didn't show up so the case was dismissed."

"Why would she go through all of that and not show up?"

"Cause I told her she'd regret it if she did. I told that bitch she wasn't about to break up my family!" Simone said.

"Damn, that's deep. You alright?"

"I'm fine now. But Shelly had the nerve to meet us in front of the court house wanting to talk to us."

"What'd she say?" Tricia picked up her drink.

"She said that the only reason she didn't come to court is because she need to get herself together before she get her daughter back. She said she was only asking for visitation but since I threatened her, she was getting ready to get her shit together and seek custody of her daughter."

"Simone, what did you and Kareem say?"

"We told that bitch good luck!" Simone saw how Trish looked at her and decided to explain her position. "Trish, I ain't worried about Shelly. If she wanted Sabrina, there couldn't have been anything that anyone said to keep her from coming to court. Our attorney told us that she most likely would have won the petition, so I'm sure her lawyer told her the same thing. Shelly never wanted Sabrina and she still don't. I'm not letting her come into that baby's life and screw it up! And I told her just that." Simone took a deep breath. "Damn girl, I'm getting all upset just talking about it."

"I see," Trish said, "you drinking?" She asked as she went into the kitchen to get another bottle of wine.

"Nah, I'm good," Simone said, "I need to eat something first."

"Well, I can offer you a sandwich but you know I haven't had time to go food shopping," Trish said.

"Let's order something?" Simone suggested.

"Can't, I don't want to spoil my appetite. I have a date a little later and I think we're going to dinner," Trish blushed.

"Who you going out with?" Simone asked.

Trish tilted her head, "why you all up in my business?" She chuckled.

"You better stop playing with me! Who are you going to dinner with?"

"My husband." Tricia dragged the latter word and winked before she fell out laughing."

"Tarik? What the hell?"

"We've been talking ever since the party. He came over to discuss the separation papers and we've been kickin' it, taking it one day at a time," Tricia said.

"Are y'all back together?"

"No, it's only been a week, we're just hangin' out."

"When did this happen?" Simone asked.

"When I saw him at the party…"

"Did he being with Tashi have anything to do with it?" Simone asked.

"Not really."

"Tricia?" Simone smirked.

"Ok, seeing her with him did remind me that Tarik is a good man and I'd be a fool to let anyone take my place."

"Good for you! I'm so glad you came to your senses because Ms. Tashi is playing for keeps." Simone gave Tricia a high five and fell out laughing. "But really, Trish, what was it that made you reconsider? You were head strong about moving on without him and now all of a sudden you're getting back together with him? And don't get me wrong, I'm ecstatic for you. I'm just asking because I don't want you to get back together and then realize this is not what you really want. It won't be fair to you or Tarik."

"I think you're jumping the gun just a little. Tarik and I aren't getting back together. We're just building a friendship right now. Like I told him, I don't know how to get back together with him."

"Sweetie, you know I wish you nothing but the best. I love you and Tarik and like I've always said, you two were meant for each other. Just keep taking it one day at a time. You'll find your way." Simone got up and hugged her friend. "I gotta get going. I need to run some errands. But have fun tonight. And don't do anything I wouldn't do." Simone laughed.

"Please, I'm ready to fuck him every which way but right but we're not there..."

"Good, call me tomorrow. I want details," Simone said.

"I know." Tricia said as she walked Simone to the door. "And keep ya mouth shut, we didn't tell Moms yet."

"I got you. See ya later."

Tricia waved as Simone pulled away from the house. She then went back inside to take a bubble bath and prepare for her date.

Chapter 47

Connie followed Joseph as he led her to the kitchen for breakfast. This was his first day off all week and he spent it cooking breakfast for Connie. She really appreciated all that he was doing to help her but she knew she had to get her own place real soon. Connie was drawn to Joseph and being so close to him didn't help her at all. What Connie didn't know was that Joseph requested the day off so that he could spend it with her. He knew she didn't have to work and he wanted to hang out with her.

"Joseph, you didn't have to cook."

"I know but you've been working so hard doing all of that overtime, I wanted to do something for you," he replied.

"But you've been working just as hard," she said, "you're going to spoil me." She sat at the table.

"I'm just making you comfortable. What kind of friend would I be if I let you starve? Besides, I know you could use a home cooked meal." He sat opposite her at the table.

"Well I appreciate this. Thank you. It looks delicious and I am hungry." She began to fix her plate.

"Constance lets go out for drinks tonight. We both could use a little relaxation."

Connie thought about it and then agreed. She was long overdue for a drink. She thought about Shelly and tried to erase her from her mind but it was easier said than done. It had only been a couple of weeks and it was hard. "Yeah, we could go out for drinks. No place fancy, I don't feel like dressing up. I just want to be casual and chill."

"Ok, let's say we meet in the TV. room at seven? We'll go right to the hotel and drink for free," he smiled.

"That's fine. I'll meet you there. Now get outta here so I can clean this kitchen." Connie said after they were done eating.

"No, you don't have to do that."

"It's the least I can do, I'll clean it," Connie insisted.

"You don't understand, I have a cleaning lady that comes twice a week and she'll be here any moment. Now you don't want to offend Maria by letting her see you cleaning, do you?" He chuckled.

"I've never seen a cleaning lady here before."

"Because you're usually at work when she comes."

"Well I don't want to offend anyone. But next time I'm cooking and cleaning. And it's not up for debate!" She walked back into the bedroom that she occupied.

* * *

Connie sat at the bar while Joseph excused himself to the restroom. She stirred her drink and swayed to the music. She really felt nice and relaxed. She was glad that Joseph invited her out. She drank the last of her drink and ordered another for herself and for Joseph. She looked towards the restroom and saw Joseph walking towards her smiling.

Shelly walked into the bar and sat at a table. She looked around for a waitress and spotted Connie sitting at the bar. Shelly perked up and smiled. She thought it was fate. There was no way for her to get in touch with Connie and now she saw her sitting at the bar. Shelly stood and smoothed her blouse and straightened her skirt. She smiled and looked in Connie's direction. Shelly was walking towards Connie the suddenly stopped in her tracks. She followed Connie's eyes and landed right on Joseph. Connie smiled as Joseph walked up to her and stood behind her holding her by the waist. He whispered something in her ear and she faced him and kissed him on the cheek.

Shelly walked up to them with her hands on her hips. "Ain't this a bitch? So the joke's on me, huh?" Shelly yelled over the music.

"Shelly, it's not what you think," Connie said as she jumped off the bar stool.

"Oh please Connie. I invented that! How long you been fucking him?" she demanded.

"Shelly, please keep your voice down. I work here," Joseph said through clinched teeth.

Connie took Shelly by the arm and pulled her outside. She held her hand up to Joseph to let him know she'd handle the situation.

"Shelly are you crazy? You don't come and accuse me of anything! We are done. Whatever I do from now on is my business!" Connie yelled.

"I'm concerned about what you were doing while we were together! You knew him all along, Connie?" she asked.

"No, we met him together, remember?" Connie retorted.

"Connie, were you fucking him before we broke up?"

"Shelly, there's only one person out here who is a cheater and that's you. You're the reason we aren't together not me and not Joseph!" Connie brushed past her and walked towards the hotel. Shelly grabbed her by the arm and spun her around.

"How you just gonna walk away from us? I said I was sorry and I promised that it'll never happen again," Shelly sobbed.

"Shelly, this is about me. I needed to come to terms with who you are. You're a bi-sexual woman that wants what she wants when she wants it. I'm looking for a relationship where I'm enough to keep my spouse from creeping. We are not meant to be together. I'm moving on!"

"With Joseph?" Shelly asked.

"Joseph and I are friends. Don't take that to mean anything else. You may not believe this but men and women can be platonic friends-even after they have sex." Connie walked away from Shelly.

Shelly pushed Connie and she almost fell to the ground. "You bitch! You and Joseph set me up, Connie?"

"Nobody set you up. You wanted to fuck a man and you did, what's the problem?" Connie walked in Shelly's face.

"Apparently you wanted to fuck a man too…"

"Why? Because you see two friends here having a drink? You feeling some type of way because you saw Joseph whisper in my ear? You're jealous because he's showing me a little attention or because I look sexy? Whatever it is, it doesn't taste good does it. I felt the same fucking way when you were all over Kareem! Now leave me alone Shelly. It's over!"

Joseph walked outside the hotel and grabbed Connie from behind. He escorted her to his car and Shelly yelled and screamed profanity behind them. Connie turned back to face Shelly. She walked towards her and pointed her finger in her face. "I'm not Simone, don't try that shit with me. I will beat your ass out here."

Joseph came around the car and gently pushed Connie in the car.

"Fuck you Connie!" Shelly shouted.

"Not any more, Shelly," she winked from the window as Joseph sped off into the night air.

Chapter 48

Connie sat in the car after Joseph turned off the ignition. She looked over at him and tried to smile. They drove to his house in silence.

"Joseph, I'm so sorry about what happened. I'm sorry we caused a scene at your job," Connie apologized.

"It's not your fault, Constance. Don't worry about it," he replied. Connie held her head down and began to cry. She didn't think it would hurt so much to see Shelly. She knew in her heart that it was over but she couldn't turn her emotions off like a faucet. "I'm sorry. I'm just sitting here boo-hooing like a baby."

"It's ok. I know what a break up feels like. You're entitled to shed a few tears." He hugged her for a few minutes and then went to her side of the car and helped her out. They went into the house and Joseph left her in the TV. room to deal with her emotions.

Connie sat on the sofa and closed her eyes. She tried not to think about what had become of her life. If it weren't for Joseph, she'd literally be homeless.

When she and Shelly met, Connie was staying with her mother. Her mother moved to Pennsylvania once she moved in with Shelly. She promised herself that she'd never let herself be in this predicament again.

Connie kicked off her shoes and turned on the television. She tried to watch TV. to get her mind off of her problems. She went to Joseph's mini bar and fixed herself a drink. Connie wrapped the throw blanket around her and lay across the sofa. She drifted off to sleep while watching a re-run of I Love Lucy.

At four twenty am, Connie stretched and sat up on the sofa. She realized that she'd dozed of on the sofa and jumped up. She quickly folded the throw blanket and took her glass in the kitchen and washed it out. She picked up her shoes on her way to her room and crept upstairs trying not to wake Joseph.

Connie went into the bathroom and took a quick shower. She didn't bring her bathrobe so she tied the towel around her body when she was done. As she tip-toed down the hall to her room, she dropped her shoe. She bent down to pick it up and her towel fell to the floor. "Oh damn!" she said. Connie was standing directly in front of Joseph's door and couldn't get the towel before his door swung open.

"Are you ok? Oh I'm sorry," Joseph said. He turned his back to Connie when he realized she was naked.

"I'm fine." She hurried into her room and closed the door. Joseph continued into the bathroom.

When Joseph finished, he stopped at Connie's door. "Are you okay, Constance?" he tapped on the door.

"I'm good." She opened the door wearing a nightshirt.

"Are you feeling any better? Do you need anything?" he asked.

"I just didn't know I would react that way when I saw her. Of course it'll take time to get over her but I know this is the best thing for me." She said and eased behind the door to cover her body.

"I understand. I know what you need to help you get through this," he said.

"What's that?" Connie asked.

"You need a hug." Joseph walked into the bedroom and pulled Connie towards him. He hugged her and stroked her back.

Connie's breast instantly poked through her nightshirt. She closed her eyes and enjoyed his touch. Joseph ran his hands through her hair and gently pulled her head back. He bent down and kissed her on the mouth. Connie opened her mouth and welcomed his tongue. She tilted her head and sucked and kissed his lips. Connie moaned as Joseph's hands roamed down to her ass.

Joseph backed Connie over to the bed and then fell on top of her. He slid up her nightshirt and found her hardened nipples. He massaged them while Connie squirmed underneath him and let her hands explore his body. Joseph began to kiss her neck. And rub between her legs. She trembled a little but she felt comfortable. Connie loved the way Joseph made her feel. "Are you okay?" Joseph asked.

"Umm hmm," she moaned.

"Can I have you, Constance?" Joseph asked. He kissed her passionately and pulled her face close to his. "Do you want me?" he asked.

"Yes," she panted, "I want you." She opened her legs and invited him into her warm and wet place. Joseph inched down and licked her nipple. He teased it ever so gently before he divulged it into his mouth. Connie moaned louder and sucked on his neck. She rubbed his back and tried to guide him inside of her. Joseph got on his knees and pulled Connie to the middle of the bed and slowly slid inside of her. She gasped and a moan escaped. He pushed in and out of her until he felt the urge to explode. Joseph pulled out of Connie and switched positions. He flipped her on top of him.

"Joseph, I…" she began.

"Just do what you feel." He slipped inside of Connie and lifted up so she could feel his soldier. Connie felt the pleasure Joseph was sending her and she met him stroke for stroke. Joseph held Connie's waist as she rode him like a pro. He felt himself about to come again so he flipped her on her back. He got on top of her and thrust deep strokes in and out of her. She became soaked and wet. She moved to his rhythm as she grabbed his ass and pushed him deeper and deeper inside of her. Connie wrapped her legs around his waist and came all over his dick. "Mmmm…hmmmm," she moaned.

Joseph bent down and kissed her as he pumped faster and faster. "Ohhh Constance…ohhhh…ahhhhh…ughhhh!" He pulled out of her and exploded all over her stomach. He collapsed on top of her and they lay basking in the glow.

Fifteen minutes later, Joseph got up and went to the bathroom. He brought back a soapy wash cloth and wiped his unborn children off Connie's stomach. She smiled when she felt the warm cloth on her body. Joseph stopped and stared at her.

"I hope you didn't do anything you'll regret," he said.

"Don't worry about me. I'm fine," she smiled.

"That's the problem. I do worry about you."

"But you don't have to, Joseph. I've always taken care of myself. I'm just going through a rough patch right now, but I'll bounce back. I always do." Connie pulled the sheet over her body. Joseph looked defeated. He stood and kissed her on the cheek.

"I'm sorry for this." He pointed to her then to himself. "I didn't plan for it to happen. It won't happen again. I don't want you to feel uncomfortable while staying here." He walked towards the door. "Get some rest. I'll see you later."

"Joseph?" Connie called.

"Yeah?" He turned to face her.

"Thank you," she smiled, "for *everything*."

Joseph smiled and closed the door behind him and proceeded down the hall to his bedroom.

Chapter 49

Tarik opened the car door for Tricia and then proceeded to the driver's side. She was nervous but happy to be out with her husband.

"What would you like to eat?" Tarik asked.

"I really don't feel like going anyplace special. Let's just go to the Olive Garden."

"Cool, so how was your day?" he asked.

"My day was tiresome that's why I needed to come out and relax," she answered, "how was yours?"

"My day was good. I looked forward to hanging out with you tonight."

"Is that right?" Trish asked.

"Absolutely! I miss us just hangin' and chillin'."

"Yeah, me too. I hope it's not crowded. I don't want to wait too long," she said. Tarik agreed as he pulled into the parking lot of the restaurant.

They went inside and were told that there was a twenty minute wait.

"You feel like waiting?" Tarik asked.

"I guess twenty minutes isn't that long. We can wait." The hostess handed Tarik a pager to let them know when their table would be ready.

"We could sit at the bar and have a drink or we can wait in the car," Tarik said.

"It's too crowded at the bar. We can sit in the car."

"Ok, let's go." Tarik held the door and followed her to the car. Once they were inside, Tarik put on a Luther Vandross cd and turned it down so that they barely heard the lyrics. He knew that's what Trish did to relax.

"This is nice." Tricia said and grabbed his hand.

"Yeah, it is." He looked into his rearview mirror and saw a figure walking towards them. He squinted his eyes trying to make out the person.

Tricia looked at his facial expression and became worried. "Tarik, what's wrong?"

"I thought I saw someone out here," he said.

"Well I'm sure we're not the only ones waiting for a table," she said.

"No, but I saw someone heading towards us."

"Let me find out you're hallucinating," she laughed. Tarik turned back to the window and was startled by the person dressed in black staring at him.

"Oh shit! What the fuck?!" he yelled.

"So you thought you could just tell me it's over because she feels like being bothered again?" Tashi asked while pointing at Tricia.

Tricia was caught off guard. She didn't know what to expect. Tashi had a deranged, distant look on her face.

"Tashi, what are you doing here? Did you follow me?" Tarik asked. He opened his car door. "Trish, stay here. I'll be right back." He passed her the pager in case they were called for their table.

"How you just gonna play me like that? I thought I meant something to you, Tarik."

"Tashi, what are you talking about? You knew I was married from the beginning."

"But you said that you were getting a divorce!" she shouted.

"I never told you that. I said that my wife wanted a divorce. I told you that I'd be with her tomorrow if she said the word. You said you understood," he frowned.

"Tarik you told me that you loved me. How you gonna just walk away from that?" Tashi cried.

"Tashi, if you're talking about what I say in the heat of the moment, you can't hold that against me." Tashi looked at

Tarik like he was crazy. She bent down and picked up the baseball bat she'd hid there before she walked up to Tarik's car. She swung the bat but Tarik ducked. He backed away from her and held his hands in front of him.

"Tashi, what the hell is wrong with you?"

"You lied to me! You gonna choose that bitch over me?" She pointed to Tricia. "She dumped you and you sitting here acting like a little bitch chasing her around!"

Tricia saw the commotion and reached in the back seat and grabbed Tarik's club. She got out of the car and ran towards Tarik.

"Tricia, stay back!" Tarik yelled as he leaned against the car. Tashi swung the bat again and this time she landed on Tarik's right shoulder and the driver's side window went crashing down. Tricia saw Tarik fall to the ground and ran towards him. She saw Tashi getting ready to swing again so she swung the club at her. Tricia hit Tashi on her arm just before the bat landed. The bat was going straight at Tarik's head. Tashi grabbed her arm from the pain and ran off.

"You punk bitch! Don't let me catch you!" Tricia yelled behind her. "Tarik, are you ok?" She bent down to check on him. He had pieces of glass sticking out of his neck and arm.

"My shoulder is killing me." He cringed in pain.

"We gotta call an ambulance. Somebody please call an ambulance!" She said as she rubbed Tarik's other arm.

People had begun crowding outside the restaurant when they heard the window crash. A woman dialing 911 came close to Tricia and told her not to move him. Tricia cried and put her head on his shoulder. Tarik lay on the ground grimacing in pain.

By the time the ambulance arrived, Tarik was weak and sleepy. He barely had any feeling in his right arm. The ambulance informed Tricia that it looked as if his shoulder and collarbone were fractured but they would know more when a doctor ran some tests. Tricia cried uncontrollably.

"Ma'am, we're ready to take him to the hospital. Will you be riding with us?" An attendant asked.

"Of course," she replied.

"Trish, take the car and follow us." Tarik slurred. Tricia grabbed his hand and smiled.

"You're gonna be ok, baby. I'll meet you at the hospital." She let go of his hand and ran to the car. She called her mother on the way to the hospital.

* * *

Tricia arrived at the hospital ten minutes after the ambulance. She parked the car inside the parking garage and ran into the emergency room.

"I need to find my husband...Tarik Hammond," she said to the nurse sitting at the desk.

"Calm down ma'am. I'll look into the system." The nurse punched a few keys on the keyboard and looked up at Tricia. "Ma'am, your husband is here but he's being attended to as we speak."

"Yes, I know that. I want to be with him."

"I'm going to need you to fill out some paperwork while you wait," the nurse said.

"You don't understand. I need to be with my husband. I'm not filling out anything right now!" Tricia stated.

The nurse looked at her watch and realized that she would be getting off in half an hour. She didn't want to deal with any drama before she went home.

"Go in the back, he's in the third room on your left."

"Thank you," Trish said. "I'll be back to fill out the forms as soon as I know my husband is ok." She ran in the back.

When Tricia came from behind the trauma doors, she saw Moms and Simone sitting in the waiting area. Moms ran up to her and hugged her. She squeezed Tricia so tight that Trish had to pull away from her mother.

"Are you ok, baby?" Moms asked.

"I'm fine. Tarik is the one who was hurt."

"Trish, what happened?" Simone asked.

"Tashi followed us to the Olive Garden then she crept up on us and caught us off guard. Tarik tried to talk to her but she wasn't trying to talk. She had a bat and she…she hit him and the window crashed. I got the club. She ran… we…Tarik got a fracture…his neck swelled up…"

"Whoa Trish, sit down. You're not making any sense. Calm down and take a deep breath," Simone said and embraced her friend for a much needed hug. Tricia laid her head on Simone's shoulder and cried for a few minutes.

Moms walked over to the vending machine and bought three ginger ale's. "Here Trish, drink this." She handed Simone a can and sat next to her. "Is Tarik ok, Tricia?"

"The doctors say he's going to be fine. His collarbone and shoulder are fractured. They're fixing him up now. He's still under the anesthesia now but they said he'll be fine." She exhaled and closed her eyes. "This is not happening."

"What happened to Tashi?" Simone asked.

"Nothing yet. But when I catch that bitch…"

"No Trish. You can't be thinking about that chile. She'll get what's coming to her once y'all press charges. You just be thankful that you and Tarik are ok. It could have been a lot worse," Moms said.

Tricia paid no attention to Moms. She was thinking about how to catch up to Tashi. Simone was reading her friends' mind. She squeezed her hand and rubbed her arm to calm her down.

"Mrs. Hammond, your husband is awake. He's asking for you." The doctor said when he entered the waiting room.

"Simone, you and Moms can go on home. I'm going to stay with Tarik tonight. Thanks so much for coming." She hugged them both.

"Make sure to call us in the morning," Moms said.

"And if you need anything," Simone added.

"I know, thanks." Tricia disappeared behind the doors.

"I know this may not be the time, but what the hell were they doing together?" Moms asked.

Simone smiled as they walked out the door.

Chapter 50

Tricia asked Kareem to go with her to Tarik's apartment to pick up a few things. She didn't feel safe going alone.
Tricia insisted that Tarik stay with her at Marvin's house until he was better. She bought him there as soon as he was released from the hospital three days after the incident. He'd been there for four days.

Kareem walked into the apartment ahead of Tricia and made sure no one was there. He stood outside the door while Tricia grabbed some of Tarik's items. Tricia looked around the apartment and had flashbacks. She thought about all the good times they shared in the apartment. She touched the sofa and thought about when they first brought it home. They made love on that sofa then fell asleep. They woke the next morning and had another sex-capade. Tricia smiled at the memories.

She walked past the bathroom and peeked inside. She could have sworn she saw herself bent over in the shower while Tarik fucked her from behind. She shook the image and walked into the bedroom. Tarik kept the same comforter set on the bed. He still had her picture on his nightstand. Tricia picked up the picture and smiled. "Seems like a lifetime ago." She placed the picture back on the nightstand and proceeded to the closet and grabbed some clothes. She went to his drawer and scooped up underwear and t-shirts. She bent down to the bottom drawer and grabbed socks.

On her way out of the bedroom, she stopped in the bathroom and grabbed his toiletries. She packed the bag until she couldn't fit anything else. Tricia turned off the lights and walked outside the apartment.

"I have everything," Trish said.

"Ok, I'm almost done changing the locks." Kareem said and began drilling a new lock on the door. It took him half an hour to change the locks. "You ready?" He asked Tricia.

"Yep, let's go." They hopped in the car and Trish drove back to Marvin's house.

They walked in the house and Simone was feeding Sabrina. Tricia went into the bedroom to check on Tarik. He was asleep so she pulled the covers up to his chin and walked back out of the room.

"Kareem, I'm gonna stay with Trish for a little while. Can you take Sabrina with you?" Simone asked.

"She can roll with me. Get her stuff together." Sabrina finished eating and ran to her father's arms. She jumped in his lap and rubbed her nose on his. Simone packed Sabrina's bag then handed her coat to Kareem. Sabrina didn't want to put on her jacket. She ran to Tricia and jumped in her arms laughing.

"What did she have?" Kareem asked. "She can't keep her little butt still."

"All she had was juice. Why don't you take her out to the park or something? She just needs to run around for a little while." Simone said.

"Sabrina. Come on. You gonna go with daddy." Kareem said. Tricia carried Sabrina over to Kareem and continued into the kitchen.

"How was she while y'all were out?" Simone asked.

"She seemed ok. I was changing the locks while she was inside grabbing Tarik's clothes." Kareem said as he struggled with Sabrina to put on her jacket.

"Well, I'll be over here for a while. Can you handle dinner for you and Ms. busy body?"

"Don't worry about it. We'll be fine." Kareem picked up Sabrina and grabbed her bag. Simone walked them to the door and gave Sabrina a kiss on her cheek. She then kissed her husband on the lips.

"Thanks, Kareem. I owe you one," Tricia said. She walked over to them and said goodbye to Sabrina.

"You don't owe me anything. If you need anything else, just call me." Sabrina reached for Tricia to pick her up but Kareem pulled away and headed out the house before she started whining. "See y'all later. Tell Tarik I'll call him tomorrow." Kareem and Sabrina got into his car and sped away.

Simone sat on the sofa while Tricia sat in a chair.

"Simone, I was so scared that I was going to lose him."

"I know, sweetie. But Tarik is fine," Simone said, "how are you adjusting to him staying here with you?"

"Honestly? I love it. I miss him so much, Simone." She looked down in her lap.

"What is it?" Simone urged.

"I finally accept and understand that Tarik is my husband for better or for worse. I have to check myself and get my man back," Tricia said.

"Are you sure this is what you want? Or is this just sympathy because of what happened?" Simone asked.

"I've thought about it for a while and I want my husband back. But once I finally talked to Melissa, I saw how foolish I was being. Then Tarik brought to my attention that everyone else has moved on except me. And now to think that I could have lost him over some stupid crazy woman with a crush – that I pushed him to anyway? No. I feel really stupid right now. It's time for me to follow my heart. I can't see myself with anyone else. I can't move on without Tarik," she admitted. "The first time I saw him in his car, I knew he was the one for me. I have to make this right. But I don't want him to think it's because of this incident."

"He's not going to think that. You two were already discussing the idea of reconciliation anyway. This may be a blessing in disguise," said Simone.

"Yeah maybe you're right. But I know I'm not leaving him available for the next bitch!"

"That's my girl! Now about Tashi, did Tarik press charges yet?"

"Yeah, a couple of officers came up to the hospital before he was released. I know they better find her before I do!" Tricia said.

"Trish, you need to be concentrating on Tarik, not Tashi."

"Aren't you being a little hypocritical? You was just beating Shelly's ass but I can't defend my husband?" Trish stared at Simone.

Simone wore a blank expression and then looked up at her friend, "Oh that was different." Both women fell out laughing.

Chapter 51

Tarik had been staying with Tricia for over a week now. She made sure he was comfortable and that he didn't want for anything. While she was working, she made arrangements for Moms and Sabrina to spend their days with him. Tarik had gotten used to Sabrina jumping on the bed waking him every morning.

He was doing much better. His arm wasn't in as much pain and his shoulder was wrapped tightly in an ace bandage. The doctors told him that because of the location of the fracture on his collar, it wasn't possible for him to have a cast but they did put a neck brace on him. He was free to remove it when he needed to.

"How do you feel?" Tricia asked as she tapped on the door.

"I'm good." He sat up and waved her over. Tricia went over and propped pillows behind his back to help him sit up better. "Did I mention that I am most appreciative that you volunteered to let me stay here so you could take care of me? A brutha could get used to this."

"Yeah, I think you mentioned it but I won't stop you from saying it again," she smiled.

"But seriously, thank you. How was your day?" he asked.

"It was fine. I'm just so glad it's Friday." She touched his leg. "Umm can we talk?" she asked.

"Sure, what's up?"

"Tarik, I don't know exactly how to say this so I'm just gonna come out with it." She exhaled and looked him in the eyes. "I am ready to accept your action for what it was- a mistake. I'm not perfect and neither are you. But we are perfect for each other." Tricia looked up at her husband and moved in closer as he opened his arms for a hug.

"Baby, you don't know how this makes me feel," Tarik said.

"It's not going to happen overnight, so I need you to be a little patient with me. Can you do that?" she asked.

"If you don't call waiting for almost a year patience then I don't know what to tell you," he chuckled. He pulled away from Tricia and looked her in the eyes. "I love you."

"I'm tired of running away from us. I love you too." She rubbed the back of his head and stroked his back. Tarik inhaled her scent and smiled.

"Trish, I'm glad that you are able to put your stubbornness aside and follow your heart. I think you forgot that I know you just as well as you know yourself. That's why I didn't sign those papers. I knew you needed time and I was willing to give you all the time you needed. I still am."

"I'm glad you do know me as well as you do," she paused, "I don't know what I would have done if something would have happened to you while I was being so stubborn. I'm so sorry for everything I put you through."

"I'm sorry, too. But I do have one question for you. Will you be able to forgive what I did?" Tarik asked.

"I just told you that I accept your mistake."

"Yeah, but will you be able to let it go? I don't want to have you throw it up in my face whenever you feel like it."

"Tarik, I know better than that. The reason I couldn't move on before was because I knew I wasn't able to let it go. But after this," She pointed to his shoulder. "I'm not going to waste any time backtracking. I'm ready to move on."

"Good, so am I. But there is one thing that I want to clarify. I'm not sure if you wanna hear this or not but I need to say it. It may not mean much but it may ease your mind a little. Melissa and I were not in a relationship. We were both drunk and in the heat of the moment we had a quickie, it was over three minutes after it started. It didn't mean anything. It was a one time thing and I regret that it happened. But I need you to believe that it'll never happen again." Tarik was sincere. He almost slipped and told her that they had sex in his truck. But he knew that was something that he'd take to the grave.

"Do you think about me and Simone?" She asked shyly. "I mean would it be a problem for us all to hang out like we used to do?"

"Not at all. I've accepted a long time ago that it was an accident and I don't want those images in my head." Tricia was offended. Tarik read her facial expression and continued before she went off. "And I say this because you and Simone are still friends. I don't want to see her and only think about what happened between you two. She's been in your life for a long time and if you can move on then so can I."

"So we agree to leave all that drama in the past?" Tricia asked.

"Absolutely!" Tarik said.

"Ok, I'm going to start dinner. You wanna lay here while I cook?" Trish asked.

"No, I'm tired of lying in the bed. I can get around. I feel so much better. There's hardly any pain at all." He followed Tricia out of the bedroom.

Chapter 52

Shelly waited outside of IHOP for Connie to get off work. She had been sitting in her car for an hour. She had called earlier to make sure Connie was working. Once Connie was called to the phone, Shelly hung up before she answered. All she wanted to do was make sure Connie was there before she made the trip to her job.

Connie walked outside with a co-worker and they talked in front of the building. After ten minutes, Connie walked towards her car. As she turned the key to open the door, Shelly pulled her car a few spaces away from Connie. Connie drove to Joseph's house without noticing that she was being followed.

She pulled the car into the driveway and then headed inside the house. Shelly sat at the end of the block, where she had the perfect view of the house. She was able to see who entered and who exited the house. Shelly twisted the top of her Smirnoff Ice and sat back and waited.

* * *

Joseph walked into his house about 2am. He saw Connie sitting in the TV. room and walked in to check on her.

"What are you doing up so late? Is everything ok?"

"Yeah, I waited up so we could talk."

Joseph kicked off his shoes and removed his suit jacket. He plopped down next to her on the sofa. "What's up?"

"Joseph, I really enjoyed being with you," she began.

"But?"

"But I need time to get over Shelly. I can't do that if I'm acting on the feelings I have for you," Connie replied.

"I'm sorry. I didn't mean to..."

"No, it's not you. This is about me being able to sort things out. Anyway, we both know that we could never have anything more than sex."

"What makes you say that, Constance?"

"Because I'm gay. I love women. You're the first man I've ever been with and I'm having feelings for you that I can't control. I just broke it off with Shelly because she was undecided. I couldn't possibly get involved with you when I'm so confused."

Joseph didn't know what to say. He knew what she said made sense but he really cared for Connie and wanted to take a shot at a relationship.

"Joseph I care too much for you to get into anything and not be sure. I know how it feels first hand to be on the receiving end of that," she said.

"I know. It's just that I feel like we have a strong connection. I guess I deserve this."

"No one deserves to be hurt."

"Remember when we first met and you said something about me being like other guys and thinking I could change you?" Joseph waited for her to respond.

"Yeah, I remember."

"Well that's what I thought. Then when I found out that I was your first, I knew I was in there. But I wanted you to see for yourself and come to me. I never intended to force you into sex or make you feel obligated to do it."

"Joseph, I'm not completely stupid. I knew what you were thinking but I never expected to feel for you like I do. I just need space," Connie said.

"You're right. From now on, our relationship will be platonic. I respect and agree with your decision. It's not fair for me or anyone else, for that matter, to try and build something while you're vulnerable."

"Thank you for understanding. I'll try to be out of your space in a few weeks."

"Constance, there's still no rush. Why don't you get it through your head that I want to help you? I know you're having a hard time accepting that but it is what it is. You need someone and I'm here for you." He picked up his jacket and headed out of the room. "Just go with the flow, Constance."

As Joseph took a step upstairs, the doorbell rang. Constance walked from the TV. room. "Who could that be at this hour?" she asked.

"I have no idea. Let's find out." Joseph placed his jacket on the banister and turned around towards the door. Connie pulled her robe closer together and stood in the doorway of the TV. room. The doorbell rang again and again. The person on the outside was persistent.

Joseph looked out the curtain then turned back to face Connie. "It's Shelly."

"Shelly? What the hell is she doing here?" Connie asked.

"I don't know but she's not going away," he said. Shelly began yelling for them to open the door. Joseph swung open the door and let her inside. He didn't want her to cause a disturbance.

"Well well well...what have we here?" She raised her arm at Connie.

"What are you doing here, Shelly?" Connie asked.

"The question is what are you doing here?" She asked.

"How can I help you, Shelly?" Joseph asked.

"You've helped enough...thank you very much. Connie, I wanna talk to you."

"Shelly do you know what time it is? I don't have anything to say to you. Get the hell out of here!" Connie shouted.

"Ok, you heard her, she doesn't want to talk to you. Please leave my house!" Joseph said sternly.

"I'm not going anywhere until Connie talk to me!" Shelly yelled.

"Joseph could you give us a minute please?" Connie asked as she turned to face him.

"Are you sure?" Joseph was surprised.

"Yes, I'm sure. I'll be fine. Just let me talk to her alone for a minute."

"If you say so," he paused, "If you need me, I'll be right upstairs," he said.

"Thank you." Connie walked him to the door and closed it behind him.

"Connie please, just come back home. We can work this out. I'm so sorry for what I did," she cried.

"Shelly, it's over! You need to go and leave me alone!" Connie said.

"Joseph got you all turned out, huh?" She pulled a gun from her waist. "You better keep ya mouth shut! Don't say a fucking word!" Shelly demanded through clenched teeth.

"This has nothing to do with Joseph. This is about me. I don't deserve this and you know it." Connie had tears rolling down her cheeks.

"Con, I would never do anything to hurt you. I love you. Why are you crying?" Shelly asked.

"You bust up in here pointing a gun and you ask me why I'm crying? You claim to love me but I'm scared for my life right now," Connie said.

"I'm not going to hurt you, Connie. I just came to take you home."

"I'm not going anywhere with you, Shelly," she sobbed.

"Take off your robe!" Shelly demanded.

"Shelly, please calm down," Connie begged.

"Take it off!"

Connie untied her robe and let it fall to the floor. She was wearing a pair of boy shorts that exposed most of her ass and she wore a sports bra that barely housed her breasts.

"Why are you dressed like that if you ain't fucking him?" Shelly asked.

"This is what I sleep in, you know that."

"Why are you up at this hour? Did y'all just get finished fucking!"

"Shelly what difference does it make? You and I are over! What I do is no longer your concern!" Shelly pointed the gun at Connie's head and moved closer to her.

"Shelly, are you crazy?" Connie asked.

"Get away from that door. Let's go." Shelly ordered Connie to move to the sofa.

"Shelly, Joseph and I are just friends," Connie pleaded.

"You set me up, Con. Why would you do something like that? I love you and you choose him over me?" Shelly pulled Connie's shorts aside and stuck her finger in her cave. Connie winced in pain and jumped back.

"Shells don't do this, please," Connie begged.

"Oh now you don't like it when I do this? You never had a problem with me doing it before."

Shelly held the gun with her right hand and moved closer to Connie. She rubbed Connie's breast with her left hand while Connie stood there shedding tears. Shelly rubbed her hand up and down Connie's belly and then made her nipples erect. She slid her hand between her legs and felt her moisture. Connie tried to squeeze her legs together to block Shelly's hand.

Shelly pushed Connie on the sofa and sat on her lap and straddled her. "If you scream, I will shoot you!" Shelly said as she noticed Connie open her mouth to yell.

Connie knew the only way to get out of this would be to let Shelly think she was giving in to her. She sat there and let Shelly do what she wanted. Her body responded to Shelly's touch but her mind was busy trying to figure out how to take the gun.

Shelly played in Connie's nest while she looked her in her eyes with the gun still pointed at her. Shelly was feeling good as she felt Connie's juices running down her fingers. She closed her eyes and held her head back.

Connie used the opportunity to push Shelly to the floor as hard as she could. Shelly fell and the gun went off. Connie jumped on Shelly and began punching her in her face. Joseph burst in the room when he heard the gun. He looked around and spotted the gun. He kicked it out into the living room. He tried to pull Connie off of Shelly but Connie was too strong.

The loud bang from the front door being kicked in startled them all. "Don't move!" A policeman stood in the doorway. He and his partner waved their guns as everyone stood still and looked at the policemen. An officer pulled the half naked Connie off of Shelly and told her to sit on the sofa.

"I'm Officer Patrick; this is Officer Dobson, we were called about a disturbance at this address. We heard the gunshot, is anyone hurt?" He looked around the room.

Connie looked up and tried to cover herself. She was scared to move with all the guns still drawn. "Can I please put on my robe officer?" She asked and pointed to her robe.

"Sure." He threw her the robe.

"She had a gun," Connie said.

"I kicked it in the living room," Joseph added.

"I want to press charges. She came in here and threatened to kill me," Connie said.

"Connie, I love you! Please don't let him break us up," she pointed to Joseph. Officer Dobson went to Shelly and put her in handcuffs.

"All of you need to come down to the station to straighten this whole mess out. Please get dressed, ma'am." Connie ran to Joseph and cried in his arms. Joseph soothed her and told her it was going to be ok.

Officer Dobson went into the living room and saw the gun lying on the floor. He pulled out a latex glove from his pocket and picked up the gun and carried it to the squad car.

When they went outside, there were more police cars. Shelly tried to hide her face as she was being pushed inside the car. She yelled for Connie as she was being driven away.

Chapter 53

Simone jumped up when Kareem walked into their bedroom. "Damn, you scared the hell outta me." She placed her hand on her heart.

"What were you doing that you didn't hear me coming?" He went up to her and kissed her on the lips.

"I was just finishing up some paperwork. This is the last day of the weekend and I haven't done anything I was supposed to do. What you so happy about?"

"About the fact that we can get our house."

"Kareem, are you serious? We got the loan?" She asked excitedly.

"Yeah baby, we have enough for a down payment and we got approved for the loan. All we have to do is find a house, now," he said.

"Oh my goodness! I can't believe it! We've waited so long for this. I can't believe it's finally happening." Simone jumped in his arms and kissed his face. They fell on the bed with Simone on top.

"Wait a minute, where's Poopy?" he asked.

"She's with Moms and Marvin. They came and got her this morning. They said they were going to the mall."

"That girl is going to be high maintenance. Everybody keep taking her to the mall and when she get older, that's all she gonna want to do. Wait until she gets older and her clothes cost more. You gonna try and take her to the ten dollar spot and y'all are gonna have problems," Kareem said.

"Ain't nobody gonna be high maintenance. Anyway, did you forget that you took her to the mall for her birthday and brought half the store?" Simone laughed.

"That was a special occasion. You take her to the mall all the time. You'll see what happens when she gets older."

"Anyway, where was I?" Simone tilted her head. She bent down and kissed her husband. He groped her ass and hugged her tightly. Simone sat up and pulled her shirt over her head. Kareem fondled her breasts as they were exposed. Simone pulled back and undid his jeans. She slid them down to his ankles. Kareem slid back and rested his back against the headboard.

Simone pulled her pants down and slowly hopped on top of her husband. Kareem ran his fingers through her hair as she slid down on his shaft. She put her feet next to his hips and began a slow grind. Kareem rested his head on her shoulder while she worked her hips. Simone teased him by pumping faster then slowing it down when she felt him get excited.

Kareem gripped her ass and assisted her in moving faster. Simone slowed her pace and grabbed the back of his neck for support. She hopped up and down on her husband until she reached an orgasm. She held her head back and moaned as she moved faster.

Kareem grabbed her and laid her on her back. He took her left leg and placed it on his shoulder. He dove inside of her and pumped. Simone grabbed his ass and met his strokes. Kareem moaned and took her other leg and placed it around his neck. He gripped Simone by the ass and pulled her to him while he sat still. He moved her back and forth until he exploded. He lay on top of her and played with her breasts.

"Get up baby I have to use the bathroom." Simone pushed him up. Kareem rolled over and let her up.

Simone breathed heavily as she got off the bed and went to the bathroom. She sat on the toilet, with her legs gapped open, and pushed. As much as she loved Sabrina, she did not want to have another baby right now. She couldn't use birth control because Kareem would never understand.

Simone walked back into the bedroom and looked at Kareem. He lay sprawled on the bed wearing his boxers. She wrapped her robe around her body and walked back towards the bathroom to take a shower.

"Kareem, can you call Moms and see what time they're gonna bring Sabrina back?" Simone asked.

"Oh, she called when you were in the bathroom and said Sabrina could stay over so we could save a trip in the morning."

"You said it was ok for her to stay over?"

"Yeah, why? You want her to come home?" Kareem asked.

"She's never stayed out before. She may act up over there," Simone frowned.

"Simone, she'll be fine. She knows Moms and Marvin and Moms knows what she's doing. You know if she has any problems, she'll call. And we could use the time alone. I'll be ready for round two in about an hour."

Simone smiled and walked out of the room. She called Moms from the living room to check on Sabrina. Moms confirmed that they were ok and told her that she'd see her tomorrow evening. Simone felt better about Sabrina spending the night. She went to take a shower and prepare for round two.

Chapter 54

Tricia woke to the smell of bacon, eggs and toast. She tossed and inhaled as the smell of coffee entered her nostrils. She smiled and looked up. Tarik was preparing a tray of food for his wife. She got up and joined him in the kitchen.

"You want some help?" she asked.

"I was trying to show my appreciation by making you breakfast," Tarik said.

"Tarik, you can only use one arm. Why didn't you wake me?" Tricia asked.

"You looked so peaceful and I wanted to show you that I'm feeling a lot better."

"Tarik, I don't mind helping you. You are supposed to take it easy." She took the tray out of his hand and placed it on the table.

"Trish, I may have limited range of motion but I can still use my hand and carry things. I've been taking it easy all week," he said.

"Babe, I love that you wanted to do something for me but come over here and sit down. I'll finish breakfast." She escorted Tarik to the sofa. She pulled up the sheets that she slept on to make room for him to sit down.

"Trish, I want to talk to you about something," Tarik said.

"Ok."

"I'm going back home tomorrow."

"Why, am I getting on your nerves already?" she smiled.

"No, it's not that. It's time for me to go. I promised that I would stay here until I was better. I'm better. I can take care of myself now."

Tricia sat the tray in front of him and went back to get a glass of orange juice. She was disappointed at Tarik's decision but she couldn't stop him from leaving if that's what he wanted.

"I want you to come home with me," Tarik said.

"Wow, I didn't see that coming."

"I don't see why not. We're getting along fine and we both want to stay in this marriage. I want you to come home with me."

Tricia exhaled before she spoke. "Tarik I would love to come back home. I just think that we need a little time to date again. I'm not changing my mind about us. I just think that we need to date while we're not living under the same roof."

"Come on, Trish, what are you doing?"

"Think about it. We've been apart for almost a year and when we do decide to go on a date, you get attacked by some crazy chic. I'm not talking about staying apart forever. Just a few more weeks."

Tarik shook his head. Tricia grabbed his hand and assured him that she was sure she wanted to be with him.

"Tarik, don't you think it's kind of sudden to move back in together? I want to be sure I can handle it. I want this to work; I don't want to lose you again," Tricia said.

"I guess I can't change your mind, huh?"

"And I know what you're thinking. I'm not being stubborn, I'm being careful."

"Ok, I'll go with that if you agree to go out on a real date next weekend."

"No problem. Where are we going?"

"You don't get to ask where. Just go with the flow," Tarik said. "Can you handle that?"

"You think you're slick don't you? But I look forward to it," Trish said.

"I'm going to call a cab so I can get out of your hair."

"You don't have to call a cab. I'll take you home after breakfast."

"No, you've done enough. I need to get used to doing things for myself since I'll be home alone for the next few weeks."

"Oh stop." Tricia threw a pillow at him. He used his good arm to block it. "You know I'll be over to check on you. And I know Moms won't mind coming to the apartment with Sabrina."

"No, Moms don't have to come by. I don't want her to go out of her way anymore. She did enough for me already." Tarik's cell phone rang and he flipped it open to talk.

Trish went to the kitchen to get more juice. When she went back into the living room, Tarik was ending his call.

"That was the police. They went to Tashi's apartment and arrested her. They want us to come down so we can identify her or something like that. I know they want us to come down there."

"What time?"

"They want us to come now. You feel like going? Cause they said they can send a car to get me," Tarik said.

"No, give me a few minutes to get dressed. We can go now. And I'll drop you off at the apartment when we're done."

"Ok cool."

Chapter 55

Tarik and Tricia walked into the police station and asked for Officer Milton. They were instructed to have a seat in the waiting area.

"I hope we won't be down here all day. I have to get ready for work tomorrow."

"He said on the phone that it shouldn't take more than an hour," Tarik said.

"Is there a Tarik and Tricia Hammond here?" Officer Milton asked.

"We're right here." Tricia stood. Tarik got up when the officer approached them. "Would you please come with me? We need you to go inside and identify the person who attacked you."

They walked down a hall with cells on both sides. Tricia was a little nervous about being in a precinct. She stopped dead in her tracks when she looked over in a cell and saw Shelly sitting on the bench.

"Tarik, that's Shelly."

"Who?"

"You know, Sabrina's birth mother. What the hell is she doing here?" Trish asked in a whisper.

"Damn, that is her. But we got other things to deal with. Let's go." He pushed her along.

The officer let them in the room one at a time to identify Tashi. Tricia went first and Tarik went last. They were escorted back to the Officer Milton's desk to sign some papers when they were done.

Tricia drove Tarik back to the apartment they once shared. She grabbed the bags out of the backseat and carried them upstairs. She gave Tarik the keys so he could open the door.

"I forgot to give you the new keys."

"Thanks." He opened the door and walked inside the apartment. Tricia followed and put the bags in the bedroom. She began unpacking the bags and putting the clothes away.

"Trish, you don't have to do that. I'll take care of it later. Sit down and relax."

They sat and talked for two hours before Trish gathered her things to leave.

"So how about dinner tomorrow? I can get dinner on my way home and cook when I get here," Tricia suggested.

"I would say you don't have to but I miss your fried chicken," he laughed.

"I'll see you tomorrow then." She pecked him on the lips and headed out the door. "Do you need anything before I go?"

"I'm good. Call me when you get home to let me know you're in safely."

"I will," she said.

"I love you," Tarik said.

"I love you, too."

* * *

Tricia called Simone as soon as she got to work the next morning. She forgot to call her when she got home. But as she was looking through the paper, she saw the article on Shelly.

"Hey Simone."

"What's up Trish?"

"So what happened with Shelly?" Tricia asked.

"What are you talking about?"

"You don't know? She's in jail. It's all in today's paper."

"What? What happened?"

"Tarik and I went to the police station last night to identify Tashi in a line-up and we saw Shelly sitting in a cell. I meant to call you last night but I forgot. But when I saw the article in the paper, I gave you a call," Trish explained.

"What does it say?" Simone asked.

"She went to some man's house with a gun looking for her ex-lover. She was arrested and charged with a bunch of charges including aggravated assault and sexual assault." Tricia read from the article.

"Get out of here! So she's in jail now?" Simone asked.

"It says that she's being held with a fifty thousand dollar bond."

"Wow. I knew that girl was losing her damn mind. At least me and Kareem won't have to worry about her trying to get Sabrina."

"I know that's right! But make sure you get the paper so you can read what it says."

"I'm going to run out and get one right now. Thanks for calling and letting me know. I have to call Kareem first," Simone added.

"You're welcome. I'll call you later." Trish ended the call.

Chapter 56

Almost a week later…

Tricia beamed all day at work. It was Thursday and she was preparing for her four-day weekend. She took a personal day for Friday so that she and Tarik could get away. Tarik suggested that they go away and spend some time together without any distractions. Tricia was ecstatic at another chance to spend time with her husband.

Tricia signed the last of the papers that her assistant placed in front of her. She then began packing her bag so that she could leave for the weekend. She double checked the work she had delegated to her subordinates to complete while she was gone. Everything looked to be in order.

She picked up her cell phone and dialed Tarik's number. She got a busy signal but at the same time, the phone in her office rang. She picked up the line and smiled, "I was just calling you."

"Really, you're not calling to say that you've had a change of heart are you?" Tarik asked.

"Not at all. As a matter of fact, it's just the opposite. What time you are coming to pick me up?" She smiled.

"I'm downstairs now. I was calling to tell you to hurry up. I can't wait to get you to myself."

"Oh really?" I'm on my way down." Tricia disconnected the call and headed down to meet her husband.

Once Tricia stepped in front of the building, Tarik grabbed her luggage and placed them in the back of his jeep.

"Should you be lifting that?" Tricia asked.

Tarik opened the door for her and then he jumped in the driver's seat and sped off. He turned the music down after he'd put in his favorite Jazz cd. As the soft words of Billie Holiday echoed through the car, he smiled. Tricia glanced over and caught him smiling.

"Tarik you really should take it easy on your arm. I can drive."

"Trish, my arm is fine. I can drive. Now sit back and enjoy the ride."

"So where are you taking me?" She leaned back in the seat defeated.

"It's still a surprise. You'll see in a few. It's no place fancy, just a place for us to go and chill and be alone."

An hour and a half later, they had reached their destination. They pulled up into the Poconos in Pennsylvania.

"Here we are." Tarik said as he put the jeep in park. He looked around and noticed the beautiful scenery. He looked at Tricia and smiled, "You like?"

"It's beautiful here. My gosh, I haven't been here since we came five years ago," Tricia beamed. She opened her door and exited the car. Tarik was already in the trunk retrieving their luggage.

He led Tricia to the lobby of the Paradise Stream Pocono Palace. As Tarik approached the check-in counter, Tricia noticed how exquisite the lobby was.

The welcome counter was at her left and to her right was a contemporary style living room decorated with red and white flowers and stone. Natural was the color scheme. Tricia went to Tarik's side and hugged him from behind. "This place is more gorgeous than I remember." Tarik smiled as the hostess checked them into their suite.

The bellhop opened the door and Tricia gasped. The room was amazing. The color scheme matched the lobby to a tee. The décor of the room was in natural, gold and red colors. And it was lavished with fresh flowers.

Tricia noticed a balcony and the heart shaped whirlpool bath tub. She walked through the Roman style villa and noticed the king sized bed. She stood in front of the log fireplace in thought. Tarik knew Tricia so well that he was reading her mind.

"Baby, I hope you don't mind that I booked the Lakeside Villa. I just really wanted us to have some privacy and enjoy each other. Since we didn't get to go on our honeymoon, I thought this was a good place for us to start. I promise you that I have no ulterior motive." He said as he playfully threw his arm in the air.

"Tarik, I know you as well as you know me. And I'm not worried about spending the weekend with you. It's not like we're strangers. We'll be fine," she smiled.

"I'm glad you feel that way. We do have memories here. And I am hoping that we'll make more." He said as he gently tilted her face to kiss her. "I didn't plan any activities but if there's something you want to do. I'm game."

"Well, we did come up here to work on us. I say we just play it by ear. Let's just take it one minute at a time and if we feel like doing anything, then we'll do it. What you think?"

"Sounds like a plan to me," he winked.

"But first, we need to get us something to eat," Tricia smiled.

"Did you wanna go out or order room service?"

"Let's get changed and go out. I think it may be the only time we'll get out of this beautiful room."

Tarik blushed. He was hoping Tricia would want to consummate their new beginning but he was excited that she was just there with him. "Fine by me, Mrs. Hammond." Tricia stopped in her tracks at the mentioning of her name. It did something to her to hear her husband call her that. She smiled and continued unpacking something to wear to dinner.

Tricia and Tarik were seated at a restaurant and hour later. They ate their dinner and talked for most of the night. They went back to the room after dinner and sat in front of the fireplace. Tarik didn't realize how tired he was. He dozed off on the giant sized sofa with Tricia lying in his arms.

Chapter 57

Tricia woke early the next morning and walked through the room wrapped in a towel. Tarik was still asleep on the sofa and she wanted to go for a swim in the whirlpool. She tiptoed past Tarik trying not to wake him. As she turned the doorknob, Tarik sat up.

"Where are you sneaking off to?"

"Oh I'm sorry. I was trying not to wake you. I wanted to jump in the pool," Tricia turned and faced him.

"It's ok, I wasn't sleep. I've been up for a while now," he stretched.

"You ok?" She asked.

"Yeah, I just had some things on my mind. Nothing major, though," he replied. Tricia shook her head up and down. She looked at her husband and smiled. She wanted him so bad.

"You want some company in the pool?" Tarik asked.

"I thought you'd never ask," she smiled. Tarik got off the sofa and followed his wife into the next room. She had already come out earlier to make sure the water temperature was just right. She dropped her towel and revealed a two piece brown bikini.

Tarik smiled and then excused himself, "Baby, give me a minute. I'll be right back." Tarik went into the bathroom inside the bedroom to brush his teeth and wash his face. He wasn't sure if anything sexual was going to happen but he sure wanted to be ready.

Tarik returned to the pool as Tricia was stepping in. He had no idea that she was listening for him. She'd timed her actions perfectly. She wore the bikini for Tarik and she wanted him to get a full view. She turned her back towards him and stepped down the three steps and eased into the water. Tarik got a full view of her thong. He instantly brushed his hand over his penis as it stood at attention. Trish knew exactly what she was doing. She was ready to be with her husband. "Oh my goodness, the water is perfect," she smiled.

"Perfect for me would mean that it's ice cold; and I know you did this on purpose." He walked around to the steps.

"Did what?" she blushed, "all I did was get into the pool."

"Yeah, ok. Well all I'm doing is getting into the pool, too." Tarik pulled his shorts off and stood on the top step. He faced Trish to make sure she got a full view of his hard-on and then he stepped into the water.

"Wow, didn't know I still had that effect on you."

"Yes you did, that's why you did this." He said as he stood face to face with her pushing his body against hers. Trish responded to his touch and slid her fingers up and down his chest.

"It's been a long time," she said.

Tarik leaned in and kissed his wife with so much passion that he didn't feel the pain in his arm. Although it hardly bothered him, he jumped and moved it out of reflexes.

"Don't worry baby, I won't hurt you," Trish said. She then moved around him so that they could switch positions. She pushed Tarik against the wall of the pool and sucked his lips as he used his left arm to palm her ass.

Trish felt down at his erect soldier. She knew the effect water had on a man's penis so she led him out of the water. She wanted him to be fully ready for what she had in store. They made it to one of the lounge chairs by the pool.

Tarik sat on the chair and Trish crawled up and caressed between his legs. She skillfully used her hands to keep his soldier standing at attention. Tarik closed his eyes and enjoyed the pleasure he received. Trish licked his chest from top to bottom while he played in her hair. She eased down and let her tongue roam around the tip of his penis. Tarik jerked at the moisture of her tongue. She teased him in this position for a few minutes.

Tarik grabbed the back of her head and tried to make her cover his entire penis. Trish stayed in control. She moved Tarik's hand from her head and held it against his side.

She let her wet mouth cover part of his shaft while he moaned out loud. Tricia worked her head up and down until Tarik began to meet her by forcing himself into her mouth. She moaned and deep throated him until he exploded in her mouth.

Trish looked at him and let his juices run out of her mouth as she continued to bob her head up and down. She was glad to get his first orgasm out of the way. Now she was ready to have some long lasting fun.

"Turn around," Tarik said. He guided her to the position that he wanted. She was on all fours with her ass pointed towards him. Tarik got on his knees and stuck his tongue inside her canal and let her juices flow down his mouth. Trish moaned and backed up for more pleasure. Tarik loved the sounds she made as he licked her inside out. He took his finger and stuck it inside her to prepare her for what was to come.

"Mmm…mmm…hmmm…" Trish moaned.

"Baby, I want to fuck you right now!" Tarik stated.

"Come on baby, fuck me." She lay on her stomach and spread her legs. Tarik entered her and eased in and out until at a slow steady pace. After a few minutes, he went in a little deeper. Trish felt incredible. She wanted Tarik to pump faster and harder. She placed her hands on the edge of the chair and pumped into Tarik. She was able to meet his strokes and turn the tables. He began to moan and roll his eyes to the back of his head.

"Damn baby…I miss…you! Mmm…mmm…" Tarik moaned.

"I miss…you too," Trish replied. She got back on her knees and let Tarik enter her from behind. He grabbed her hips and pulled her into him as he pumped in and out of her.

Trish backed him up so that his back was against the back of the chair again. She fucked him while he sat there and watched. She began to gyrate her hips and move up and down.

"That's it baby, work that body," he said. Tarik bent over and caressed her nipples. This drove her wild and he knew it. Trish spread her legs wider and used her hands to lift herself up in the air. She rode her husband and worked up an orgasm. She pumped faster as Tarik held her leg to make sure she didn't lose her grip.

He moved in a little off the chair and helped his wife into heaven. Tricia continued to grunt while she buried her face into the cushion on the chair. Tarik hit her spot over and over until she called his name. He slowed his pace as she released her juices all over him.

Tarik pulled out of her and sat on the chair. Tricia moved up on top of him and lay in his chest. She played with his chest and tried to control her breathing. "You don't know how much I missed you," Trish said.

"Yeah I do, you just showed me. But we're gonna make sure we don't miss each other this much again." Tarik rubbed her shoulder.

"Is your arm ok?" Trish asked.

"Yep, and so is everything else," he winked.

"Hey, you wanna watch a movie?" Trish asked.

"I don't mind. What do you want to see?"

"I feel like laughing, have you seen *Martins'* latest movie? *Welcome Home Roscoe Jenkins*?"

"Nah, I didn't make it to the movies so I was waiting for it to come on DVD," Tarik said.

"Ok, we'll order that. I didn't see it either but I heard it was funny as hell."

Chapter 58

It had been two weeks since Shelly went to prison. Connie felt bad but she knew in her heart that she did the right thing. Connie read the paper and saw that Shelly was being moved to another correctional facility. She wanted to know how Shelly was coping. Since Connie wasn't an immediate family member, they wouldn't release any information just yet.

Joseph walked past the TV. room, where Constance sat.

"Are you ok, Constance?" he asked.

"I'm fine. I'm just thinking about some things," she stared at nothing in particular.

"I hope you don't regret pressing charges."

"No...well yes...but that's not what I'm thinking about. I don't regret what I did but she doesn't have anyone else. And I feel really bad that it had to end this way. Shelly is usually a sweet person."

"Ok, we're going out to eat in order to get your mind off of this. I don't want you to regret your decision and start second-guessing yourself. Get dressed, I'll call around and see if we can get a reservation." Joseph walked out of the room.

"Joseph," Connie called.

"Yes?"

"Well, I didn't know how to tell you this, but...I'm moving in two weeks. That apartment I looked at will be available soon," she began.

"Oh, I didn't realize that you were interested. I thought you said it was a little small."

"Yeah, it was small but it's in my budget and I'll adjust."

"Constance, I don't want you to rush and take the first thing you see. You have other options, take your time," Joseph said.

"With my budget, I don't have many options. But it'll be a place to call my own."

Joseph didn't want to see Connie leave but he knew she had to do what was best for her. "I got used to you being here. I really wish you didn't have to leave but I understand that you have to move on." He grabbed her hands.

"Thank you, Joseph. I appreciate everything you've done. I owe you big time," Connie said.

"I know that you don't want to hear me say that you don't owe me anything so I'm going to tell you how to repay me. Just take care of yourself and please call me if you ever need anything."

"I will. Thank you." She rubbed the back of his hand.

"Now, may I please take you out to dinner?"

"Of course. I can be ready in an hour."

"No problem." Joseph stepped out of the room and closed the door behind him. He leaned against the door and closed his eyes. He was trying to prepare to watch the woman he love walk out of his life.

* * *

Joseph poured champagne in Connie's glass and then in his own. He reached for her hand and looked into her eyes.

"I have something to say to you, Constance."

"Yes?" she replied.

"I'm so happy that you're moving on after your break-up with Shelly. You have come a long way in terms of getting yourself together and getting your own place. And I understand that you're a strong independent woman…but,"

"But what, Joseph?"

"I really want you to stay with me. I love you, Constance and I want us to be together." He sipped his drink out of nervousness.

233

"Joseph, I'm flattered that you feel this way. I've never tried to hide my feelings from you and I'm not trying to deny them. I'm gay, Joseph. I can't be with you knowing that. You see what I just went through with Shelly? I don't want to be with you and still lust for women. It's not fair and I love you too much to put you through that. Please understand that it's nothing personal. However, I would love to continue our friendship," Connie explained.

"Thank you for being so honest. I'd like you to keep in touch. You deserve to be happy, even if it's not with me." He ran his hand over his jacket pocket which contained a diamond ring. He held his glass up and clinked it with her glass. "To friendship."

"A long-lasting friendship," Connie finished. They drank the rest of the champagne and headed back to Joseph's house.

Chapter 59

Tricia made sure all of she and Tarik's things were packed before she closed the bags. Tarik had gone to a gift shop to get a few things. Trish had called for assistance with the luggage. The bellhop loaded the four bags on the cart and asked if that was everything. Trish told him yes and called Tarik on his cell phone.

"Babe, are you almost done because everything is in the car and I'm waiting for you."

"I'm on my way now, I'll meet you at the car," Tarik said and closed his phone.

Tricia was in the driver's seat when Tarik arrived. They drove home recalling the events of the weekend. They both seemed to have enjoyed themselves.

"Thank you so much for taking me away. It felt good to turn off the cell phone and not be interrupted by anyone about anything."

"I'm glad I could do something to help you enjoy yourself. I miss being the reason for that look on your face." He touched her chin.

Tricia smiled and grabbed his leg. "I also miss the other look on my face that you were responsible for. Tarik, I really enjoyed lying in your arms again. I felt like I found that missing piece to my puzzle."

"Well we could get together again during the week."

"How about tonight?" Trish asked.

Tarik was delighted that she suggested what was on his mind. "Tonight's good."

"But tomorrow we have to go to Marvin's house and bring some of my things home."

Tarik looked at his wife and squeezed her hand. He leaned over and kissed her on her lips while she tried to keep control of the jeep.

"I love the way this jeep drives." Trish said.

"It's ok but I'm getting ready to upgrade to something else."

"But why? It rides so smooth."

"New beginnings." He kissed her hand.

Chapter 60

Kareem took Sabrina from Simone while she signed the papers for Sabrina to legally be her child. Shelly's year was up and the courts decided that she abandoned Sabrina so Simone got legal maternal rights as her mother and not just her step-mother. Kareem and Simone got sole custody of Sabrina. Their lawyer explained a few minor legal details before they left the office.

"Kareem, I'm so excited! We should go out to celebrate."

"I know but we both have to work in the morning. And Sabrina needs to go home and lay down for a nap. She's tired and hungry. We could go out next weekend."

"Yeah, I guess so. I'm just happy we don't have to worry about when Shelly's going to pop up and stir trouble in Sabrina's life. And ours, for that matter. You know how she always trying to throw shit in the game," Simone added.

"Yeah, but I ain't worried about her. We're too strong to let anyone come between us. I love you and Sabrina too much to let anything or anyone try and break up my family!"

Simone strapped Sabrina in her car seat and got in the passenger side of the car. Kareem buckled his seatbelt and drove home.

He thought about what happened between him and Shelly and smiled on the inside. He came so close to losing his family. That was his wake up call. He would do right by Simone and his daughter.

Chapter 61

Shelly was just transferred from the county jail to a women's correctional facility. An officer escorted her to her cell and closed the gate behind her. She was the only person in the cell so she chose the top bunk. She didn't want a roommate that was overweight sleeping overtop of her.

Shelly lay on her bunk and cried. She wondered how she ended up in prison. She still couldn't believe that Connie pressed charges against her. She cried for Sabrina. She really wanted to do right by her but now she wouldn't get the chance. She knew that she missed her deadline to get her daughter; she held on to the fact that Simone and Kareem loved Sabrina enough to give their own lives for her. She wiped her tears and went to unpack her bag.

Her cell gate opened and an attractive woman walked in with her belongings. She looked around and saw that the bottom bunk was empty so she threw her things on the bed. She sat down and put her head in her hands. She looked up a few times when Shelly wouldn't stop crying.

"Hey, are you ok?" the roommate asked.

"Not really, but ain't nothing I can do about it in here," Shelly said.

"I can tell you now that crying ain't gonna help. I'll show you the ropes around here. I've been here for four years and looking forward to going home."

"Wow, you did four years?" Shelly asked and hopped off of her bunk.

"Yep, so I can show you a few things. I requested to be moved so I'll be here for the next year until I go home," she smiled, "by the way, I'm Tammy," she extended her hand.

Shelly hesitated before she shook her hand. She noticed the tattoo on her middle finger that read Simone.

"What's wrong?" Tammy asked.

"I just used to know a woman name Simone," Shelly said.

"Maybe one day you can tell me all about her," Tammy winked.

Also by Ty

With Friends Like That…
ISBN # 0-9758602-2-4
$14.95

Sinful Desires
ISBN # 0-9758602-0-8
$14.95

His Baggage Her Load
ISBN # 0-9758602-1-6
$14.95